HARLEQ

Harlequin
Big Sisters
Sisters of Canada in April 1988. Since then,
we have become the largest single sponsor of
Big Sisters Programs and related services in
North America.

This fitting association between the world's
largest publisher of romance fiction and a
volunteer organization that assists children and
youth in achieving their highest potential is a
wonderfully different kind of love story for
Harlequin. We are committed to assisting our
young people to grow to become responsible
men and women.

Brian Hickey
President and CEO

For more information, contact your local
Big Brothers/Big Sisters agency.

Dear Reader,

Out on a Limb is special to us because it's about something very close to our hearts—friendship. In addition to writing books together, we've been close friends for a long time. We know how important it is to have someone to listen, to help, to laugh with and to cry with. But most of all, it's important to have someone who accepts and loves you just as you are. And that pretty much describes a Big Sister.

The Big Brothers/Big Sisters organization has been making special friendships possible for more than eighty years. For a motherless girl like Kacie, who is crossing the threshold from childhood to adolescence, having a Big Sister makes all the difference in the world. A Big Sister is someone who has been there before. She is someone who can understand the first bra and the first kiss in a way no father can.

And as often happens, Big Sisters like Suzanne receive even more than they give. That's something we've discovered about friendship, and something we hope you will take with you from *Out on a Limb*.

With love,

Sally Bradford
(Sally Siddon/Barbara Bradford)

Sally Bradford

OUT ON A LIMB

Harlequin Books

TORONTO • NEW YORK • LONDON
AMSTERDAM • PARIS • SYDNEY • HAMBURG
STOCKHOLM • ATHENS • TOKYO • MILAN
MADRID • WARSAW • BUDAPEST • AUCKLAND

"The Prayer of the Dog" from PRAYERS FROM THE ARK
by Carmen Bernos de Gasztold, illustrated by Jean Primrose,
translated by Rumer Godden, Translation copyright © 1962
by Rumer Godden. Original Copyright 1947, © 1955 by
Editions du Cloitre. Used by permission of Viking Penguin, a
division of Penguin Books U.S.A. Inc.

Published October 1992

ISBN 0-373-70518-2

OUT ON A LIMB

Printed in U.S.A.

"He hurt you, Suzanne,"

Jed exploded. "Why are you covering up for him?"

"I'm not covering for anyone," Suzanne said. "I hit my head on the stair rail, that's all. Everything is just fine."

"Is it, Suzanne?" Jed stood up, willing her to look into his eyes. "I don't think so."

"You're being ridiculous," Suzanne said angrily. "I'm engaged and I'm going to be married in April. And that's the way it is, whether you like it or not, Jed Parker!"

"And do you love this man with your entire being? Would you lose part of yourself if you lost him? And do you trust him? Totally and absolutely, even beyond reason?" Somehow he had to get through to her. "If you can't answer yes to those questions, you sure as hell shouldn't be marrying him."

"Stop it, Jed! I don't want to hear any more." Suzanne grabbed his jacket and thrust it at him. "Get out. Get out of my life. I don't want to see you again."

Lord,
I keep watch!
If I am not here
who will guard their house?
Watch over their sheep?
Be faithful?
No one but You and I
understands
what faithfulness is.

From "The Prayer of the Dog"
by Carmen Bernos de Gasztold

To Maggie and Krissie and Misty
who have kept watch over our lives
and the lives of those we love.

CHAPTER ONE

BY ANY REASONABLE standards the puppy should be put to sleep. He was just another stray that had been hit by a car and thrown to the side of the road to die. His coat was caked with mud from rain the night before, and his broken foreleg hung limp. His gums were pale, his breathing shallow and rapid. A long gash in his side oozed blood onto the stainless steel surgery table.

Veterinarian Suzanne Peterson looked directly into Kacie's brimming eyes. "I don't think this dog is going to live." Her voice was controlled, even and thoroughly professional.

The thirteen-year-old swallowed hard, understanding but not accepting. "But he's still alive now, isn't he?" she whispered.

Suzanne nodded.

"Then make him better, please. At least try."

Suzanne stroked the puppy's muzzle gently. This was the hardest part of being a veterinarian—the painful struggle to determine if an animal could recover and lead a full life, or if it should be mercifully put out of its misery. Each animal was different, and there were rarely any easy answers. Slowly Suzanne shook her head. "There's no one who loves this dog, no one to take care of him," she told Kacie. "He doesn't even have a name."

Lady, her black Labrador retriever, whimpered and nuzzled the side of her leg. Suzanne bent down and gave the dog a pat on the head. "What do you think, old girl?" she asked. "Is this puppy strong enough to make it?" Lady's dark, trusting eyes gazed at Suzanne.

"Lady thinks you should operate," Kacie said firmly.

Suzanne looked at the puppy stretched out on the table, at Kacie and at the puppy again. She'd been practicing in Cartersburg, Virginia, for more than a year now, and three months ago she and Kacie had been paired as Big and Little Sisters by the Big Brothers/Big Sisters of America organization. She'd grown very close to Kacie, and she knew Kacie trusted her. That made her decision even harder.

"I think he's part German shepherd," Kacie continued. "His fur is really a nice brown color under all the mud." She reached over and carefully stroked the stray's ear. "He's so soft...." Her voice broke. "And besides, I love him."

For a long minute there wasn't a sound in the austere surgical room. Kacie continued stroking the puppy's ear. Lady settled on the floor underneath the stainless steel table and rested her muzzle on her paws. The stray was barely breathing. Only God knew why he was still alive. Suddenly, without even being aware of having made a decision, Suzanne reached for an IV drip and a catheter.

"Out, Kacie," she ordered. "I've got work to do if I'm going to help this poor animal. You'll have to wait in the reception room."

"Okay." Kacie broke into a grin of relief. She got as far as the door then stopped and looked at Suzanne. "You should know he does have a name. I'm going to call him Lucky."

"Out!" Suzanne ordered again. Hearing the dog's name didn't help the situation at all. It was much simpler to deal with a nameless stray than with a puppy named Lucky.

Jed Parker heard the door open and looked up from a magazine as his daughter came into the reception room. From her expression, he figured she had persuaded Suzanne to operate on the dog. He hoped they weren't just prolonging the agony. "How is he?" Jed asked hesitantly.

Kacie folded herself into a worn lounge chair. "Suzanne is operating on him now." She stared at an aquarium full of tropical fish. "I named him Lucky, because I think he's going to be. I know Suzanne can make him better."

"Now wait a minute," Jed cautioned. "When we found that dog on the highway I told you he didn't have much of a chance. Suzanne is a good vet, but she can't work miracles."

"She's going to make him better," Kacie repeated stubbornly. "I know she can do it."

Jed opened his mouth to respond, but seeing the determined thrust of Kacie's chin, decided against any more warnings. There were some things kids had to believe. And a lot of things they had to learn for themselves. He watched Kacie for a moment. Even though she was a typical thirteen-year-old—all arms and legs with dark hair forever falling in her face—she had the promise of one day being as beautiful as her mother had been. Elizabeth would have been pleased.

Kacie picked at the torn arms of the lounge chair and continued to stare at the fish. She tried not to think of the puppy lying so still on the shiny table and Suzanne working on him. She liked Suzanne. She'd been lonely sometimes after her mother died and had really wished she had somebody to talk to besides her father. When her dad had taken her to the Big Sisters agency the first time, that's what she had told the caseworker. The lady obviously understood, because she'd paired her with Suzanne.

Kacie picked up a magazine, flipped through it, then traded it for another. She was having trouble not thinking about the puppy. His fur was nicer than brown, sort of caramel colored with some black patches mixed in, although it was hard to tell with all the mud and dried blood on him. She'd noticed his feet were big, which meant he still had a lot of growing to do. If he lived to grow up. Kacie stared unseeing at the magazine. After what seemed forever, she hoisted herself out of the lumpy chair and wandered over to look out the window.

"Suzanne has been working on Lucky for a long time. I guess that's a good sign, isn't it? I mean, if he was already—already...." Her voice faltered.

"Waiting is hard, Kacie," Jed answered.

"Yeah, it sure is." She continued to stare out the window. Even though it was only October, there was a carpet of red leaves under the maple trees. She thought about running with Lucky in those leaves—if he lived.

Jed wanted to go across the room and put his arms around his daughter, but he wasn't sure how she would react. She had changed so much in the past year. She must have grown nearly six inches. He'd have to remember to measure her and put another mark on the kitchen wall. And her clothes—she insisted on wearing torn jeans and old T-shirts that even the Salvation Army would probably reject. But at least they were baggy and covered up most of her budding shape. Jed hated to admit it, but he wasn't altogether comfortable hugging Kacie any more. She wasn't exactly the little girl who used to burrow in his bed with the comics on Sunday morning. Sometimes that seemed like a long time ago, and sometimes it seemed almost like yesterday. It was hard for a man to raise a kid by himself. Especially a girl.

The door opened, and both Jed and Kacie looked up expectantly as Suzanne, with Lady at her heels, came into the reception room.

"Well, the puppy—" she glanced at Kacie "—Lucky," she amended, "is still unconscious, but he seems to be doing a little better. He's hooked to an IV now, and the heating pad is bringing up his body temperature." Lady walked over and stood by Kacie, who was hanging onto every word. "I cleaned up his injuries and put a cast on his broken leg," Suzanne continued. "Fortunately, that laceration on his side didn't penetrate the chest wall."

"Then he's going to be all right?" Kacie's eyes were wide with a mixture of hope and fear.

Suzanne wished she could say what she knew Kacie wanted to hear. "I'm afraid I can't make any promises yet," she answered gently. "He was hurt pretty badly. And even if everything does go well, he's going to need a lot of help and love over the next few weeks."

The answer was enough. "I'll give him all the love he needs," Kacie promised, already halfway to the door of the clinic. "I'll stay with him day and night. Can I see him now?"

Suzanne smiled at Kacie's stubborn determination. "You may see him, but remember, he's still unconscious and has an IV. He's a very sick puppy, Kacie."

"Yes, but he's alive." Kacie disappeared through the door, heading toward the back of the clinic where the cages for sick animals were kept.

Once Kacie had gone, Jed turned to Suzanne. "That dog looked pretty bad to me," he said slowly. "If you worked on him because of your relationship with Kacie, I'm not sure you did any of us any favors."

Suzanne hesitated, mostly because Jed was at least partly right. At one point, Lucky's heart had stopped. At that moment, Suzanne had been sure her professional judgment had been swayed by the sight of Kacie's eyes brimming with tears. But then the dog's heart had started spontaneously, and as the arrhythmias had responded to medication, Suzanne's optimism had grown. Sitting in the chair Kacie had vacated, she looked squarely at Jed. "It's hard to resist a child's belief in life. I'm sure that had something to do with my decision, but I wouldn't have gone ahead if I hadn't thought the puppy had a chance."

"I hope not."

She could see he wasn't convinced.

"Kacie adores you, you know," he added after a moment. "She places a lot of importance on having a Big Sister."

"No more than I do." Suzanne remembered nearly every one of the talks they'd had and the confidences

Kacie had shared. From the beginning there had been so few awkward moments that it seemed almost like they really were sisters. Suzanne thought again about the stray and hoped she'd made the right decision. If the puppy didn't make it, Kacie was going to be devastated. Lady wandered across the waiting room and put her head on Suzanne's knee. She scratched the old dog behind the ears. "Kids and dogs." Suzanne laughed. "Guess I've got a soft spot."

"Especially for Lady."

"No question about it. She's my best friend, and the only family I have."

An odd way of putting it, Jed thought—her only family. He knew Suzanne was twenty-eight, and that her mother and father were dead, but that was about all he knew. He scrutinized her face. The artist in him was intrigued by her finely chiseled bones and misty gray eyes with thick, sweeping lashes. Gentle, compassionate eyes, yet intelligent, too. Her dark brown hair, pulled back into a single braid, emphasized her eyes. She was wearing faded jeans and a pink oxford-cloth shirt with the sleeves rolled partway up. The shirt happened to be the same color as the blush in her cheeks, he noticed. As usual she wore no makeup, and he couldn't imagine that she would need any.

"Why are you staring at me?"

"Because I'm fascinated," he answered. "You have a beautiful, almost classic face. I'd like to sketch you—" Jed stopped abruptly when he realized he was making her uncomfortable.

Suzanne turned away. "I didn't know cartoonists did other kinds of drawing."

"Most cartoonists are cartoonists partly because they say things better with pictures than with words, just like any artist. I get into trouble with words. I shouldn't have said anything."

His eyes drew her in, dark brown, sensitive eyes, which suggested feelings far deeper than those his words expressed. He had sandy-colored hair, often tousled by the wind, and the lean, angular frame of a man who worked and played hard. As he watched her now, Suzanne tried to assure herself that he wasn't as perceptive as he seemed. But she knew better. Anyone who had read "Out on a Limb," his syndicated cartoon strip, knew about his insight and the humor that went with it.

Jed shifted his gaze toward the window and the darkness beyond. "It's getting late. Maybe you'd like to go get a pizza with Kacie and me."

Suzanne started to accept, then she remembered: Marty was coming at eight. She was genuinely sorry she couldn't go with Jed and Kacie. "Maybe we could do it another night," she suggested. "I've got a date with Marty."

"Oh, yeah, the pharmaceutical salesman. You told me about him a few weeks ago."

"He's not actually a salesman. His father owns the company, and in a few years Marty will take over as vice president. Right now he's working his way through the various divisions to learn how everything operates."

"I see." Jed watched her closely for a moment. "Is this thing with him serious?"

"Well, I don't know...." What she did know was that she felt happy inside whenever she and Marty were together. She wished he didn't travel so much and she could see him more often.

"None of my business, anyway." Jed stood up. "Come on, Kacie, time to go," he called.

Kacie appeared in the doorway almost immediately. "I'm going to stay here tonight," she announced. "I heard what Suzanne said about going out, and I don't want Lucky to be alone."

"I don't think so," Jed answered. "It isn't safe."

"Oh, Dad, you're always so sure somebody is out to get me." Kacie's voice rose. "We live in Cartersburg, Virginia, remember? It's not exactly the crime capital of the nation."

"That's enough, Kacie."

"But Daddy—"

Suzanne listened curiously to the exchange. She knew how much it would mean to Kacie to be there when the dog woke up. And Kacie was right about Cartersburg. It was a little rural town in central Virginia where not much ever happened. The population barely reached five thousand, and rush hour meant more than two cars were stopped at the red light at the intersection of First and Main. Surely a thirteen-year-old would be all right, and besides, she wouldn't be alone. "My part-time assistant will be here watching the puppy," she told Jed. "If you'd like, Kacie could stay here with her for a few hours, and then Marty and I would bring her home."

"Thanks, Suzanne, but Kacie has to get up early in the morning for school. This just isn't the night for her to be out late." Jed started toward the door.

Kacie stood her ground. "At least can I say good-bye to Lucky?"

"Hurry."

Instantly Kacie darted through the door. Once inside the surgical room she looked hastily around until she spotted a ground-level window near the back. Quickly she unlocked it.

"Come on, Kacie," Jed called from the reception room.

"Coming right away," she answered. She quietly raised and lowered the window just to make sure it would open. Then she ran to the back room for a quick glimpse of Lucky. She reached into the cage and patted him on the head. He was totally still except for his steady breathing. "See you later," she whispered, then hurried out to join her father and Suzanne.

"I'm sure Lucky will be all right while I'm gone," Suzanne reassured her.

"I hope so," Kacie answered. She glared at her father's back and followed him outside.

Before she left the clinic, Suzanne checked on Lucky once more. He seemed stable, and her assistant would be there in a few minutes. Suzanne leaned down to pat Lady. "Why don't you stay here and help watch the puppy?" Lady whimpered softly. Sometimes Suzanne thought Lady understood her completely. As she walked across the wide yard toward her small frame house, she felt slightly guilty about leaving Lady behind, but with Marty coming she knew it was best. She had never understood why Marty didn't like Lady or why Lady stayed so close to her side whenever he was around. Maybe they were jealous of each other, she thought, laughing softly.

After allowing herself the luxury of a long shower to wash away the day's tension, Suzanne dried her thick, wavy hair and slipped into a gray knit dress that matched her eyes. Marty especially liked the gray dress on her. He said it made her look like a little dove. Suzanne had chosen it tonight because Marty had told her on the phone to prepare for a very special evening. Suzanne wondered what he meant. Her hands shook slightly as she applied her makeup. She wanted everything to be exactly right. Patiently, she brushed the shining brown waves that spilled over her shoulders until all the tangles were gone. She always left her hair down for Marty. He liked it that way. After stepping into a pair of gray suede pumps, she put on her shimmering moonstone earrings and checked the mirror once more. Her eyes glistened, her cheeks were pink, and she was as nervous as she had been the day she started her veterinary practice. That was stupid, she told herself as the doorbell rang. It was just a date. But it wasn't just a date. She was going out with Marty.

"You look beautiful tonight, sweetheart—like a soft little dove." He handed her a bouquet of roses.

"Marty, you shouldn't have—"

"Of course I should. The world's loveliest flowers for the world's loveliest woman."

He flashed a dazzling smile, and Suzanne thought for the hundredth time that he was the most charming man she had ever met. She glanced at him as she arranged the roses in a vase on the hall table. His wavy blond hair was brushed back from his face, framing piercing blue eyes. And that smile—he could melt an Arctic glacier with that smile. He was tall, with broad shoulders and an easy demeanor that reflected wealth and privilege. She'd never known a man like him.

"I hope you don't mind a bit of a drive," he said as he helped her into a lightweight wool coat. "We're going to a French country inn not far from Richmond." He slipped his arm around her waist and guided her into the crisp October night.

"Le Château?" Suzanne had read about it although she had never been there.

"Precisely. It's the ideal place for tonight." With a flourish he opened the door of his red Firebird.

Suzanne hesitated. If they were going all the way to Richmond, they wouldn't be back until late. She was worried about Lucky. "I did surgery on a stray puppy this afternoon. If we're going so far, maybe I should run over to the clinic and check on him."

Marty's hand tensed slightly against hers. "Is it really necessary? I'd hate to have us miss our reservation."

"Well—" She wasn't sure. She knew Kacie was counting on her, and she felt an enormous responsibility toward her Little Sister. But she had done all she could for the puppy, and her assistant was there to keep an eye on him. "I guess it's not absolutely necessary."

"Good," Marty answered, his smile returning. "You're not exactly dressed for animal doctoring, anyway. Besides," he continued, slipping behind the wheel of the Firebird, "you need to get away from your job and have some fun."

He was probably right, and she couldn't do anything more for Lucky right then anyway, she reminded herself. Her assistant would watch him, and she'd call from the restaurant. By the time they pulled onto the highway, Suzanne had only a few lingering misgivings, and by the time they walked into Le Château, she was totally absorbed in conversation with Marty. Their table was tucked into a quiet corner with candlelight, fresh-cut flowers and a soft, rose-colored linen cloth. Soon after they were seated, the waiter brought a bottle of Pouilly-Fuisse 1981, which Marty had obviously ordered ahead of time.

"You think of everything," she told him, and she could see that her admiration pleased him. But it was absolutely genuine. He was so polished and attentive to every detail.

Marty raised his wineglass, and she followed suit. "To a lovely lady on a very special night."

Lowering her eyes, Suzanne sipped the light, dry wine. "You said that before. Why is tonight special?"

But just then the waiter arrived with the menus, and Marty didn't answer her question. He ordered sole amandine for both of them, and while they ate he talked to her about the pharmaceutical company and his hopes for the future. "I should be in that vice president slot in two or three years, and then I'll really be able to move. I've got some plans for expansion that will have a big impact on the balance sheet."

Suzanne smiled. Marty's excitement was contagious. He was used to having money, and he liked to make it almost as much as he liked to spend it. Suzanne had never known that kind of luxury. She took another sip of her wine. Not that she minded all the presents Marty bought her or the places he took her. She could see that having money could be quite nice.

When they finished their entrées, Suzanne excused herself to phone the clinic about the puppy. After learning that his heartbeat and respiration were stable and his gum color substantially improved, she told her assistant to go ahead and cap off the IV and leave at midnight. She'd be home soon afterward.

At Marty's insistence, they ordered crème brulée for dessert followed by a cup of rich, fragrant coffee topped with heavy cream. When the waiter had gone, Marty reached across the table and took her hand. "Now it's time to talk about why tonight is special."

Suzanne's mouth was suddenly dry. He seemed so serious.

"I have a present for you, Suzanne." He reached into his suit coat pocket, and took out a small, square blue velvet box.

Her eyes were riveted on it as he raised the lid. Then she gasped. A large pear-shaped diamond, set in gold, sparkled in the candlelight. "A ring?" Her throat was tight, her voice no more than a whisper.

"An engagement ring," he confirmed. "To symbolize the beginning of our life together."

"Oh, Marty..." She stared at the ring. Our life together, he had said. The thought was overwhelming. With Marty she could do so much. He had money, sophistication, everything a woman could want. She would have a lifestyle that had always been beyond even her dreams. Their children would never know the deprivation and fear that had hauntd her childhood. But was she ready to marry him? Did she really know him? He was waiting for an answer. She swallowed hard. "Marty..." She hesitated. "I don't know—"

Marty's expression changed suddenly, and he leaned across the table. "Is there someone else?"

"No, of course not," Suzanne quickly reassured him.

"Then why are you reacting like this? You don't want to marry me?"

Now he was upset. She tried again. "It's not that I don't want to marry you, Marty. It's just, well, I wasn't expecting—"

The tight lines in Marty's forehead disappeared as quickly as they had come. "I surprised you."

Suzanne laughed uneasily. "You certainly did."

"Well, if that's all it is—" He removed the ring from the box and took her left hand in his. His eyes locked with hers. "Suzanne Peterson, will you be my wife?"

She searched his face, looking for her answer. Getting married was a big step, an enormous step. Maybe she should think about it. On the other hand, what was there to think about, really? He was offering her all the things she'd always wanted, home, family, security. Suzanne took a deep breath. "Yes, Marty, I will marry you."

No sooner had she said the words than he slipped the ring on her finger. Then he cradled her face in the palms of his hands and kissed her lips. "How about a Christmas wedding?" he whispered.

"Marty, that's too soon! It's less than three months away." She stared at the diamond sparkling on her finger. It would take that long to get used to being engaged, let alone actually being married. "Marty, I need more time," she told him.

He looked disappointed and tried to persuade her to change her mind, but she held firm. By the time they had finished their coffee, he was laughing and promising to buy her a trunkful of gorgeous lingerie for their honeymoon. Suzanne found herself laughing with him and thinking about how wonderful their life was going to be.

KACIE HAD BARELY SLEPT between worrying about Lucky and waiting to go back to the clinic. The alarm had been set for midnight, but she had shut it off before it rang. She dressed in navy blue sweats, pulled on a pair of sneakers, and then slipped silently out her open bedroom window to the porch roof.

"You're late," Billy whispered from below.

"I'm not late. You're early," she retorted as she climbed down the branches of the big pine tree to where Billy Hankins was waiting. She'd known Billy forever—he'd always lived next door. Until a few months ago, he had been half a head shorter than Kacie, with chubby apple cheeks and red hair that fell into his eyes. Now, suddenly, he was tall and skinny, and sometimes he even tried to tame his hair, without much success. The fact that they were boy and girl had never mattered. Kacie hoped it never would. "Let's get going," she whispered. "I want to see Lucky."

Quickly she and Billy headed down the sidewalk toward Main Street. The sky was pitch black with only a sliver of a moon, but she and Billy hadn't brought a flashlight. They never used one when they sneaked out at night, because it might attract attention. "Did you have any trouble getting out?" Kacie asked.

"Nope. Piece of cake, just like always." Billy kicked at a rock on the sidewalk. "Are you sure Suzanne's assistant will be gone by now?"

"Yeah." Kacie wasn't sure, but she figured they'd find out when they got there.

"You think the dog will still be alive?"

"Of course, he'll be alive." Kacie wasn't willing to consider any other possibility. "I named him Lucky, like I told you."

"And I suppose you think your dad will let you keep him?"

Kacie didn't answer. She'd deal with that problem later.

They had gone two blocks when Billy grabbed her arm. "See that car?" he whispered, pointing to a late-model sedan parked along the curb. "There are people in it."

They flattened themselves behind a broad oak tree and waited. "Bet it's somebody making out," Kacie whispered. "They're probably too busy to notice us."

"Wonder who?" Billy moved two trees ahead and waited for Kacie.

"Beats me. Miss Henniker lives down here, but she sure wouldn't be in a car making out in the middle of the night." They both giggled at the image of their school librarian, an unmarried woman in her fifties, making out. As much as they liked her, they couldn't imagine her kissing a man.

Just then the car doors opened, flooding the interior with light. Kacie gasped. Not only was Margaret Henniker getting out of the passenger seat, but the man in the driver's seat was Ed Arnold, the school principal. Kacie clung to the tree, praying that they wouldn't see her or Billy. She watched them walk up to the front door of the house. Miss Henniker unlocked it, then both of them went inside. A thin shaft of moonlight illuminated them as they slipped into each other's arms.

"Billy." She poked him. "Did you see them? Did you see who that was?"

"Did I ever. Just wait till I tell the guys."

"Billy!" Kacie exclaimed. "You can't tell anyone. Miss Henniker could lose her job."

"Maybe." Billy looked disappointed. "Right now, let's get out of here."

For the next two blocks, they ran as fast as they could. When they finally slowed down, both of them were out of breath.

"I still can't believe it." Kacie glanced over her shoulder. "We have to be careful. Mr. Arnold will be going home any minute."

"I bet he doesn't go home," Billy said smugly.

"He can't just stay there all night. Someone would find out."

"I don't mean all night. Just long enough."

Kacie stared at him. "You mean you think they do it? They're pretty old."

"They were kissing. If they do some of it, they probably do all of it. Miss Henniker seems really comfortable talking about sex, you know, like in the book discussions, all that stuff she says."

Kacie thought that over as they walked along the shoulder of a two-lane country road just outside of town. Miss Henniker did talk very frankly during the book discussions about all sorts of issues, including sex. That was why the discussions were so popular and why a lot of parents were starting to object. "I don't think just because she talks about sex necessarily means she does it," Kacie ventured.

"Bet ya."

Kacie didn't answer. They turned onto the gravel drive approaching the clinic, and she started thinking about Lucky again. She hoped he was all right. Beside her, Billy's pace was slowing. "Come on, hurry up," she urged.

"Do you really want to go through with this?" he asked.

"You mean seeing Lucky? Of course. That's why we came."

"You're sure you fixed that window so we can get in?" Billy still sounded hesitant.

"No sweat." Kacie gave him an impatient look. "Don't tell me you're going to back out now, when we're almost there."

Billy scuffed his sneaker on the gravel. "What if the assistant is still inside? Or what if Suzanne is there? And what if they get us for breaking and entering? Sneaking out is one thing, but breaking in some-where—"

"Quit worrying, will you?" Kacie led him through the trees to the back of the clinic. "Even if we got caught, Suzanne would never turn us in. She'd under-stand why I had to come—I know she would."

They peered in the window for a full minute, but saw no sign of people. The reception room light was on, casting an eerie glow. Otherwise the clinic was dark. Kacie tried the window, and as she had promised, it slid open easily. Billy found an old wooden crate to stand on and had his knee on the windowsill when they heard the low, menacing growl. He pulled back. "What's that?"

"It's got to be Lady," Kacie said. "Here, let me go first. She knows me."

"I'm not going in there," Billy announced. "We'll get bit for sure."

"No, we won't." Kacie wished she was as certain as she pretended to be. Lady knew her, but that was in the daytime with Suzanne around. Going in the window at night with a stranger was different. "Lady, it's me," she said softly. Lady growled again.

"Told you."

Kacie ignored him. "Here, Lady, here, girl. Come here, Lady, it's all right." Slowly she raised herself up until she was poised on the sill, half in and half out of the window. All the time she kept talking. "I'm just coming to see Lucky," she crooned. "It's all right, girl, it's really all right." Summoning all her courage, she eased cautiously into the clinic and held out her hand, palm up below Lady's head, like Suzanne had told her.

"Here, girl, come see me," she pleaded. "Come here, Lady."

The old dog hesitated for a moment then walked slowly toward her and sniffed her hand. The growl was replaced with a soft whine of welcome. Kacie bent down and wrapped her arms around Lady's neck.

"It's okay, Billy," she said victoriously. "You can come in now."

Billy threw his leg over the sill and dropped inside, closing the window behind him. Lady looked him over without much interest and stayed close to Kacie.

"I told you it would be okay."

Billy didn't answer. With Lady at her heels, Kacie led him across the room, past the stainless steel table and the supply cabinets that lined the wall, through the door that led to the kennels. Lucky was in the first cage, lying in the same position as when she'd left him. The leg with the cast was stuck straight out in front of him. Kacie approached slowly with fear catching in her throat. What if he was dead? Dead animals were cold and stiff. She had read that somewhere. She didn't want to touch the dog. Then she heard a muffled whimper. She reached out, still frightened, and stroked his head, feeling the sticky, matted fur behind his ear. With great effort the puppy opened his eyes.

"Billy, he's alive," Kacie exclaimed.

"Not by much," Billy observed.

"Yes, but he is."

Billy scrutinized the animal carefully in the dim light from the reception room. "He looks pretty awful."

"Yeah." Kacie was near tears. "But he's got to be okay. He's just got to. I love him."

"You don't even know him. How could you love him?" Billy asked pragmatically.

"I don't know," Kacie answered. "I just do." Very gently she touched the puppy's muzzle. He raised his head slightly and, exerting maximum effort, weakly licked her hand. "Oh, Billy—" Kacie began.

"Shh," he commanded. "I think I heard a car." Lights seared the darkness then were gone. Lady scampered toward the reception room, barking all the way. "Somebody's coming," Billy warned. "We've got to get out of here."

Desperate, they looked around, realizing they were trapped. By the time they got to the window in the other room, it would be too late. "We can't make it," Kacie said. "We'll have to hide here. Quick, get in a cage down at the end.'' Kacie scrambled into a kennel cage and pulled the steel mesh door shut. Her heart pounding, she curled into a tiny ball at the back of the cage and held her breath.

CHAPTER TWO

SUZANNE'S VOICE cut through Lady's frantic barking. "Lady, settle down! It's just Marty and me." Lady growled. "Lady!" Suzanne reprimanded.

"That dog doesn't like me. I've tried to tell you that."

"That's not true, Marty." Suzanne patted Lady's head and looked at the man behind her. "She's probably just jealous. She'll get used to you when you're around her all the time."

Marty eyed the dog warily. "You're damn right, she will." As Suzanne slipped her lab coat on to protect her dress, Marty paced across the clinic. "How long will it take to check this stray dog?"

Suzanne could tell from his voice he wasn't pleased she had work to do. She glanced at the diamond glistening on her finger and sensed a looming problem. They'd talked about the wedding and a honeymoon in Bermuda, but they hadn't discussed how their lives would fit together. She had assumed he would accept her job, just as she accepted his. She looked at him. "You're going to have to be patient with me, Marty. Being a rural vet isn't a nine-to-five job."

"But your job can't be your life. You need time for yourself—and time for us." Marty reached out and stroked her cheek. "You work too hard, Suzanne. If you were in a small-animal group practice in Richmond instead of in a clinic here by yourself, you'd make good money and have lots more time off.''

''But that's not what I want.'' Suzanne picked up her stethoscope from the examining table and hung it around her neck. ''I like being in practice by myself, and I like treating large and small animals. It took me a long time and a lot of hard work to get where I am. I've saved almost enough money to expand the clinic. I can't give all that up.''

Marty put his hands on her shoulders and looked directly at her. ''I'm not asking you to give up everything. You'd still be working as a vet if you were in a group practice.''

Suzanne looked at him for a long minute. ''Marty, when you asked me to marry you tonight, I assumed you understood about my work.''

Marty's eyes narrowed. ''I do understand. I just want us both to be happy. If that means a few sacrifices, well—that's the way it is.'' He tightened his hands on her shoulders.

From the floor beside Suzanne, Lady growled.

''Stop it, Lady!'' Suzanne commanded.

Marty made no attempt to hide his irritation. ''We can't even have a conversation with that damn dog around.''

''I'm sorry, Marty.'' Suzanne looked at her fiancé. ''Let me give Lucky his antibiotic, and then we can talk.'' She checked the refrigerator, sensing Marty behind her, watching her. She wished he wasn't so impatient, but then again, when a man asked a woman to marry him she could understand why he might expect her full attention. After inspecting several small bottles, Suzanne couldn't find what she was looking for. "I'll have to go get some out of the truck," she said. "It'll just take a minute."

"Hurry up," Marty prodded, as Suzanne headed out to the portable clinic unit that filled the bed of her pickup.

From the corner of the cage where she was hiding, Kacie heard the door slam behind Suzanne. For a brief minute she relaxed, knowing she was safe until her Big Sister came back to the clinic. She wished she could whisper to Billy, but with Marty still there, that was too risky. Then she heard Marty's voice again.

"Damn dog," he muttered. "Always underfoot. There are going to be some changes once we get married, and the first one is going to be you, you dumb black mutt."

Kacie heard Marty's footsteps pound across the floor and stop. Lady growled, then there was a thud, and Kacie heard Lady's sharp yip of pain.

"Serves you right, mutt," Marty said in a harsh voice. Lady began barking ferociously, and the front door of the clinic opened.

"What's the matter?" Suzanne called. "I heard Lady barking and—"

"She just started barking like that," Marty answered. "Probably saw a squirrel out the window or something."

"Lady, come," Suzanne said firmly. The dog came to her side, whining softly. "I'm really sorry, Marty," Suzanne apologized. "I can't imagine what's wrong with her."

"Probably just mean-tempered. Some dogs are." He picked up his coat from the chair. "Listen, as long as you've got work to do, I'll take off. I've got an early day tomorrow.''

''You're leaving already? I thought we were going to talk some more.''

Marty kissed her cheek briefly. ''We've got all the time in the world, now,'' he told her. ''In a few months you'll be all mine.''

As Suzanne stood watching Marty's red Firebird disappear down the gravel road, Lady nuzzled against her leg. Minutes passed. Suzanne looked at the diamond ring on her finger, took it off, looked at it again, then put it back on. ''I don't understand,'' she told Lady. ''He hardly even kissed me goodbye.'' Lady gazed at her. ''What is it, old girl?'' She rubbed Lady's ears and looked into her eyes. ''Is there something you want to tell me? Sometimes I really wish you could talk.'' She stood up, and with Lady following close on her heels she went to check on Lucky.

Still huddled in the corner of the cage, Kacie watched Suzanne flip on the overhead light and open the door to Lucky's cage. The puppy whimpered softly.

''Still hurting a lot, I'd guess,'' Suzanne said sympathetically. She examined the sutures and felt the strong, even pulse. The puppy's respiration was steady, and she didn't hear any fluid sounds in his chest. His gums were a good pink color. ''I'd say Lucky is a good name for you,'' she observed, giving him his injection. ''It looks like you may make it after all. I'll be back to check you in a couple of hours, and we'll see if we can't get you cleaned up tomorrow before Kacie comes.''

Suzanne turned off the lights and started through the clinic, calling to Lady as she went. When the dog didn't come, Suzanne turned to see her sitting at the far end of the room in front of the empty cages. "Come on, girl, what's the matter with you?" Lady barked once and held her ground. Suzanne shook her head and opened the door. "Let's go, girl." Lady barked again. "All right, have it your way," Suzanne said finally. "You keep an eye on the pup, and I'll see you in a couple of hours." She closed the door behind her.

Inside the kennel room, Lady woofed and wagged her tail hopefully in front of the cages where Kacie and Billy were hiding.

"Shh," Kacie warned the dog as she crawled out.

Billy appeared beside her, moving stiffly after being curled up in the cramped cage. "Boy, that was close. Let's get out of here."

Kacie barely paused to pat Lucky as they ran through the clinic, opened the window and climbed out in record time. Billy shoved the window down and they both took off. All Kacie wanted was to get home to her own bed. She had heard more than she wanted to hear between Suzanne and Marty, and she didn't like any of it. Especially when Marty had hurt Lady. How could Suzanne want to marry someone who was so mean?

SUZANNE SPENT the next several days trying to adjust to the idea that she was engaged to be married. In the middle of inserting a drain in a cat's abscess she caught herself staring into space, trying to imagine herself as Mrs. Martin Lanning instead of Suzanne Peterson like she had been for twenty-eight years. She finally decided that the idea seemed overwhelming because Marty's proposal had been such a surprise.

Even wearing the ring required some getting used to. On Saturday, when she went out to Pickett's dairy farm to help with a difficult calving, she forgot to take the diamond ring off before pulling on her obstetrical gloves. Her left glove split inside the cow, and when she pulled the glove off afterward, the ring slid off her wet, slippery finger and was lost in a pile of hay. They spent half an hour looking for it, and all the while she agonized about how she'd explain its loss to Marty.

First thing Monday morning she took the ring down to Thornberg's Jewelry to have it made a size smaller. With an indulgent smile that implied he was used to dealing with young women who had just become engaged, Mr. Thornberg promised her she could have the ring back that afternoon.

When Suzanne returned to the shop later in the day, she found a note on the door saying Mr. Thornberg had gone for coffee and would be back in fifteen minutes. Suzanne checked her watch. There was just enough time to stop by the hardware store down the street and pick up a new lock for her kitchen window. Suzanne hurried to the store. She was walking past the hammers looking for the locks when she saw a familiar figure studying a can of paint. Jed Parker. She rarely saw him without Kacie, and she couldn't ever remember seeing him in a jacket and tie. Granted, Jed was wearing a brown corduroy blazer, not gray pinstripes, but on him it had the same effect. He looked extraordinarily handsome, with his thick, sandy-colored hair carefully combed back from a high, broad forehead. She hesitated only a moment before she approached him. "Hello, Jed," she said softly, not wanting to startle him.

"Suzanne." The smile on his face clearly said he was pleased to see her. "What are you doing here?"

She met his eyes and realized for the first time what a rich, dark brown they were. For a moment she almost forgot why she had come. "Well, I—I stopped to buy a window lock." Yes, that was it. "How about you?" she asked him, wondering if he was dressed for a date. Kacie had never mentioned that he was dating, but then maybe she wouldn't.

"Just picking up some paint." Jed looked down at his blazer and slacks. "I'm on my way to a Chamber of Commerce dinner, and I had a little extra time."

For some reason, that answer made her feel relieved. "Kacie came in to see Lucky this afternoon," she told him.

"Yes, that's what she said."

Suzanne saw a flicker of concern in his eyes.

"Is the puppy really doing as well as she thinks he is?"

Suzanne nodded. "Really well, Jed. Even better than I'd hoped. He should make a full recovery."

"Then I guess I owe you an apology."

She searched his face, but found no clue to what he meant. "An apology for what?"

"I said if you'd only operated on him because Kacie is your Little Sister, you weren't doing anyone any favors. I shouldn't have said that, Suzanne."

Intuitively she reached toward him and rested her hand on his arm. "You were partly right, Jed." She paused, sensing his closeness and feeling connected to him, wanting very much for him to understand. "I did do it for Kacie. But I believe in preserving life, too, sometimes maybe more than I should, and so I guess I also did it for the puppy.''

He looked at her for a long moment, his eyes locked with hers, and she knew that although her words had been inadequate, he really did understand.

''You're a very special person, Suzanne,'' he said softly. ''You've done something for Kacie and me. Now, what can I do for you?''

His question took Suzanne totally by surprise. ''You don't need to do anything for me, really, Jed—''

''There must be something,'' he insisted.

''Well—'' At first she couldn't think of a thing. ''I know—help me find a lock for my kitchen window. I'm looking for the kind that will let me leave the window open partway but still not let anyone get in.''

Jed looked at her curiously, then burst out laughing. ''That's the easiest request I ever heard. Come on.''

She followed him down the center aisle to the other side of the store and, when she saw the array of locks hanging in plastic covers on the wall, she was glad she'd asked for help.

''Maybe this one,'' he said after studying the display for a few moments. They both reached for it at the same time and ended up clasping each other's hands instead of the lock. For an instant neither of them moved. Suzanne felt suspended in time. She was totally aware of him, the texture of his skin, the warmth of his hand, the faint, spicy scent of his after-shave. Their eyes met once more, and they both smiled and moved their hands apart. Then Jed gave her the lock. As he explained how it worked, she listened to him, but what she heard was the timbre of his voice, not his instructions. The lock, which had been so important when she walked into the hardware store, didn't seem to matter much at all.

"Well, I guess I'd better go if I'm going to get to the dinner on time," he said as he glanced up at the clock on the back wall of the store.

"Thanks for helping me with this." Suzanne looked at the lock. "I'd have been totally confused."

"No, you wouldn't," Jed assured her with a smile. "But I was glad to help you anyway."

Not until he went to get the paint he'd been looking at did Suzanne realize that she'd totally forgotten to tell Jed her news. All the time she'd talked to him, she hadn't said anything about getting engaged to Marty. She wasn't sure how she had forgotten, and she wanted Jed to know as soon as possible. And Kacie, too. They were good friends, and they'd both be so happy for her.

"Jed, wait just a minute," she called to him as she hurried up to the counter to pay for the lock. He stood by the door until she joined him, and as they walked outside together, she opened her mouth to speak, but she wasn't sure how to begin. "I have some news," she finally said, feeling awkward.

"What's that?" He was looking at her, smiling, and she realized he had the barest hint of a dimple that she'd never noticed before.

"Well—" The best approach, she'd always believed, was to simply say what you had to say and be done with it. "Marty and I are engaged."

The smile faded from Jed's lips. "You're engaged? When I asked you about Marty the other night, I thought you said it wasn't serious."

She felt the change in him, saw the disbelief in his eyes. Then it was gone, and in its place was a neutral expression that said nothing. "I said I didn't know if it was serious," she corrected him. "I guess everything happened all at once and, well.... I'd show you my ring but I'm just going to the jewelry store to pick it up. It was too big, and Mr. Thornberg is going to cut it down a size." Suzanne realized she was rattling on to fill the silence that settled whenever she took a breath.

"Well, I should congratulate you." Jed's expression didn't change. "When's the big day?"

"I—we—I'm not sure yet. Next spring some time."

"Spring weddings are very nice." He looked at his watch. "I really do need to go or I'll be late for the dinner. Congratulations again."

She watched him cross Main Street and get into his car then hurried toward the jewelry store. Jed's reaction wasn't exactly what she'd expected. Actually, she didn't know what she had expected; she just knew that wasn't it. Maybe once he met Marty, Jed would be more enthusiastic.

Suzanne reached the jewelry store just as Mr. Thornberg was pulling down the shade on the front door. "I've been waiting for you, young lady," he said, patting her on the shoulder. "I knew you wouldn't want to be without that ring for a whole night."

No, Suzanne thought, as she slipped the ring on her finger, she wouldn't want to be without it. After all, she'd be wearing that ring for the rest of her life.

THE SUN WAS BARELY UP, glowing red outside the kitchen window, as Jed sat at the table poring over a book Kacie had left there. Since the week before, when they had found the injured puppy, Kacie had been preoccupied. He'd thought it was because of the dog, but now he'd found this book. He ran his fingers through his hair, which was still damp from his morning shower.

The story seemed to be about two teenagers' attitudes toward having sex. There was lots of talk about condoms and where people might go to "do it." His eyebrows tightened into a frown. He turned the book over and noticed the school library sticker on the spine. The book, by an author named Allison Craig, appeared to be one of a series and, after checking the titles listed at the back, he thought he remembered seeing a few others around the house.

He read for several minutes more, until Kacie came flying into the kitchen for breakfast and dropped her backpack on the chair. Jed took a careful look at her. She had on her standard outfit—a faded University of Virginia sweatshirt and a pair of jeans torn at the right knee. She certainly didn't look ready to have any burning interest in sex. "Kacie, where did you get this book?" he asked her, holding it up.

"From the school library," Kacie answered casually. She hadn't meant to leave it lying around. She knew how her father would react. It was just that she had been thinking so much about Suzanne and Marty since that night in the clinic that she hadn't paid much attention to where she had put the book.

"Have you read it?" he asked.

Kacie poured her cereal. She wasn't in any mood to have a heavy discussion at seven-thirty in the morning.

"Well?" he prodded.

"I've read most of it," Kacie answered, her tone guarded. Actually, she'd read the entire book twice, and she'd been going to read it again except Billy had been bugging her for it.

"What did you think of it?" Jed asked.

Kacie shoveled in two quick bites of cereal. She couldn't tell him how much she liked it. He'd never understand that wanting to know about sex and all the feelings that went with it didn't mean she was going to do it. "It was okay, I guess," she answered carefully. "A little far out in places."

"Is this the first book of this series you've read?" Jed felt like he was conducting an inquisition, and that wasn't what he wanted at all. Talking to Kacie, especially about sex, wasn't easy, but if information about sex was the reason for her interest in these books, they needed to discuss it.

"No, I've read some of the other books."

"And your teachers approve of them?"

Kacie quickly finished her cereal. She needed to get out of the house before the conversation got any more involved. "I guess so. I don't know. The librarian runs the book program. What's the big deal, anyway? It's just a book."

"It may be just a book," Jed replied, "but I think there are other books that would be more appropriate for the seventh and eighth grades. What's the librarian's name?"

Kacie sighed. "You know her name, Dad. It's Miss Henniker, and you won't need to call her because she's having a meeting Thursday night to explain the books and the program." She had hoped to keep her father out of the controversy. Miss Henniker was going to have enough trouble without him making it any worse. And no matter what the parents thought, the books and the discussions were really good, probably the best thing going at Cartersburg Intermediate. Kacie held out her hand. "Can I have the book now? I promised to give it to Billy."

Reluctantly, Jed handed her the paperback. "I'll make it a point to be at that meeting."

I'll bet you will, Kacie thought. Then an idea began to grow. Maybe this was exactly the opportunity she'd been waiting for to show Suzanne what a jerk Marty was. Kacie couldn't tell Suzanne about Marty hurting Lady because she'd have to admit being in the clinic. But if Marty had hurt Lady, he probably did other rotten things, too. Maybe if Suzanne spent some time with her dad, she'd see what a nice man was like and ditch Marty. Miss Henniker's meeting might be the perfect excuse to bring them together. "Why don't you ask Suzanne to go to the meeting with you?" she asked innocently.

"Why would she want to go?"

"Well, she's my Big Sister and all, and so she might like to see what kind of stuff I'm reading."

"Maybe." Jed turned to the morning paper and began reading.

"I've got to call her anyway," Kacie said, picking up the phone. "I want to check on Lucky before I go to school." Which was half true. Over the past week, Lucky had improved so much that Kacie didn't have to call every morning, but she still felt good when Suzanne said he was fine. Her Big Sister answered on the second ring, and Kacie smiled at the report that Lucky had wolfed down his breakfast and wanted more. "One more thing," Kacie added before they hung up. "There's a meeting at school Thursday night about some books we're reading. Dad wondered if you might like to go with him."

"Kacie!" Jed exclaimed, suddenly aware of what his daughter had said.

"You would? Great! I'll tell him. See you this afternoon."

"Kacie, what did you do that for?" Jed demanded after she hung up.

"Do what? You said you wanted her to go, and I had to call about Lucky anyway."

"I said maybe," Jed corrected.

"You don't want her to go?"

Jed hesitated. How could he answer that? He liked Suzanne, liked her a lot, actually, and he'd been damn disappointed when she told him she'd gotten engaged to that pharmaceutical salesman. But he certainly couldn't explain that to Kacie. "I didn't specifically *say* I wanted her to go. That's the point. I'd appreciate it if you would let me issue my own invitations from now on."

"Sure, Dad. Sorry." Kacie picked up the book and her backpack. "I've got to go now." She rushed out the door just in time to catch Billy.

"I did it," she announced proudly, as she fell in step beside him. "I solved the problem."

"What problem?"

Billy wasn't too swift first thing in the morning. "Suzanne being engaged to Marty, dummy. She's going to the school meeting with my dad, and any other things I can think of to get them together in the next couple of weeks. It shouldn't take her very long to see what a creep Marty is."

Billy scuffed through a pile of leaves. "That'll be a real great evening. They can sit and listen to Miss Henniker defend books about sex and divorce while a bunch of angry parents yell at her."

"So, I did the best I could."

"You really figure Suzanne will dump Marty just because she spends time with your dad?"

Kacie shrugged. "You got any better suggestions?"

"Nope."

She hadn't thought he would.

"Hey, how about that book?" Billy said as they walked into the school. "You promised you'd bring it."

Kacie took the book out of her backpack and Billy shoved it under his arm. She watched him swagger down the hall toward his locker trying to look cool. Actually, he really did look kind of cool.

The day dragged for Kacie. She had more pressing things on her mind than the metric system and the proper punctuation of complex sentences. When she stopped in the library after lunch, she found herself staring at Miss Henniker, trying to imagine her as a sexy woman instead of a school librarian. Billy was right. If they hadn't both seen her with Mr. Arnold, she'd be convinced it had been only a dream.

After school, Kacie went to visit Suzanne and Lucky at the veterinary clinic. As she walked through the door, Lady barked in welcome, and Lucky was waiting for her, his tail thumping the cage in excited rhythm when she came to him. He whimpered with funny, hoarse little sounds that Suzanne had told her were a result of his injuries. She wasn't sure his voice would ever be quite normal, but Kacie didn't care.

"Hi, Lucky," Kacie said happily, and the puppy wiggled with excitement.

"He's really getting attached to you." Suzanne smiled at the two of them. "You can take him out of the cage today, but don't let him get too wild. He's not quite healed yet."

Kacie had no sooner opened the cage door than the puppy was all over her, whimpering happily and licking her face. "Lucky, stop! That tickles!" She gathered the puppy in her arms carefully so she wouldn't put any pressure on the bandages and carefully set him down.

As soon as his feet touched the floor, Lucky was in motion, scampering awkwardly around the clinic, dragging his right front leg, which was still in a cast. With his feathery tail wagging furiously, he sniffed everything, including Lady, who lay quietly at Suzanne's feet.

"Lucky's really almost well, isn't he?" Kacie said hopefully. "I mean, look at his eyes, how bright they are and how well he's walking even with the cast still on. And his fur is really soft and fluffy now."

"He certainly has made a remarkable recovery," Suzanne agreed. She wouldn't exactly describe Lucky's motley brown coat as soft and fluffy, but she did agree that his recovery had far exceeded anything she'd anticipated. She watched him scamper into the examining room and suddenly realized the door to the supply cabinet was open.

"You'd better get him, Kacie, before he—"

Lucky burst forth with a hoarse bark.

"No, no, Lucky," Kacie called as she dashed into the adjoining room, but the puppy had already sent a box of sterile gauze dressings flying off the cabinet shelf by the time Kacie grabbed him. He jumped up, licked her nose, knocked her to the floor and climbed on top of her. "No, Lucky," Kacie said, giggling. "No, no."

"We need to put him in the cage, I'm afraid," Suzanne said, leaning down and gathering the puppy in her arms. She held him firmly for a moment until he settled down. "He's getting pretty tired, and he's too young to know when to stop."

Kacie sat up amidst the white gauze squares strewn across the floor. "He sure doesn't look tired to me."

"He's got a lot of energy and a lot of character," Suzanne said as she carried Lucky to his cage and gently laid him inside. "With the right kind of training, he'll make a fine friend."

"Like Lady," Kacie said, reaching through the cage doors to stroke the puppy's head, which was resting quietly on his paws. He looked as though he were about to fall asleep.

"Well—" Suzanne hedged. She wasn't willing to go that far. No dog would ever be quite like Lady.

"How soon can I start to train him?" Kacie asked.

"Probably a couple of months before you can get very serious about it. You'll need to housebreak him first." Suzanne looked into Kacie's excited face and asked the question she'd been avoiding for a week. "Is it all right with your father for you to keep Lucky?"

Kacie looked at her feet. She had wanted a dog for a long time, but her father had been reluctant. She hadn't asked him about Lucky directly, mainly because she'd been afraid he would say no. She had hoped every-thing would somehow work out.

"I gather you haven't talked to him about it yet?"

"No, not exactly," Kacie admitted. "But how could he say no? I mean, after we saved Lucky's life—well actually, you saved his life, but we found him, and he doesn't have anybody except us..."

"You probably need to mention it to your dad pretty soon." Suzanne patted Kacie's shoulder. "You'll know when the time is right."

"Yeah," Kacie leaned her head against the cage, close to the sleeping puppy. Somehow she'd convince her father. She stayed there a long time while Suzanne stood at the sink washing feeding dishes. Slowly Kacie became aware of something staring at her. She glanced sideways and found herself looking into the face of a huge cat, which was solid black except for its startling green eyes. She moved toward the cage, fascinated, but the cat hissed and backed away.

"That's a real mean cat," Kacie said. "Whose is it?"

"That's Othello, Margaret Henniker's cat," Su-zanne answered. "He's not really mean, just angry be-cause he's used to being king of the neighborhood and now he's caged."

Kacie stared into the cat's cold green eyes. "You mean Miss Henniker, the school librarian?"

"That's the one. In fact, she was supposed to pick up Othello today after school. I don't know what's keep-ing her."

Maybe she had a date with Mr. Arnold, Kacie thought. But she didn't say it. After she'd warned Billy not to tell, it wouldn't be fair if she did. "Miss Hen-niker is running the meeting you're going to with Dad next Thursday," she volunteered. "I'm really glad you can go. I was afraid Marty might be coming or something."

"No, he's going to be gone for the next two weeks," Suzanne replied absently as she dried a stainless steel bowl.

"Will you miss him after you just got engaged and all?"

Suzanne looked up. "Of course I will. But he has to travel because of his job."

"Do you love him?"

Startled, Suzanne stared at Kacie. What an odd question for her to ask. Of course she loved Marty. "You don't plan to marry someone unless you love him, Kacie."

"Is he nice to you?" Kacie knew she was on treacherous ground, but she asked anyway. She had to make Suzanne understand that Marty wasn't a nice person. She wished she could tell her about Marty hurting Lady.

"Marty is very nice to me." Suzanne was increasingly uncomfortable with the discussion. It seemed almost as though Kacie knew the intimate details of her relationship with Marty, but that was impossible. "I'll have to get you and Marty together—I'm sure you'll like him," she added. "Now, tell me about this meeting Thursday night."

She's changing the subject, Kacie thought triumphantly. She doesn't want to talk about Marty. That means she's uncomfortable, so maybe she isn't so sure about him after all. "I guess the meeting will be pretty good," Kacie answered. "Miss Henniker is going to talk about this series of books that deals with how life really is for kids growing up. Some of the parents are kind of upset."

Suzanne listened carefully, relieved they were no longer discussing Marty. Kacie was a very perceptive child, and it was easy to forget she was only thirteen. "The parents don't like the books?"

"The books and the discussions after school," Kacie explained. "You can talk about anything you want in the discussions, and Miss Henniker never criticizes you no matter what you think about something. One girl said she thought everyone should get into sex by the time they're thirteen because it's a good way of exploring feelings, and Miss Henniker asked her what other ways were good to explore feelings."

Suzanne nodded, quickly getting the picture. Obviously that kind of approach could cause heated controversy. "Do you have one of the books I could read, Kacie?"

"No, but I can get one from Billy tomorrow."

The bell on the door jingled, and Lady barked once. They looked up to see Margaret Henniker walk in, followed closely by Ed Arnold.

"I'm so sorry I'm late," she apologized, "but my car battery was dead and Mr. Arnold was nice enough to offer me a ride."

Mr. Arnold, is it? Kacie thought. She was willing to bet that Miss Henniker hadn't been calling him Mr. Arnold that night last week. She greeted them politely and dried a few feeding dishes while she listened to the adults discuss Othello, who seemed to have recovered completely from being neutered.

"I know he'll be glad to come home," Miss Henniker said as she and Suzanne wrestled Othello into a large blue cat carrier, which they handed to Mr. Arnold.

"Come on, Othello," he said jovially. The cat hissed at him.

As they turned to leave, Kacie watched carefully to see whether Mr. Arnold touched Miss Henniker at all. He didn't. Kacie was rather disappointed.

"I'll see you tomorrow at school," Miss Henniker said, as she picked up her purse. "Will your father be at the meeting Thursday?"

Kacie nodded. "Suzanne's coming, too."

"I'm glad to hear that." Miss Henniker smiled. "We can use all the open minds we can find."

"That doesn't include my dad," Kacie warned her.

Miss Henniker's smile faded. "Maybe it will after Thursday."

"Don't count on it," Kacie replied.

WITH THE CLINIC DOOR safely closed behind them, Ed reached over and squeezed Margaret's hand. "Don't worry so much. You'll convert them."

Margaret didn't answer. She'd once thought that, too, but now she was wondering whether she had made a mistake. Practically all the feedback she was getting was negative. She was beginning to wonder how many parents had any idea what was really on their children's minds. "I'm frightened, Ed," she said after they got into his car. "That bunch of parents Thursday night is going to be a lynch mob."

Ed frowned. "Why don't I come and give you some support? If I advocate the program, too—"

"You're wonderful, Ed," Margaret interrupted, taking his hand, "but no. You're already taking enough flak about this."

He turned on the headlights and drove away from the clinic. "Are the books really that important to you, Margaret?"

"Not the books, Ed. The children. I wish you could hide in the closet some day when we have one of our discussions. Children I've never seen voluntarily read a book are there debating ideas. Every time I have a discussion, more of them come. In fact, I've had more kids in the library checking out books in the past month than I did during the whole fall semester last year."

Ed watched her light up as she talked, her voice animated, her eyes bright with enthusiasm. He hated to tell her the bad news, but he had to. "Margaret, I've been hoping this would die down, but it hasn't. The opposition to that reading series is growing daily. I got a letter from the PTA board yesterday. They're demanding that I take the Allison Craig books off the shelves."

"And what are you going to do?" She looked at him, dismayed that he was being dragged into the controversy. He was such a gentle man and so warmhearted. She reached over and touched his arm. His hairline had receded some and he carried a few more pounds than absolutely necessary, but he was still terribly handsome. His eyes were such a clear blue and so often twinkling with laughter, and his eyebrows were thick and slightly unruly. She really liked his eyebrows.

Ed patted her hand. "I don't know what to do about this, Margaret. Hold out as long as possible, I guess, and see if we can get people to listen to reason." He pulled the car into her driveway and turned toward her. "I want to get this solved because it's complicating both our lives."

"Ed, I can't back down on this."

"I understand that," he answered gently. He took her hands in his. "But I love you, Margaret. I want to marry you—I've told you that a dozen times. I'm tired of sneaking around."

She looked at their hands twined together. It would be so easy if she would simply give up, resign from her job and marry him. "Oh, Ed, I do love you. Please be patient a little longer," she pleaded, meeting his eyes. "If I back down now, these kids are going to get the message that books dealing with real issues are somehow wrong or dirty."

"Then let me help you, Margaret."

"And jeopardize your job, too? Some of these parents are very angry. You know what they'd say if they found out about us."

Ed sighed. He knew all too well. In conservative Cartersburg, where a husband and wife weren't allowed to teach in the same school, their relationship could be a problem even without the books. "Let's take Othello inside," Ed suggested, "and then I'll move the car. I want to be with you tonight, Margaret."

A little shiver ran through her and she smiled at him. "Come the back way. I'll unlock the door."

CHAPTER THREE

ALTHOUGH TEN DAYS had passed since Marty had
asked her to marry him, Suzanne hadn't told anyone
about her engagement except for Jed and Kacie and the
few people who had noticed the ring and asked. She
was still trying to get used to the idea herself. But when
Janet Sawyer, Kacie's caseworker from the Big Sisters
agency, stopped by on her way through Cartersburg,
Suzanne wanted her to know.

They picked up box lunches at Aunt Emma's Pan-
try, which had a well-deserved reputation for serving
the best food in Cartersburg, and took them to the
park, settling themselves on a bench where the warm
sun poured through an opening in the trees. "I love
October," Suzanne said as she looked at the perfect
blue sky.

"So do I," Janet agreed, "but that's not what you
wanted to tell me. Your news couldn't have anything to
do with the diamond sparkling on your finger, could
it?"

"It could." Suzanne was glad that Janet had asked
because she seemed to have trouble bringing up the
subject. "Marty and I are going to get married."

Janet took Suzanne's hand and admired the ring.
"It's really beautiful. When is the big event?"

"Sometime in the spring," Suzanne told her. "When Marty called last night, we talked about April." As she said it, April sounded so close. She peeled a crust of rye bread off her sandwich and tossed it to a squirrel that sat watching hopefully nearby. She was certainly excited—brides-to-be were always excited—but she was slightly overwhelmed, too.

"How is Kacie reacting to the news?"

Suzanne hesitated a minute before answering. "Well," she said tentatively, "I'm not sure."

"Not real enthusiastic, I gather." Janet unwrapped a large fudge brownie. "That's not unusual."

"It isn't?" She was glad for Janet's perspective. Janet had the benefit of experience with dozens of Little Sisters, and she had recently been married.

"Not unusual at all. It's perfectly normal for Kacie to be a little jealous. Has she met Marty yet?"

"No, he travels so much, and when I do see him—" Suzanne stopped. That was only partly true. She had suggested to Marty once or twice that he might like to meet Kacie, but he had told her that their time was so limited he wanted to spend it only with her. Maybe now that they were engaged, that would change.

"I understand," Janet answered. "Probably what Kacie needs most is just some reassurance that your relationship with her won't be any different."

Suzanne nodded thoughtfully. "You're probably right, Janet. Thanks."

"No problem." Janet took a large bite of her brownie. "By the way, I finally remembered to ask Kacie's dad about her name the other day. You know how we've both been curious? Well, it seems Kacie comes from the initials K.C., and is short for Katherine Caroline, a combination of her grandmothers' names. I guess Katherine Caroline was too much of a mouthful, so it got shortened to K.C., and when her first grade teacher objected to initials, she became Kacie.''

Suzanne laughed, thinking of how ingenious Jed could be in handling problems.

"How are you getting along with Kacie's dad?" Janet asked.

"He's really special," Suzanne answered softly, a smile lighting her face when she thought of Jed. "He invited me to go along with him to a meeting Thursday night to find out about a book program at school."

"How did Kacie feel about that?"

"She seemed very pleased when I said I'd go," Suzanne answered.

Janet nodded but didn't answer. "I'm sorry I have to eat and run," she said as they deposited their lunch boxes in a nearby trash can. "I have a mountain of paperwork waiting at the office."

"And I have about two dozen holsteins to service this afternoon."

Janet gulped. "You what? Never mind," she added quickly. "Don't try to explain inseminating cows. I don't think I really want to know. I guess we each have our own little niche in the total scheme of things."

Suzanne laughed. Sometimes she forgot that there were aspects of her job that seemed foreign to most people.

IT WAS ONLY NINE-THIRTY, but Kacie felt like Suzanne and her dad had been at Miss Henniker's book meeting forever. Finally a key rattled in the front door lock and she heard muffled voices in the hall. Quickly she burrowed deeper under the covers. If her dad had brought Suzanne home, she wanted them to think she was asleep. She waited until he came to check on her, lying perfectly still and breathing slowly and steadily until he was gone. Then she slipped silently out of bed and, taking her pillow with her, tiptoed into the bathroom and curled up against the heat vent so she could listen.

"Would you like a cup of coffee or a glass of wine?" she heard her dad saying, his voice coming through the vent practically as clear as if she'd been standing next to him.

"Coffee would be fine—just black," Suzanne answered.

Good, Kacie thought. *They're having coffee. That means Suzanne is going to stay for a while.*

"I'm glad Kacie is asleep," Jed observed as he searched the cabinet for a coffee filter. "Otherwise she'd want a blow-by-blow account of the meeting, and I don't want to go through it again. Once was enough, especially since nothing was decided."

Suzanne laughed. "That's for sure. Some of those parents were really up in arms. You could tell by their faces that they weren't really listening when Margaret Henniker gave her explanation. They were just waiting till the discussion period when they could have their say about taking the books off the library shelves."

"I still can't figure out why that Henniker woman is so determined to push these books," Jed continued. "Especially when the majority of the parents seem to be so against them."

"Are you really that opposed to the books, too?"

"For kids Kacie's age, yes," he answered without turning around. "I think they're inappropriate."

Upstairs at the heat vent, Kacie grimaced. She knew exactly how her dad felt about the Allison Craig books. She just hoped he hadn't made a real spectacle of himself at the meeting.

Suzanne was quiet for a few moments, thinking about the book Kacie had given her to read. Her immediate response had been that it was sensitive and rather well written. The explicit sex talk had been woven skillfully into a story about a search for values that Suzanne was pretty sure reflected what was going on in most kids' minds. "Kacie's growing up, you know," she said cautiously. "If she didn't have questions, she wouldn't be interested in the books."

"Well, maybe you're right. But whatever's bothering her, these books aren't the answer." He set two mugs down hard on the counter, like a giant punctuation mark.

"Are you concerned about Kacie?"

"I'm always concerned about Kacie, especially in the past year or so. That's one of the reasons I wanted her to have a Big Sister, a woman to provide some balance." He smiled at Suzanne. "And I think the relationship is working pretty well, don't you?"

"I certainly do." Suzanne leaned her elbows on the table and watched Jed for a few moments as he moved around the kitchen. He was a wonderful father, but he was also a very attractive man. Instead of his customary jeans and sweatshirt, he was wearing a sandy brown crew-neck sweater just about the color of his hair and a pair of dark brown slacks. His body had the trim, lean lines of a runner. She liked him and she felt com-

pletely comfortable with him. "Jed, I've been meaning to ask you if it would be all right for me to take
Kacie shopping on Sunday. I thought we might go over
to the big mall near Richmond."

Jed turned to Suzanne with a huge smile. "That's the
best idea I've heard in weeks. Shopping with a teenage
girl isn't exactly my favorite activity."

"I'd enjoy it," Suzanne said, "and I want to spend
the time with her." She hesitated, then decided it was
best to explain everything to Jed. "I know Kacie isn't
very enthusiastic about my getting married, and when
I talked to Janet the other day at lunch, she suggested
Kacie might be jealous. I want her to know that nothing is going to change between us."

Jealous! Kacie could barely choke back her outrage. She couldn't believe Suzanne had said that. *I'm
not jealous,* she wanted to shout. *I just don't want you
to marry Marty. He's a creep and he's mean!*

Jed stopped in the middle of pouring the coffee and
listened intently. "I'd have sworn I heard a noise upstairs. I'd better go check."

Disappointed, Kacie hurried into her room. She'd
blown it, and she didn't dare go back to listen any more
because if they caught her, she'd lose one of her best
sources of information. She was under the covers
breathing slowly and regularly by the time her father
arrived.

"Everything's quiet," Jed reported as he returned to
the kitchen. "Must have just been the furnace shut-
ting down."

Suzanne had heard the noise, too, and to her it had
sounded more like a muffled cough, but she accepted

Jed's explanation. "It must be hard, handling all this by yourself," she said as he joined her at the table.

"Sometimes it is," Jed admitted. "I thought everything would be easier as Kacie got older, but I was wrong. The problems just get tougher. I keep finding myself wondering what Elizabeth would have done."

"That's Kacie's mother?" Jed had never talked about her, and Suzanne knew Kacie had been only six when she died, too young to remember her well.

Jed nodded. "She was killed in an automobile accident. Kacie probably told you."

"Kacie talks about her sometimes," Suzanne answered. "Her memories seem happy."

"Except the last one. I took her with me to the hospital the day Elizabeth died." Jed stood up and walked to the counter for a spoon. "It's damn hard when somebody dies so young. Elizabeth was only twenty-seven when—" Jed stopped, embarrassed. He never talked to anyone about Elizabeth.

"You must have loved her very much," Suzanne said gently.

"Yes, I did. Very much." Jed was quiet for a minute. "But, you know, our marriage wasn't perfect. Nothing's perfect. I always wanted things to be better for her. We were still in college when we started out, and we never had any money. I went to classes and worked at a gas station in the daytime and drew cartoons at night." Jed smiled, remembering. "The few times I sold something, we blew the check on a couple of steaks and a bottle of wine, even if the utilities weren't paid yet that month. We were young and naive. I guess we didn't realize how tough it really was."

Suzanne stared at the ring on her finger. Jed and Elizabeth had obviously been very much in love, to the point where nothing mattered but each other. Suzanne had always dreamed of a marriage like that.

"I don't mean to bore you with the past," Jed said, noting her silence as he set their coffee on the table. "I see the jeweler fixed your ring. It's very pretty. Tell me about your wedding plans."

Suzanne followed his gaze to the diamond that sparkled on her finger. "We're going to be married in the spring in Richmond. When I talked to Marty last night on the phone, we pretty much settled on April. Marty wants to have a big wedding." She was slowly getting used to that idea, although she'd have been just as happy to elope. "I hope you'll have a chance to meet him soon," she added, looking at Jed. "It's hard because he travels so much that he can't be here as often as we'd like."

"That's too bad," Jed sympathized. "I hope it won't always be like that for you. Maybe once you're married and he moves here—" He realized he was making an assumption. "You are staying in Cartersburg, aren't you?"

Suzanne remembered her discussion with Marty about her changing to a group practice in Richmond. Although they hadn't talked about it again, she'd thought about it a lot. She was willing to make practically any other concession Marty asked, but not that one. She looked squarely at Jed. "I'm definitely staying right here."

"Good." Jed smiled at her. "Kacie would be very unhappy if you moved away." He looked at her eyes, soft gray and gentle, set in clear ivory skin framed by thick, wavy brown hair down to her shoulders. He was glad she was going to be around. Not that it really mattered, except, of course, to Kacie.

"You're staring at me again," Suzanne told him.

Jed's smile broadened, and he didn't look away. "I told you before—you're an artist's dream. I really would like to sketch you some day if you wouldn't be uncomfortable."

This time, Suzanne considered his proposal. The idea of Jed sketching her did make her uncomfortable, though probably not for the reasons he imagined. It was just that Jed seemed to look not *at* her but *into* her, and she'd never let anyone see inside. Yet, at the same time, there was something exciting and tremendously flattering about his suggestion. "I don't know, Jed." She knew she was stalling. "Let me think about it. Right now, show me where you work. I'd like to see your studio—that is what artists call it, a studio?"

Jed laughed, standing up. "That's stretching it. In my case, it's a converted sun porch."

Suzanne was enchanted with Jed's studio. The sun porch was small, but, when Jed turned on the outdoor floodlights, a broad expanse of windows opened the room to a yard surrounded by oak trees. Jed's drawing table was near the front of the room, facing the windows. Behind it were a beaten up leather couch and two mismatched chairs set randomly around an old trunk that was used as a coffee table.

Suzanne felt Jed behind her, his hand on the small of her back, lightly guiding her inside. He was no closer to her than he had been before, but he felt closer. She smelled his after-shave ever so faintly and felt a warmth where he was touching her. She sensed suddenly that he was becoming a good friend, and she realized how much she needed someone in Cartersburg that she could talk to.

"This is it," he said, taking his hand away. "Not exactly a studio as you call it, but I'm happy here."

Suzanne walked across to the drawing table, which was littered with rough sketches and clippings representing unfinished ideas Jed was working on. He stood back and watched her, surprised that he didn't feel invaded by her presence. Except for Kacie, no one ever went into "Daddy's room," as Kacie had christened it long ago.

"It's a marvelous place to work." Suzanne turned toward the window, her eyes sparkling, and looked high into the spreading limbs of the oak tree. "That must be the squirrel's nest that was in 'Out on a Limb' a few weeks ago. And the tire swing. That's where the little girl goes when she's mad."

"You must read the strip regularly."

"I read it every day."

"I'm surprised it interests you," he said. "'Out on a Limb' is about the life of a single parent." Jed's eyes were on her, studying her.

Suzanne looked at him curiously, but his expression told her the remark was genuine. "'Out on a Limb' is funny whether you're a single parent or not. And besides being funny, it's poignant." She paused, trying to phrase the question that had been on her mind for some time. "Just one thing I've wondered about—probably everyone asks you this. Does it all come from your experiences?"

"The strip isn't really autobiographical, but I can't deny that my experiences with Kacie sometimes generate ideas."

Suzanne already knew that, because Kacie had complained more than once that the comic strip was an invasion of her privacy. But apparently she was either supersensitive or Jed didn't realize how much his work reflected his daughter. "How did you come up with the title?" Suzanne asked.

"Actually, I was sitting at my drawing table one day, staring at that tree right over there." Jed pointed to a tall oak near the house. "Suddenly I spotted Kacie, who was only seven years old at the time, almost hidden in the leaves. Somehow she had managed to climb the tree and get all the way out on the end of that crooked branch. She was terrified and hanging on for dear life. I realized that was exactly how I felt with Elizabeth gone. I was out on a limb all alone, and hanging on any way I could. So, after I retrieved Kacie, I started sketching and the strip just sort of evolved."

"But you still say it's not autobiographical?"

Jed smiled. "Not really. I won't say I don't identify with Morgan, the man in the strip—"

Suzanne nodded. She knew very well who Morgan was.

"—and sometimes his daughter, Jennifer, has experiences similar to Kacie's. But that's just because some situations are universal. If I do it well, lots of readers see themselves."

"That could be why it's so popular," Suzanne commented. She looked again at the drawing table, and at the room, and back at Jed. She was finally ready to answer his question. "I guess it would be all right if you wanted to sketch me," she said hesitantly. "I'm flattered that you'd want to."

Jed was surprised and pleased. "There's something very special about you Suzanne," he told her. "I don't know if I can capture it, but I'd like to try."

His words whirled in Suzanne's mind long after he took her home. He was unlike any man she'd known before, attractive not only physically but in a far deeper sense. He had the makings of a very good friend. She wondered if he and Marty would like each other. She thought about that for quite a while, hoping they, too, might become friends, but knowing deep inside that they were two very different types of men and, like oil and water, they probably wouldn't mix.

WHEN SUZANNE TOOK KACIE shopping the next Sunday, she didn't have to wait long to find out why her Little Sister had been so anxious to make the trip. The big mall near Richmond was crowded with shoppers, some of them trying to get a head start on Christmas, some of them passing a leisurely afternoon. But Kacie paid little attention. She headed straight for Mabley's Department Store, where she surveyed the racks of filmy lingerie. Then she looked at Suzanne. "This sure is easier with you than with my dad."

"There are some things men have difficulty relating to," Suzanne said diplomatically.

"You're not kidding." Kacie fingered a black lace teddy curiously. "When Dad brought me to buy my first bra, he kept looking around and shuffling his feet a lot. Then he turned me over to a big, fat saleslady and said he had to go buy some drawing pencils."

Suzanne had no trouble imagining the scene. Although Kacie had probably been secretly excited, she no doubt had also been embarrassed and apprehensive. And for Jed it must have been even worse. Men always had trouble with their daughters' developing shapes, and being forced to confront a lingerie department... No wonder he had been desperate to get away. "At least your dad found a saleslady so you had a woman to help you," Suzanne said in Jed's defense.

"Yeah. Big help she was." Kacie checked out a rack of silk bikini panties as they walked toward the bras. "That saleslady looked at my chest like she could see right through my clothes and said I obviously needed their smallest size. Then she came right into the dressing room and stared at me while I tried the bras on. I felt like I was deformed or something."

Suzanne was careful not to smile. "Is that why you like to wear big shirts, so your shape doesn't show?"

For a moment Kacie looked surprised, then she shrugged. "I suppose. But if you don't, some of the boys think it's really funny to snap your strap. I hate that." She stopped and stared at Suzanne. "You know, I never told anybody that before."

Suzanne slipped an arm around her shoulder. "It's okay, Kacie. I understand."

"Yeah."

"Now, let's see if we can find a bra you really like." Bypassing two racks of shiny satin bras with wires, Suzanne spotted a display on the back wall that appeared much more appropriate.

"None of the ones you can see through," Kacie cautioned.

"Gym class, right?"

Kacie nodded.

Things didn't change. Suzanne took down a cotton knit bra with tiny picot edging along the top. "This one closes in front. You might like that." She handed it to Kacie.

"That means I could get it fastened on the first try every time." Kacie examined it, obviously intrigued. After glancing over her shoulder to make sure there was no one around that she knew, she went a step closer to the display. "They come in colors. That saleslady said my kind only came in white. These are pretty."

"Very pretty," Suzanne agreed. "And they come with matching panties."

"Really? Could I have those, too?"

"Of course. Matched lingerie is fun." She wondered briefly what Jed would think, and then decided it didn't matter. Kacie should enjoy becoming a woman.

Looking happier than she had all day, Kacie disappeared into the dressing room with a large handful of underwear in several sizes. Suzanne waited discreetly outside.

"Do you have to look at them?" Kacie's muffled voice asked through the door.

"Not unless you want me to," Suzanne answered. "They shouldn't be loose and baggy, but don't get them too tight because they'll shrink a little in the wash."

After a few minutes, the door tentatively opened a crack. "I think this is right. What do you think?"

Suzanne realized what an enormous step Kacie had taken by asking her to look. After a quick glance, she assured Kacie that she had chosen well, and bought her four matched sets in pink, light blue, yellow and mint green.

Kacie looked enormously pleased with herself. "My dad said I should just keep getting the same kind the lady picked out for me. I'll bet he doesn't even know about these."

Suzanne grinned. She wasn't so sure.

They ate lunch at a salad bar with Kacie doing most of the talking and Suzanne most of the listening. Suzanne could see why Jed might be slightly overwhelmed sometimes. Even a simple problem like getting Kacie a bra could take on major proportions for Jed and Kacie. However old-fashioned it might sound, some things were handled better by a woman. When she'd phoned Janet to tell her how anxious Kacie seemed to be to go on their impending shopping trip, she'd heard a chuckle on the other end of the line. "I'll bet Kacie's father is at least as happy about it as Kacie," she had observed.

"Is there anywhere else you'd like to go?" Suzanne asked Kacie as they left the restaurant.

"Let's check out the bookstore." Still clutching the lingerie bag, she turned toward the far end of the mall. "Allison Craig has a new book out, and Miss Henniker doesn't have the library copies yet." She glanced at Suzanne. "Did you really like the book I gave you?"

Suzanne already had told Kacie how much she liked it, but Kacie obviously wanted to hear it again. "I think the author has lots of insight into people, and she certainly tells a good story."

Kacie nodded with satisfaction. "Yeah. She tells it like it is. Writers don't do that very much, especially in kids' books. They always write what they think we ought to read.''

They located the book quickly, in a stand-up display near the front of the store. Both of them stopped as they recognized Margaret Henniker and Ed Arnold standing to one side of the display, engaged in what was obviously a very serious discussion. Margaret had three copies of the new book in one hand. Her other hand was resting gently on Ed's arm. What struck Suzanne was the coincidence of seeing them together again. When Ed had brought Margaret to pick up Othello at the clinic, they'd explained that her car battery was dead. But that had been three weeks ago. Maybe there was something more going on.

Kacie recognized the body language immediately. She'd seen it before. She remembered Mr. Arnold kissing Miss Henniker and what Billy had said about them probably having sex. Kacie had an overwhelming desire to leave quickly before they saw her. But that would mean telling Suzanne why. Before she could make any decision, Mr. Arnold turned around.

''Why, Margaret, look who's here,'' he said in a rather loud voice.

Margaret turned, her hand moving instantly away from Ed's arm. ''Kacie, Suzanne, what a surprise.''

Kacie decided that was an understatement if she'd ever heard one.

''How nice to see you,'' Suzanne answered, starting toward them. ''How is Othello doing?''

''Just fine. As obstinate as ever,'' Margaret answered with a chuckle.

Kacie was always fascinated by how adults made small talk. Whatever the occasion, they always seemed to be able to talk about something else.

"And how are you, Kacie?" Margaret asked. "I see you've been doing some shopping."

Kacie looked at the bag self-consciously. She wasn't about to discuss her new bras with Miss Henniker and Mr. Arnold. "Actually we came in to buy Allison Craig's new book," she answered quickly.

"Same reason I'm here," Margaret said. "I thought I'd put a few copies on the school library shelves so we wouldn't have to wait for the shipment to come in."

"That's great, but I still want my own copy," Kacie replied.

Ed wished them luck with their shopping, and he and Margaret walked toward the cashier. Suzanne noticed that they were standing much farther apart than they had been initially and wondered whether Kacie had noticed the same thing. She didn't want to give her Little Sister any ideas she didn't already have. "What a coincidence running into Mr. Arnold and Miss Henniker," she said casually.

"Yeah." Again, Kacie was tempted to tell Suzanne what she knew about them. She was sure she could trust Suzanne. But she and Billy had agreed. "Really a coincidence," she muttered, picking up one of the books.

As they left the store, Kacie stuffed the sack with the lingerie into the bag with the book. "I'm really glad I came with you," she told Suzanne. "Dad would never have let me buy the book."

Suzanne felt suddenly uncomfortable. She didn't want to challenge Jed's authority. He was, after all,

Kacie's father. At the same time, she knew that Kacie would read the book whether or not she was allowed to buy it. After all, they'd just watched Margaret Henniker buy three library copies. Suzanne made her choice quickly. "Have you ever really discussed these books with your dad, Kacie?"

"He doesn't discuss; he lectures."

"Try again," Suzanne advised, making a mental note that she would talk to Jed, too.

CHAPTER FOUR

JED WAS STILL on Suzanne's mind when she and Kacie walked past the bridal shop. Of course Jed would come to the wedding—he had become a friend in addition to being the father of her Little Sister. She paused, looking into the window of the bridal shop. "Come on, Kacie," she said on a whim. "Let's go look at wedding gowns."

Reluctantly Kacie followed Suzanne into the shop. She had often walked by and gazed in awe at the satin and lace creations in the window and wished she could go inside and take a closer look. But now she didn't want any part of it. She didn't want Suzanne to marry Marty. He was mean and he would make her unhappy. And not only that, he wanted Suzanne to leave Cartersburg. She had heard him say so that night in the clinic.

"Maybe we should leave now," Kacie suggested tentatively as she caught up with Suzanne just inside the door. "We were going to go back and see Lucky...remember?"

Suzanne checked her watch. "We've got plenty of time, and I'd love to have you look at wedding gowns with me. You don't mind, do you, Kacie?"

Kacie swallowed hard. What could she say? Her Big Sister had helped her pick out bras, bought her lunch and gone with her to buy a book. Now Suzanne was asking her to do something special, something she would have loved under other circumstances. "No, of course not. It would be nice to look at wedding gowns."

Suzanne couldn't quite figure out Kacie's reaction. Any thirteen-year-old girl should be thrilled to go into a bridal shop, but she sensed no enthusiasm at all in Kacie. Maybe she was just anxious to see the puppy. They wouldn't stay too long, Suzanne decided, but she did want Kacie's company.

Several other customers were in the shop, mostly young women with their mothers. A striking blonde stood on a raised platform at the far end of the display area with what appeared to be three sisters and a mother fluttering around her, examining a heavily beaded, low-cut satin gown with a long, swirled train. Kacie stared at the dress. "Are you going to get one like that?" she asked.

"Not exactly." Suzanne turned to the display of white gowns that stretched the entire length of the shop. "I'd rather have something more traditional." As she searched through the dresses, she found herself moving quickly past the shiny satin ones with heavy beading and plunging necklines and pausing at the more classic styles with long sleeves and simple lines. She glanced at the blonde and wondered how Marty would feel about her taste.

"Are you going to buy a dress today?" Kacie asked from behind her.

"No, I'm just looking." She held out a gown with delicate lace sleeves and a sweetheart neckline. "How do you like this one?"

Kacie shrugged. "It's okay, I guess."

Suzanne turned toward her Little Sister. "You really don't want to be here, do you?"

"Sure, it's fine." Kacie's face reddened.

"No, it's not. Tell me the truth, Kacie." Suzanne waited patiently.

"It's just..." Kacie shifted uncomfortably. "Are you really sure you want to marry him?"

Suzanne turned away from the dresses and studied Kacie carefully. "What makes you ask that?"

Kacie shuffled. "I don't know," she mumbled. "I just wondered. I mean—how can you really be sure?"

"Well..." Suzanne tried to be honest. "I guess I'm as sure as anyone ever is, Kacie. Marty is a nice man. I'm anxious for you to meet him."

Kacie didn't answer. As far as she was concerned, Marty was a jerk.

"Let's give up this project for today." Suzanne slipped her arm around Kacie's shoulder. "Why don't we get an ice-cream cone and go see how Lucky is doing?"

Kacie brightened considerably. "All right!" She headed quickly for the door before Suzanne could change her mind.

On the way to the clinic Suzanne was quiet, lost in thought. Kacie decided it was as good a time as any to ask the question that had been on her mind for more than a week. "Suzanne, do you think Lucky is ready to go home?"

"I sure do. He's walking fine without his cast." Suzanne smiled. "But how about your dad, Kacie? Is he ready?"

Kacie didn't look at her. "I think so."

"You have discussed this with him?"

"Yeah, we've talked about it," Kacie answered carefully. No need to mention that Jed had said they would have to discuss it further. She was certain that once Lucky was there her dad wouldn't send him away. "Can I take him today?"

"Well, if you're sure it's okay with your dad," Suzanne told her, as the pickup rattled up the gravel driveway.

"Yippee!" Kacie yelled, leaping out and running toward the clinic.

As soon as he was out of his cage, Lucky was all over Kacie, jumping on her then running in circles and bounding across the clinic. From the way he acted, he might never have been injured. "I think he's grown." Kacie dropped to her knees and grabbed him, dodging as he wiggled closer to lick her face.

As Suzanne watched the two of them, she bent to pet Lady who sat placidly beside her. She remembered the boundless love she and Lady had shared when she wasn't much older than Kacie and thought of how the bond between them had deepened through the years. She hoped the same love and trust would grow between Kacie and the puppy. "He's going to be a good-size dog," Suzanne predicted. "He'll need a lot of exercise and some training very soon."

"I'll start tomorrow," Kacie promised.

Suzanne gave Kacie a collar and leash for Lucky, but when they tried to put the collar on him, he backed away, pulling out of it. He grabbed the leash in his teeth, jerked it away from Kacie and raced around the clinic shaking it wildly. "No, no, Lucky," Kacie shouted, running after him.

"Remember, be calm and firm when you're work-ing with him," Suzanne said with a chuckle. No two words could have been farther from describing Kacie at that moment.

Once they got Lucky into the front of the truck, he sat with his nose pressed against the window watching the world whip by, and by the time they arrived at Ka-cie's house he was relatively subdued. He scurried around the yard sniffing at the piles of leaves.

Suzanne glanced up to find Jed standing on the porch, holding a rake. How handsome he looked in the fading sunlight of the warm autumn afternoon! His well-worn jeans fit snugly over lean, trim hips, and the remnants of a summer suntan were still apparent against his white polo shirt. He was watching Kacie and Lucky, his expression both amused and perplexed un-til he turned toward Suzanne. Their eyes met and held, and for several moments she couldn't look away. Something about him changed when he saw her, a dif-ference so subtle she couldn't explain it, but it made her heartbeat quicken, and she could feel the sun burning her cheeks. He took a step toward her, and she felt as though no one was there except the two of them.

Suddenly Lucky spotted a cat and bolted across the yard barking, with Kacie in hot pursuit. Suzanne came back to reality with the sense of having been awak-ened from a dream. Then they were all off after Lucky. When they finally caught him, he had run the hapless cat up a tree and was leaping enthusiastically against the tree trunk, barking all the while.

"Down, Lucky, down," Kacie commanded, and Lucky jumped higher.

"He certainly does seem to have recovered completely," Jed noted as Kacie wrapped both arms around the wriggling puppy and hauled him home. "I guess the next question is what to do with him."

"But Kacie said—" Suzanne stopped. What Kacie had said was that she and her father had discussed Lucky. "I got the impression from Kacie that you'd said it was all right to adopt Lucky."

Jed raised his eyebrows and looked at Kacie. "Just where did Suzanne get the impression we'd decided to keep the dog?"

"But, Dad, we discussed it, remember?" Kacie's eyes were wide and innocent. "We talked about how we rescued him and so we're responsible for him. And there isn't any other place for him to go."

Jed's face was sober as he faced his daughter. "A dog is a big responsibility, Kacie. He needs to be fed and brushed and housebroken and exercised regularly. And he can't be allowed to terrorize the neighbor's cat."

"I know all that, Dad, and I'll take care of it. I promise." She knelt beside Lucky, who was lying with his head on his paws, apparently tired out from his adventures. "I couldn't stand it if Lucky went to someone else now."

Jed appeared to be wavering, although Suzanne suspected he had accepted the inevitable from the beginning and was simply drawing the lines of responsibility. As Jed looked at the dog, Lucky crouched and wagged his tail. Suzanne tried hard not to smile. The puppy couldn't have managed to look any more appealing if he had understood what they were saying.

"But, Kacie, who's going to watch Lucky during the day when you're in school?" Jed questioned.

"No problem, Dad. He can stay in the backyard and we can build him a doghouse so if it rains he can go inside."

Jed stuffed his hands in his pockets and allowed himself a smile. "Sounds like you've thought of everything, Kacie."

"Then I can keep him?" Kacie leaped to her feet. "He's really mine?"

"He's really yours."

Kacie let out a loud whoop and, catching her excitement, Lucky bounded around her in circles, alternately chasing his tail and the leash that trailed behind him.

"Congratulations to both of you." Suzanne hugged Kacie then turned to Jed and felt suddenly awkward when she realized she'd been about to hug him, too. Instead she touched his arm and he covered her hand with his.

"Thanks, Suzanne," he said quietly, "thanks for everything."

She understood that he wasn't talking only about the puppy but about the way their lives—hers and Kacie's and his—had blended over the months since she'd become Kacie's Big Sister. The bonds of friendship had strengthened and grown into the comfortable feelings people have about those who are family or almost family. As she stood there with him holding her hand, she felt very close to him. A giddy happiness swept through her, and she decided it must be an outgrowth of Kacie's delight with the puppy, who was barking his distinctive bark as he romped around the yard.

"I'd just lit the grill when you came. I decided such a rare thing as a beautiful, sunny day in November was too good to pass up." Jed released her hand. "Why don't you join us for hamburgers and we'll all celebrate the new addition to the family?"

Suzanne hesitated. Marty often came on Sunday evenings. Of course he hadn't mentioned it this week because he'd been out of town, and the chances of him getting back were extremely slim. Almost nonexistent, she decided. "I'd love to stay. What can I do to help?"

Jed put her to work making a salad while he started the hamburgers, and Kacie carried milk and potato chips and assorted condiments to the picnic table in the backyard. Suzanne noticed that there was exactly enough of everything set out for three. Maybe dinner hadn't been quite so spur-of-the-moment as it appeared.

At Suzanne's suggestion, Kacie got the bag of puppy chow they'd brought and fed Lucky so he wouldn't go wild when he smelled the hamburgers. "You'll be happier, and so will he, if you don't feed him from the table," she told Kacie as they pulled the benches up to the picnic table.

"Why?" Kacie asked. "I think dogs are cute when they sit up and beg."

"In a few months, if this dog sits up to beg, he'll have his nose almost on the table," Suzanne warned. "You also shouldn't take him to bed with you. In the long run, you'll both be happier if he has a place of his own to sleep."

"I suppose." Kacie took a big bite of her hamburger. She hated it when Suzanne sounded like an adult. As soon as she finished dinner, Kacie stood up.

"I want to take Lucky over to Billy's," she announced.

"Take your dishes inside first," Jed reminded her. "And keep a tight hold on Lucky. You don't want him to get away again."

With Kacie gone, the only sounds were the two squirrels chattering in the nearby oak tree. Suzanne helped Jed take the rest of the dishes to the kitchen, feeling as comfortable with him as though the simple, everyday tasks were something they had done together many times. They took mugs of coffee outside and sat in two lawn chairs at the edge of the patio, watching the darkness gather. Suzanne had a nagging feeling that she ought to go home, but she pushed it away because there was no real reason to leave and she was so happy where she was.

"I sure hope things work out with Lucky," Jed mused, taking a sip of his coffee. "I don't know when I've seen Kacie so excited."

Suzanne shifted in her chair and curled one foot under her. "This is an exciting time for her, Jed. She's growing up."

"You're telling me." He shook his head. "Speaking of growing up, how did the shopping go?"

"We found some very pretty lingerie—"

Jed groaned.

"Not sexy, just pretty," Suzanne assured him with a laugh. "And she bought Allison Craig's new book."

For several moments Jed didn't answer. Suzanne waited, knowing how he felt about the books and hoping he wasn't angry. Finally she added, "We ran into Ed Arnold and Margaret Henniker buying some copies for the school library."

"I know, and you're going to tell me Kacie might as well have the book because she's going to get it from the library and read it anyway."

"Something like that." She sat forward, deciding to meet the issue head on. "Have you ever read one of those books all the way through?"

"No," Jed admitted. "But I've flipped through a few of them and found some sex scenes that kids this age don't need."

"Try reading one from beginning to end and see what you think."

Jed was quiet again, then he looked directly at Suzanne, his expression sober. "You're right. I've been against censorship for years, and now, when it involves my daughter, I suddenly move to the other side." His eyes asked for understanding. "Kacie is all I have."

Suzanne wanted to reach out to him, touch him, drawn by the depth of his emotion. She could feel the overwhelming love that bound him to Kacie and at the same time she sensed his loneliness.

"In some ways I envy you, Suzanne." He looked at the ring on her finger. "Beginning a marriage and the love and sharing that goes with it is the best part of life. As time goes on and you grow closer and closer to each other, it keeps getting better."

Now it was Suzanne's turn to be quiet. The chattering of the squirrels seemed louder as she sat there, thinking about Marty and the commitment they were about to make to each other. An uneasiness settled over her, and slowly her eyes met Jed's. "I hope so," she said softly, "and now I think it's time for me to go home."

WHEN SUZANNE PULLED UP the gravel drive to her house, Marty's Firebird loomed before her. "No," she whispered. She'd gambled and lost. She glanced at herself in the rearview mirror, but could see little in the darkness inside the truck. Yet she knew without looking that she wore no makeup, her hair was wild from a day outdoors, and her clothes definitely showed the effects of playing with a puppy. And worst of all, she hadn't been home when Marty came.

She jumped out of the truck and hurried toward the house. Marty had been sitting on the porch steps, but he stood up as she approached. Even from a distance, she could tell he wasn't pleased. "I'm sorry, Marty," she apologized. "I didn't expect you."

"Obviously not." His tone was cool and controlled, the voice of someone who didn't like to be kept waiting.

"I thought you were still out of town." Her first impulse had been to go to him and hug him and tell him how glad she was to see him, but now she didn't want to do that. He seemed distant, a study in controlled anger. Everything about him made her want to stay away.

"You apparently aren't here much when I am gone. What was it this time? Another emergency?"

Suzanne shook her head. "No, not tonight. Actually, I was with Kacie—you know, my Little Sister— and her dad getting her new puppy settled." Suzanne brushed some stray strands of hair out of her face with the back of her hand. "That puppy sure is going to be a handful."

"You spent the day with her father?"

Even in the moonlight, Suzanne could see Marty's expression change. Tiny lines appeared around his eyes, and his lips were set in a straight line. He obviously had the wrong impression. "I was with Jed and Kacie and Lucky," she added quickly.

"You're engaged to me now, Suzanne." He took a step toward her. "We're going to be married in a few months. I don't want you spending your time with other men."

"But Marty, Jed is just a friend and Kacie—"

"That's enough."

His voice was harsher than she'd ever heard it. She'd made him very angry, and inside she couldn't help but feel guilty. Marty did come on Sundays whenever he could, and she had thought about that when she stayed at Jed and Kacie's, but she really had believed Marty was still out of town. "I'm sorry, Marty," she said softly.

He stared at her for a moment, then his face relaxed and his mouth curved into a smile. "That's better. Now, how about a late dinner?"

"Why don't I fix you some scrambled eggs or maybe a grilled cheese sandwich?"

Marty laughed. "That's not dinner. Hurry up and get dressed and we'll go out."

She started to tell him she'd already had a hamburger, then decided not to. They didn't have much time together, and he'd be so pleased if she went. By the time they drove to wherever they were going and were served, she'd be able to eat something. "I'll only be a few minutes. Come on in." Suzanne quickly fed Lady and let her out while Marty settled himself in the living room with a glass of wine.

"Wear your black dress," he called after Suzanne as she went to the bedroom to get dressed. "I like the way you look in black."

Suzanne showered and with shaking hands managed to apply her makeup and blow dry her hair softly around her face the way Marty liked it, all in record time. Then she slipped into the black dress he had requested. When she appeared in the living room, he took her in his arms and kissed her. "You're beautiful," he said, holding her at arm's length. "You should always look like this."

He took her to an intimate Italian restaurant about half an hour from Cartersburg. Over dinner, which for Suzanne consisted of a cup of soup and a salad that she ate as much of as she could, they talked more about the wedding and decided on April third as a firm date. "We'll have to talk about what you're going to do about your practice and where we're going to live," he said as they drank a brandy after dinner.

"Marty, I've already told you, I'm going to keep my clinic in Cartersburg. We talked about that and—"

"Shh." He patted her hand. "Not tonight. We don't have to make any decisions tonight. We have a whole lifetime ahead of us."

When he had said that before, Suzanne had felt a flutter of anticipation, but this time the prospect made her slightly uneasy. Changes were always a part of blending two lives into one, but she wondered if she would be the one making most of the changes. She was afraid that the issue of where her clinic was located was only one of the problems she would have to face.

She was quiet and thoughtful during the drive home, and although Marty held her hand, he didn't push her to talk. After he pulled the car into the driveway and cut off the engine he took her into his arms. But when his lips touched hers she felt little of the surging desire she expected.

"Come on, sweetheart, relax." His breath was hot against her cheek, and he pulled her close before he kissed her again.

She responded automatically, parting her lips slightly and pressing against him as she kissed him back. Immediately his kiss deepened and he began to probe the soft recesses of her mouth. She should feel something, she thought. Some desire. At least a tiny glimmer. After all, she was going to marry this man. Then his hand grazed the side of her breast, and her body stiffened. Now that they were engaged, he would expect to go to bed with her. Always before she had been able to avoid the confrontation, but now...

Marty held her tight and groaned. His hand caressed her sensuously. "Why don't you invite me in to spend the night?" he whispered hoarsely.

Suzanne froze in his arms. "I'm not ready for that yet, Marty."

"We're engaged now, sweetheart. We're going to be married in only a few months. Don't you think it's time?" He trailed a line of kisses down the side of her neck.

Marty was right. When two people were planning to be married, sex was usually a part of their relationship. But she couldn't. She just couldn't. And she didn't understand why. "I'd really like to wait," she began.

"Wait? There's no need to wait any longer, Suzanne," he said reasonably. "If you love me—"

"Of course I love you. It isn't that," she answered quickly.

"Then what is it?" His face darkened and his eyes narrowed as he looked at her intently. "Are you a virgin, Suzanne?" he asked bluntly.

Startled by his frank question, she pulled away. "No—no, I'm not," she stammered. "I had a very long relationship with a man while I was in vet school. We were planning to be married, but then one day I came home and he was gone. He had just packed and left. He didn't leave a note or anything. My whole future was gone. I had been so sure—" Suddenly an immense feeling of relief swept over her. Of course, that was the problem. She was afraid. That was it. Afraid because of what had happened before. That was why she couldn't relax with Marty. "I've never told you all this, but do you understand now, Marty? I want to wait until we're married to make love. It's terribly important to me."

"Don't you trust me?" Marty's eyes glittered at her.

"No, it's not that," she replied hesitantly.

"Then what is it, Suzanne?" He pounded his fist on the dashboard. "You're going to marry me, dammit!"

"Marty—" Alarmed by his anger, Suzanne laid her hand on his arm and felt his hard, tense muscles. "Please understand, Marty," she pleaded. "Waiting is important to me."

"All right, Suzanne." He jerked his arm away from her. "We'll wait until after the wedding. But I'm telling you this, and you'd better remember it." His voice carried an overtone of threat. "Once I get you alone on our honeymoon I'm never going to let you out of bed."

Suzanne laughed nervously. "Is that a promise?" She hoped she sounded carefree and eager. She kissed him lightly and eased toward the car door. "You'll call tomorrow?"

"Yeah, I'll call." He jammed the key into the ignition and gunned the motor.

"Good night, Marty," she said as she climbed out of the car. She didn't wait for his answer.

Long into the night Suzanne sat wide awake on the bedroom floor, her long flannel nightgown wrapped around her legs and Lady's head in her lap. "I wish I could make Marty understand." Gently she stroked the dog's ears. But how could she, when she didn't understand herself. "I'm going to get married, old girl," she told Lady, who cocked her ears at the sound of Suzanne's voice. Suzanne listened carefully to her own words then said them again. "Married. I'm going to get married." It sounded so final. "I guess everybody gets the jitters when they make a decision this big." Lady whimpered softly. "And everybody runs into problems. We'll work it all out." But even as she said it, some part of her deep inside wasn't quite sure. She should want more than anything to make love with the man she was going to marry, so much that nothing could get in the way. But she didn't feel like that at all.

FROM THE WAY the women walked into the school library on Monday afternoon, Kacie knew they meant trouble. Billy Hankins's mother was a step ahead, followed by Mrs. Wilkes and a woman in a purple skirt Kacie didn't know. Billy would be mad as anything when he found out his mother had come to school.

Kacie took a book off the shelf and opened it, waiting to see what would happen.

The three women headed directly for the librarian's desk where Margaret Henniker had been gathering books into a needlepoint bag, obviously preparing to leave for the day.

"Miss Henniker," Mrs. Hankins said as they approached. Kacie thought it sounded more like a command than a greeting.

"Why, Mrs. Hankins." Miss Henniker seemed to draw herself up to her full height as she turned to face the women. "How nice of you to come by. Is there something special I can do for you?"

Mrs. Hankins got right down to business. "The PTA has discussed this matter at length and we have contacted Ed Arnold and we don't seem to be getting any response. Joan and Trudy and I decided it is time to confront the problem head on."

"What problem?" Miss Henniker removed the half glasses she wore for reading and calmly studied her visitors. Except for Mrs. Hankins, they seemed uncomfortable. Kacie tried not to snicker. Miss Henniker was real good at the innocent act.

"Miss Henniker, of course you are aware of the growing opposition to this series of books by Allison Craig. We were all at your meeting." Mrs. Hankins looked very determined.

Miss Henniker smiled. "That series has generated some lively discussion among both students and parents, and it certainly has increased the students' interest in reading."

Score one for Miss Henniker, Kacie thought.

"It is the position of the PTA that the material is totally inappropriate for seventh- and eighth-grade children." Mrs. Hankins looked at her companions, who nodded agreement. "We should be teaching values at this age, and books that promote premarital sex and sanction divorce aren't doing it."

"Whose values should we be teaching?" Miss Henniker asked. "Your values, my values?"

Kacie took a step closer. She wanted to be able to report the whole conversation to Billy word for word.

"We are trying to preserve the values generally held in the community," Mrs. Wilkes said, "and we're not doing that by promoting premarital sex among thirteen-year-olds."

"How many of these books have you read?" Miss Henniker asked her.

"Enough to form an opinion."

"Maybe if you read them a bit more thoroughly, you might change your opinion. They most definitely do not promote premarital sex."

"That's the way I read it," Mrs. Hankins interrupted.

"Then I suspect you didn't read the entire book."

"And you're sure the children have?"

"Absolutely." Miss Henniker grinned. "They can't put them down." She leaned her hands on her desk and turned serious. "These books capture the students because they confront the issues they're concerned about. Kids are bombarded with confusing messages on television, in videos, in advertising—practically everywhere they turn. Parents lecture them on morality—their friends dare them to try things. This series of books challenges them to think for themselves by dealing with these issues on their terms.''

Way to go, Miss Henniker. Kacie almost said the words out loud.

But then the third woman spoke in a quiet voice. ''You argue very convincingly, Miss Henniker, but nothing you say changes the material in these books or the age of the children we're dealing with. The potential problems outweigh the benefits. These books need to be removed from the shelves.''

''That sums it up, Trudy,'' Mrs. Hankins said to the woman. She turned toward Miss Henniker. ''We'll go now. We simply want to be certain you understand our position.''

The three of them left, and Kacie wished there were some way for her to leave, too. Miss Henniker looked so unhappy that Kacie was afraid she might cry. She sat at the librarian's desk and rested her head in her hands. When more than a minute passed and she didn't look up, Kacie turned and tiptoed out of the library.

CHAPTER FIVE

OTHELLO WAS WAITING on the front steps when Margaret got home, meowing indignantly as he often did when Ed was around. The door opened before Margaret touched the knob. Othello shot past her, and as soon as she stepped inside, Ed took her in his arms.

"Margaret, where were you? I was getting worried."

She collapsed against his shoulder, holding him and finding comfort in his strength. "The battle lines are drawn," she said softly. "The war is about to begin."

They made tea and took it upstairs to Margaret's bedroom, a large, bright room, which she had decorated in ivory and Wedgwood blue when she had first begun to dream of having Ed stay overnight with her. As they sat in two wing chairs across from the queen-size bed with its antique lace coverlet, Margaret relayed the conversation in the library. "I couldn't get through to those women at all," she said sadly. "I wanted them to understand that we can't impose values on children by lecturing them, but if we give them a forum to discuss these issues and stimulate them intellectually..." Margaret shook her head. "I don't know, Ed. It all seems so hopeless."

"Don't talk that way, Margaret." He reached over and squeezed her hand. "I know how much this means to you."

"It means even more to those kids. I wonder if Sue Hankins even knows that son of hers. If she could have heard Billy telling his buddies jokes that made my hair curl, maybe she'd realize he needs some direction. I wonder if she realizes that Billy is one of the most enthusiastic participants in the book discussions."

Ed grimaced. "Knowing Sue Hankins, she'd probably say the discussions were responsible for the dirty jokes. If you hadn't put those ideas in his head, he'd never even be thinking about such things."

"You don't believe that, do you, Ed?"

He stood up and pulled her to her feet, holding her against him. "Come now, Margaret, what do you think? Billy Hankins is an adolescent with all his hormones churning. He's going to have sex on his mind whether his mother likes it or not." Ed bent and kissed her on the neck. "Which isn't all bad," he added, "if he were a little older."

Margaret felt his hand moving across her back, and the familiar little shiver ran through her. "A lot older," she murmured. And then he kissed her, and for the next hour neither of them thought at all about books or Billy Hankins or the PTA.

KACIE SAT IN THE CENTER of the tree house impatiently twirling a frayed piece of rope. Billy was late. She wouldn't have waited for him, except that she wanted to tell him what his mother had said to Miss Henniker. And what she'd heard when she walked past the women as they were standing beside Mrs. Hankins's car. That had bothered her even more.

The familiar whippoorwill whistle sounded through the trees long before she could see Billy. She answered it, like always, so he'd know she was there. He came running up the path, swung onto the rope ladder and hoisted himself onto the tree-house platform. "Boy, is my mother in a rotten mood this afternoon," he announced as he flopped down beside Kacie. "I thought I'd never get out of the house."

"Do you know where she was today?" Kacie asked.

"Yeah, bugging me."

"Before that she was at school bugging Miss Henniker."

Billy's cheeks flushed and he stared at Kacie. "What do you mean?"

"She and Mrs. Wilkes and some other lady showed up in the library to demand that Miss Henniker get rid of the Allison Craig books."

"How do you know?"

"I was there."

"You're sure it was my mother?"

"Real sure. She was the ringleader."

Billy picked up the length of rope and smacked it against the tree trunk as Kacie related in detail what his mother had said. "And then I walked past them outside and I heard your mother say if something—I couldn't hear that part—then 'she would have to go.' I think she meant Miss Henniker."

Billy turned around. "You mean fire Miss Henniker?"

"That's all I heard, but that's what it sounded like."

"They can't do that. That's stupid."

"I don't know, Billy. They're really mad. And isn't Mrs. Wilkes the president of the PTA?"

Billy shrugged. "How would I know?"

"So what are we going to do?"

"What do you mean, what are *we* going to do? There's nothing we can do." Billy stared sullenly at his feet.

Kacie was silent for a moment. Billy was obviously too mad to have any ideas. "Do you think we should tell Miss Henniker?"

"Tell her what? You aren't even sure what you heard."

"Maybe you could talk to your mother," Kacie suggested.

"Are you kidding? She's so hung up on her own ideas she can't hear anything else. I don't have anything to say to her anyway."

"How about your father?"

"He goes along with whatever she says." Billy kicked at the tree trunk. "I gotta go. I sneaked out and if she catches me I'll be in more trouble."

Kacie watched him swing down the rope ladder and run off through the trees. Billy was even worse off than she was. At least she had a Big Sister to talk to. Billy didn't have anybody.

THE NEXT DAY was a school holiday. Kacie went into the clinic after lunch, and found Suzanne in the surgery room neutering a gray striped tomcat. Kacie hesitated in the doorway, scratching Lady's ears. "Can I come in? Or are you sterile, or something?"

"Hi, Kacie. Come ahead. Neutering is just minor surgery. That's why I'm not gowned." She pushed aside the tom's tail and leaned forward with her scalpel. "And, from what I understand, neutering this particular animal should reduce the future feline population of Cartersburg dramatically." When she got no response, she glanced at Kacie. "You're looking glum. What's the matter?"

As Suzanne continued working on the cat, Kacie poured out the story of what she'd overheard in the library and in the parking lot afterward. "I just don't think it's fair for them to fire Miss Henniker when she's been there so long just because they don't agree with the books she's letting us read."

Suzanne frowned. "Maybe you misunderstood, Kacie. Maybe the woman said 'they've got to go,' meaning the books."

"No chance." She took a step closer as Suzanne picked up the scalpel again. "Why doesn't he bleed when you do that?"

"Because I'm only making a superficial incision and there's very little blood supply to the skin in this area."

Kacie walked around the table and stroked the cat's head. "Will he hurt when he wakes up?"

"Not much. He may be uncomfortable for a few hours, but that's all."

"Poor kitty." As Kacie continued to stroke the unconscious cat, the phone rang.

Suzanne looked up from the cat. "Get that, will you Kacie, and take a message. I'll call back when I finish here."

The voice through the phone was male, and pleasant enough as it asked for Suzanne. But when Kacie said she was busy and offered to take a message, the voice became insistent.

"Tell her it's Marty," the man said. "She'll take my call."

Kacie could barely hide her irritation when she turned to Suzanne. "He said to tell you it's Marty," she reported in a flat voice.

"Oh, Marty...just a minute." She laid down the scalpel. She was nearly finished, and the cat had enough anesthetic in him to last a while longer. Marty got so annoyed lately when she couldn't take his calls, and of course she couldn't blame him because often he was calling from a pay phone.

"Hi," she said, as she took the phone from Kacie. "Oh, that was Kacie, you know, my Little Sister. She's watching me neuter a cat."

Lady curled up at Suzanne's feet and closed her eyes. Kacie settled on the floor and stroked the dog's silky ears as she listened to the conversation. She thought it was really selfish of Marty to expect Suzanne to come running no matter whether she was busy or not.

"The third of December," Suzanne was saying. "Yes, I know that's only four months before the wedding."

Only four months. Kacie had chills inside. Time was running out, and she still hadn't come up with any way to bring Suzanne to her senses. As far as she knew, Suzanne still didn't have a dress, and that was a good sign, but it wasn't enough. Suzanne was still planning the wedding for April third, and she always wore the diamond ring.

"Well, I had something a little smaller in mind," Kacie heard Suzanne say. "Of course it's a beautiful church, but I just thought—"

Maybe they wouldn't be able to agree and they wouldn't get married at all, Kacie thought hopefully.

"Then we can take care of the invitations that same day, and the flowers..." Suzanne paused, listening. "Marty, do you think we're rushing this? With you gone so much right now, maybe we should—"

Kacie held her breath. They were going to put it off. Maybe there was hope after all.

"All right, that sounds fine," Suzanne was saying. "We'll go next weekend and take care of everything. But, Marty, if we could scale it down just a little—"

Kacie didn't even look at Suzanne as she hung up the phone, but when she returned to the surgery table to finish the cat, Kacie asked hesitantly, "Do you think you might postpone the wedding?"

"No, I don't think so, Kacie." After carefully cleaning the incision area, she picked up the neutered cat and laid him gently on a soft towel near the wall where she could watch him as he came out of the anesthetic. Then she began wiping down the surgery table with disinfectant. "I must admit I've thought about postponing it because there seems to be so much to do in such a short time, but I suppose somehow it will all get done."

"But if you put it off," Kacie argued, "you could get married in the summer, or even next fall, and then you wouldn't have to hurry so much."

Suzanne laughed. For whatever reason, Kacie obviously didn't want her to get married. "I really do have to get you and Marty together. You'll be much more enthusiastic once you get to know him."

With her back turned, Kacie rolled her eyes. She knew Marty as well as she ever wanted to. That was the whole problem. What she'd seen of him that night in the clinic made her absolutely sure he was the wrong choice for Suzanne. And since no one else knew what a mistake Suzanne was about to make, that left everything to her. "Have you got any more surgeries this afternoon?" she asked.

Suzanne glanced at the clock. "No, I'm finished for today."

"Then why don't you come home with me? I promised Dad I'd help finish building the doghouse. You could help us, too. And you could see Lucky," she added as further enticement.

Suzanne was about to refuse when she had second thoughts. Why not go? She hadn't built a doghouse since Lady was a puppy. "Do you think it would be all right with your dad if I came?"

Kacie's assurance sent a pleasant warmth flowing through Suzanne. She liked Jed. He had called her a few times since that evening they'd eaten hamburgers together. He'd always had a reason for the call, either a question about Lucky or something he wanted to tell her about Kacie. But the conversations usually went well beyond that, often lasting half an hour or more. And more than once Suzanne had found herself thinking about Jed when she was working. The difference between friends and lovers could be very confusing, she decided.

Jed was in the yard measuring boards when the pickup truck pulled into the driveway.

"I brought Suzanne and Lady to help us," Kacie called to her father.

As Jed broke into a grin and walked toward them, Suzanne struggled with the same feelings she'd had the last time she'd seen him. His hair was tousled and he had a smudge of dirt across his cheek but he looked more handsome than most men in three-piece suits. She sensed a gentle strength about him that drew her to him and she could feel his genuine delight in seeing her again.

"Bringing help was a good move, Kacie," he answered, but his eyes were on Suzanne. "I hope you're an experienced doghouse builder, because I know Lady can't pound nails, and Kacie's skills in that area are definitely marginal."

Suzanne laughed. "I'm not really terribly experienced, but I work hard, and Lady is a fantastic sidewalk superintendent."

"Where's Lucky?" Kacie asked, looking around.

"I had to shut him in the kitchen. First he stole my hammer, and when I got that back, he spotted a cat on that tree limb over there and practically leaped the fence to get it."

Kacie took the back steps two at a time. "I'll go inside and get him."

"I'm glad you could come over, Suzanne," Jed said, moving closer to her. "I haven't seen you for a while."

Suzanne smiled at him. "You should stop by the clinic one of these days." After she said it, she wasn't sure why. There was no reason for Jed to come to the clinic, unless to bring Lucky, but having him come to see her seemed like a nice idea. She didn't have time to consider the possibility any further because a blood curdling yell came from the house.

"Lucky!" Kacie was shouting. Suzanne and Jed raced toward the steps with Lady on their heels. Inside the kitchen they immediately saw the problem. Lucky stood in the middle of the room, knee-deep in cookies, crackers, dry cereal and shredded cardboard. He was wiggling all over, his tail wagging and his tongue hanging out of his mouth in a semblance of a lopsided grin.

"That loose cabinet door. He must have pried it open." Jed sounded stricken. He looked at Kacie then at Suzanne. Lucky barked proudly and they all burst out laughing.

"Bad dog, Lucky," Kacie said, not sounding at all firm, as Lucky raced in circles spewing cornflakes behind him. Lady regarded the puppy with the dignity befitting a mature dog.

"I knew I should have fixed that door," Jed muttered as he took Lucky outside and tied him to a tree in the yard, well out of reach of the building project.

After half an hour of scooping, sweeping and vacuuming, the kitchen had returned to normal. "What a mess," Jed said as he and Suzanne carried the last of the bags outside to the trash cans. "I had no idea there was so much stuff in that cabinet. Probably needed cleaning out anyway."

"At least you have a sense of humor about it," Suzanne replied.

They dumped their bags into the garbage, and as they turned to the house, Jed put his hand on Suzanne's arm. She was aware of him in the way she had been all afternoon whenever he got close to her. She looked at him, wondering if he felt it, too, and from the intensity in his eyes, she knew he did.

"Thank you for helping clean up," he said in a slightly husky voice.

"I . . . I enjoyed it." It was a strange answer, but she meant it. She turned away from him, confused by her feelings, and saw her diamond sparkling in the sunlight. These feelings for Jed had to be the deepening of a friendship; there was no other explanation. She was about to get married. Only hours before she had arranged with Marty to go to Richmond to see the church, choose invitations and talk to the caterers. She felt Jed's arm brush lightly against hers as they walked together toward the framework of the doghouse, and she shivered lightly as the image of Marty faded from her thoughts.

For the rest of the afternoon they sawed and hammered and took turns playing with Lucky so he wouldn't either howl in frustration at being tied up or grab the tools and race wildly across the yard. Lady made a few futile attempts to subdue the puppy, but finally gave herself up to a nap on the porch. They were all very proud of what they were creating from the pieces and scraps of wood Jed had picked up at the lumberyard, and by dinnertime they were putting a coat of paint on a perfect little house with shingles and windows and an oval doorway that they hoped would be big enough for Lucky once he grew into a full-size dog. Lucky was far more interested in the process than the product, and after a near disaster with the paint, Jed sent him for a run with Kacie while he and Suzanne finished up.

"Let's order a pizza," Jed suggested, looking at his watch. "That new pizza place down on Sixth Street has started a delivery service."

"Oh, Jed, I really should go home."

"Why?"

Suzanne laid down her paintbrush. Why, indeed? Lady could eat some of Lucky's puppy chow. It was so easy being with Jed and Kacie, so comfortable. Of course there was nothing wrong with that, she reminded herself, but something kept bothering her, and she sensed that her misgivings were somehow tied to Marty. Maybe the next time Marty came she could invite Jed and Kacie to do something with them. Maybe that would help. But, for some reason, she didn't think that idea would appeal to Marty at all.

"You do have to eat dinner somewhere," Jed encouraged her. "Might as well have pizza with us."

"Might as well," Suzanne agreed. If she couldn't think of any good reason not to stay, then why not? They finished painting and Suzanne helped Jed clean up.

"I really do appreciate your help," Jed told her. "We'd have never got the doghouse painted today without you."

"It's been a lovely afternoon." Suzanne glanced at the brilliant blue sky. "Definitely a day to spend outdoors."

"It has been nice," Jed agreed, touching her arm.

The light in his brown eyes was unmistakable as were the feelings that surged through Suzanne when he touched her. He wasn't talking about the weather or the doghouse. She knew that. He was talking about their afternoon together. Again she thought of Marty, and he seemed very far away.

"Remember when we talked about my sketching you?"

Jed still was standing very close to her, and Suzanne felt no desire to move away. "Yes, I remember."

"I thought about what you said awhile ago about my stopping by the clinic. Maybe I could sit there and sketch and you could go ahead with your work if you don't think I would get in the way..."

He sounded hesitant, almost shy.

"You mean I don't have to pose?" Suzanne was surprised.

"No, you don't have to do anything," Jed assured her. "Just be yourself."

Suddenly Suzanne didn't mind the idea of having him sketch her. "Come whenever you want to," she told him. "I'd love to have you." And she really meant it.

Kacie and Lucky and the pepperoni pizza arrived at the front door simultaneously. Jed poured glasses of cola and they all sat around the picnic table. Lucky was relegated to the kitchen with a bowl of puppy chow. Lady stood guard outside the gate that blocked the doorway as if her sole job for the evening was to keep the puppy in line. Jed had taken a few minutes to tie the loose cabinet securely, so presumably the kitchen was disaster-proof—at least temporarily.

"I've been meaning to tell you both—I read that new book by Allison Craig," Jed announced nonchalantly.

Kacie nearly choked on her drink, but her father appeared not to notice.

"And you were right." He looked directly at Suzanne. "By skimming scenes I hadn't given it a fair chance. The impression is much different when the book is taken as a whole."

"You mean you liked it?" Kacie's eyes were wide.

"Well, I don't know if 'like' is the word..."

Kacie took another piece of pizza. "So you hated it."

"No, I don't hate it," Jed explained patiently. "There are still some parts of it I can do without. But overall, the book's message is different from what I thought it was. Tell me something, Kacie."

She looked at him skeptically.

"Do kids really read these books all the way through?"

"Of course."

"You mean if I got one of these books from the library and held it by the spine, it wouldn't fall open to the juicy scenes?"

Kacie giggled in spite of herself. Most kids did read those scenes first. Everybody knew that. "Maybe it would," she admitted, "but everybody I know goes back and reads the whole book, sometimes two or three times. And when Miss Henniker has the discussions, we talk about how we felt about what the characters did and why we felt that way."

Jed studied her thoughtfully. Whether or not everybody read the whole book, apparently a number of students did, and his daughter was among them. "Sounds like a reasonable approach," he replied, pouring more cola. "Although I must say, I'd still rather see all this going on in high school instead of junior high."

Kacie's irritation was immediate. "C'mon, Dad. You act like I was still a baby or something." Her voice rose angrily. "You don't have to wait till you're in high school to think about divorce or alcoholic parents or sex." Kacie stood and picked up her empty plate. "Actually it's sex that's the problem, just like in music and movies and everywhere else. Adults just can't handle it.''

Suzanne stifled a smile as she watched Kacie wind up. Her father's sudden change of heart about the books had obviously made Kacie more willing to talk. And now she was angry because she thought he was questioning her maturity. Suzanne wondered what she'd say next, and she hoped Jed was ready for it.

''I don't know why adults have this big hang-up,'' Kacie continued. ''Nobody thinks you have to wait till you get married to have sex. You just have to wait till you get old enough, and nobody really knows how old is old enough except the people doing it.''

Suzanne knew Kacie was testing her father, or maybe both of them. She could see the surprise on Jed's face, but he responded calmly.

''Is that what you really think, Kacie?''

''Well, that's how it is, isn't it?''

Suzanne sat forward and leaned her elbows on the picnic table. ''Not necessarily, Kacie.''

Kacie looked at her, startled. She had obviously been expecting a reply from her father, not Suzanne.

''I don't think you can say all adults believe that sex before marriage is a good idea.'' Suzanne spoke softly, watching Kacie's reaction. ''Of course, attitudes have become much more liberal in the past few years, but believe it or not, Kacie, some people still feel that sex is better left till after marriage.''

Kacie set her jaw stubbornly. ''Not very many. I'll bet even people like Miss Henniker don't believe that any more.'' As soon as the words were out of her mouth, Kacie wanted to take them back. She looked awkwardly at her feet, wishing she'd never started the conversation.

"I don't know about Margaret Henniker, Kacie, but I know how I feel. I think sex should wait until you get married."

"You do?" Kacie gulped and stared at her.

"Yes, I do." Suzanne could feel Jed's eyes boring into her as well. They were both obviously very surprised. She considered telling them she hadn't held that view until she'd learned the hard way, but then decided against it. "There are probably more people who feel like I do than you realize, Kacie. The saddest thing is when someone really wants to wait but goes ahead because she—or he—feels pressured."

Kacie looked at her feet. "I suppose. I guess I never thought about it that way." She picked up her dirty dishes and started toward the door, then turned and looked over her shoulder. "Anyway, I'm going to take my stuff inside and play with Lucky for a while. After that I have to read this dumb poem for English."

"Don't wait too late to start reading," Jed called after her. He looked gratefully at Suzanne. "That's more than she's talked about sex around me since . . . well, ever. Thanks for giving her the message you did."

Suzanne smiled at him, realizing again how hard it must be for a father, especially one as conscientious as Jed, to raise a teenage girl. "I just told her what I believe. Kids should know that they have choices."

After watching Kacie try to teach Lucky to fetch the ball for a while, they all went inside. Kacie shut Lucky in the kitchen, and Lady followed Jed and Suzanne to his studio to look at sketches Jed had done of the puppy. "I think you like him," Suzanne said as she flipped through pencil drawings of Lucky playing, sleeping and lying with his head on his paws, looking up with big, mournful eyes. "Oh, Jed, I love this." Suzanne held a sketch at arm's length and studied it carefully. "He looks like he's waiting for Kacie and is afraid she will never come." She turned to Jed hesitantly. "Do you suppose I could have this drawing to hang in the clinic?"

"Sure, if you want it, but it's just a rough sketch. I could make you something more finished."

Suzanne shook her head. "No, I want this one exactly like it is." She held it out to him. "Except for one thing. Would you sign it?"

Jed shrugged. "Sure." He signed it with a flourish, just as he signed his cartoon strip, then as an afterthought titled the picture "Lucky."

Kacie, who had been standing in the doorway, nodded approvingly. "That's my favorite, too. It'll be perfect in the clinic." She walked across to watch her father finish lettering the title. Then she casually flipped through some preliminary sketches piled on the corner of the drawing table. Her smile faded. "What are these?"

Jed didn't look up. "Just some working drawings for the strip."

Kacie stared at the drawings for a moment longer then slammed them down on the table. "You can't do that."

"Do what?"

"You can't put that in your strip." Kacie's face was scarlet with anger. "That's me buying a bra. You can't, Daddy, please, you just can't."

Jed laid down his pencil and faced his daughter. He'd had some misgivings about the drawings, but the idea had been so perfect—the experience of buying the first bra. "Kacie, you know I don't write the strip about you. One of the characters is about your age, and of course she's going to have some similar experiences and some similar problems."

"That sucks."

"Kacie!"

"I don't care." Kacie was near tears. "It isn't fair and you can't do it. You're making me into some kind of a freak." She stormed out of the room. They could hear her crying as she stalked up the stairs.

Jed ran his fingers through his hair in exasperation. "It really is just a preliminary idea. I didn't intend for her to see it."

He handed the sketches to Suzanne, who studied each one carefully. They were sparse drawings picking up only the detail that he wanted to focus on, but they left no doubt that his central theme was a girl buying her first bra. "They're wonderful, Jed." She handed them back. "But I can understand why Kacie is upset."

Jed nodded. "I suppose I can, too."

"She's embarrassed. These things are very important and very private for girls her age."

Jed tipped back in his chair. "That's the whole point. The experience is universal and that's why it works so well in the strip."

Suzanne could see his position, but she could also see Kacie's. "Maybe you could put the idea away for a couple of years until it isn't such an issue with Kacie.

It would still be universal, but it wouldn't hit quite so close to home.''

Jed sighed. "I guess you're right.'' He stood up and put his hands on Suzanne's shoulders. "No wonder Kacie thinks you're fantastic.''

Suzanne lowered her eyes, aware of nothing but Jed, his scent, his touch, the deep resonance of his voice. She knew his touch was to have been a quick, playful gesture, but it lasted longer than that and stirred a swirl of emotion that confused her. She looked at him, and for the barest instant she thought he might kiss her, but instead he let her go and stepped away. Of course he would have. They were simply friends.

CHAPTER SIX

"OH, MARTY, IT'S BEAUTIFUL." Suzanne spoke in a whisper that seemed to echo in the silent church. She clasped Marty's hand as she stared at the sanctuary's high vaulted ceilings and massive stained-glass windows. A seemingly endless expanse of thick red carpet ran down the center aisle, flanked on both sides by oak pews, which were intricately carved like the front doors of the church.

"A perfect place for our wedding, right?" Marty slipped his arm around her shoulders, and she leaned against him, trying to imagine herself walking down that aisle. "Come on," he said, hugging her. "Let's go down to the front." He led the way, stopping to indicate where floral arrangements and candles would be placed. "The governor's daughter was married here last month," he told her in a satisfied tone. He gestured to the marble steps leading to the altar. "We'll have velvet-covered kneelers here, and the bridesmaids will be on this side and the groomsmen over here."

"Bridesmaids!" Suzanne realized that she hadn't even decided who to ask.

"How about my two sisters?"

"Well . . ." Suzanne hesitated. She had met one of Marty's sisters, who seemed very nice, but the other one lived in California and Suzanne didn't know her at all.

"Did you have someone else in mind?"

Suzanne shook her head.

"My sisters were very excited when I talked to them about it." Marty turned to her, taking her hand again. "And my five-year-old niece could be the flower girl. How does that sound?"

"Just fine," Suzanne told him. And it did. That was one more thing taken care of, and she wasn't sure that most of her friends from school would be comfortable in the kind of wedding he was talking about. "But we might have Kacie as a bridesmaid, too," she added.

Marty looked blank.

"You know," Suzanne reminded him, "my Little Sister."

"Oh, yes..." Marty frowned. "I'm not sure how that would work. I was only planning to have two groomsmen. Is it absolutely necessary?"

Suzanne hesitated. "Not really, I guess." She wasn't even sure whether Kacie would want to be a bridesmaid.

"Good, then it's settled." Marty put both arms around her and hugged her. "I do love you, sweetheart. This wedding is going to be absolutely perfect."

Suzanne leaned her head against his shoulder, wondering why she felt so uncomfortable. Somehow their wedding had become his wedding. Then again, maybe she should be grateful, because she certainly hadn't had time to do much planning, and she had no mother or sisters to help her.

After they talked to the minister about the ceremony, Marty and Suzanne ordered the invitations, inspected the country club where the wedding dinner and dance would be held, and ordered the flowers. Then they went to a tiny, romantic restaurant where Marty had made reservations for lunch. When the strolling violinist paused at their table, Marty held Suzanne's hand and she was sure she was living a fantasy.

But when the violinist had moved on and their lunch had been ordered, Suzanne found herself still troubled by the wedding plans. "Marty, are you sure we shouldn't do something more simple?" She saw his look of disappointment as soon as she asked.

"We could," he answered, "but why not have a spectacular wedding? After all, we only do it once."

He had a point, but Suzanne still wasn't sure. "But it's going to be so expensive."

He reached across the table and again took her hand. "Don't worry so much, my little dove. That's already taken care of. My father talked to me last night. He and Mother have about two hundred people they'd like to invite. He said if we would include their friends, they'd pay for everything and we could have as big a wedding as we wanted."

"Two hundred people?" Suzanne found the number staggering. She'd be lucky to come up with thirty people she wanted to include on the guest list.

"I figure by the time we add our friends, it will be about three hundred. But don't worry. All you have to do is look lovely and enjoy it."

Suzanne didn't answer. He made it sound so easy but, somehow, something wasn't right.

As they were finishing their meal, Suzanne's napkin slid to the floor. Before she had time to retrieve it, a good-looking man from a nearby table had picked it up and handed it to her.

"Why, thank you," she said with a surprised smile.

"No problem," he replied, grinning.

"That wasn't necessary," Marty said in a low, controlled voice. He was intense and suddenly serious. "That man has been watching you, you know," he added in the same tone.

Suzanne laughed softly. "Oh, Marty, you must be mistaken."

But his expression was humorless. "No, I don't miss things like that. You have to be careful, Suzanne. You're a very attractive woman. You shouldn't do things that men might see as flirting." He stood abruptly. "It's time to go."

"But Marty, I haven't finished my coffee—" He was behind her, ready to pull out her chair. She couldn't understand what had happened. But since the coffee was too strong anyway, it seemed easier to go than to argue.

As they left the restaurant and got into the car, Marty seemed unusually quiet. But by the time they reached the bridal salon, he was in good spirits again. Hand in hand they walked inside.

The salon was hushed with faint strains of classical music floating in the background. The decor was a pastel floral theme enhanced by thick carpet in pale peach. Cut-glass chandeliers cast soft light on a seemingly endless array of wedding gowns and exquisite bridal lingerie. Standing there with Marty, surrounded by such beauty, Suzanne was almost afraid to breathe for fear she would destroy the enchantment. Before she knew what was happening, she was whisked off to a

spacious dressing room and fastened into a white lace
strapless bra. A satin gown was slipped over her head.
She found herself gliding in a pirouette on a raised
platform in the center of the salon. Everywhere she
turned she was met by her reflection in full-length
mirrors.

"Beautiful, you are absolutely beautiful, Suzanne." Marty was sitting in a velvet Queen Anne chair
just to one side of the platform.

Suzanne felt beautiful as she modeled one wedding
gown after another for Marty. At first she had been
uneasy about having him help her select a gown, but
her apprehension had vanished completely, and she
glowed from his lavish compliments. His taste was far
more elegant and dramatic than hers, and many of the
gowns he seemed to prefer were heavy satin embel-
lished with seed pearls and iridescent sequins. She had
a fleeting thought of the traditional gown with the
sweetheart neckline she had seen the day she and Kacie had been shopping, but it seemed too simple for the
grand wedding they were planning.

Finally Marty stood up and proclaimed a gown to be
perfect. Suzanne studied herself in the mirror for a
minute. The designer gown was striking and very so-
phisticated with its narrow lines and long cathedral
train. The beaded bodice was cut low, exposing the
creamy swell of her breasts. A little self-consciously,
she tugged at the top of the bodice, trying to pull it up
just a bit. When Marty laughed in amusement, she
found herself blushing. Then her hair was twisted up
into a high-fashion style, and a pouffed veil with a
beaded band was settled into place.

"You could have stepped off the cover of *Vogue* magazine," Marty told her proudly. "It's time you dressed like the gorgeous woman you are."

Suzanne gazed into the mirror in awe, hardly recognizing herself. She had always thought she had a very good sense of the woman she was, but Marty might be right. Perhaps there were facets of herself she hadn't uncovered yet.

Once the initial fitting had been done on the wedding gown, Marty and Suzanne chose bridesmaids' dresses in a deep rose color with matching picture hats. When they were finished, Marty suggested taking Suzanne to his apartment, but she persuaded him to go home with her. She didn't tell him her main reason was that Lady had been shut inside all day and would need to go out. Marty wasn't very understanding about Lady.

By the time they drove to Cartersburg, it was dinnertime. As soon as she'd let Lady out, Suzanne took some stew from the refrigerator, turned on the oven to heat a loaf of French bread and gave Marty a bottle of red table wine to open. He frowned when he read the label. "Once we're married, my dove," he said, expertly inserting the corkscrew, "I'll be the wine buyer and you stick to the stew."

"Fine by me," Suzanne agreed. She'd never known much about wine, and Marty's taste was impeccable. While the stew heated, Suzanne let Lady in and fed her then checked the answering machine for messages. She found nothing of importance, just a canceled appointment on Monday and a question about cat vaccinations. As soon as the stew was bubbling, she ladled it into two bowls and took the bread out of the oven. She went through the motions automatically, her mind elsewhere. She was disturbed about the wedding, not just the ceremony but the whole idea of getting married. She glanced over at Marty who was sitting at the kitchen table reading the newspaper. He was handsome, attentive, very concerned about her, and yet something was wrong. She wished she could talk to him about it, but she didn't know where to begin.

"Tired?" Marty asked, after she served their dinner and joined him at the round oak table in the corner of the kitchen.

She nodded. "It's been a long day."

He covered her hand with his. "But we really got the wedding together, didn't we?"

"We certainly did." She couldn't argue that. Marty had packed their day so tight that she couldn't imagine how they'd have fit in another thing. And the decision making had been easy. He seemed to know exactly what they wanted.

"Only thing we didn't get done was looking at those new town houses." He took a sip of wine. "I know you'll like them."

Suzanne stopped eating. "Marty, I don't want to live in Richmond."

"Have you ever lived there?"

"No, but—"

"Then you don't know whether you want to live in Richmond." With a flourish he filled her wine glass.

"Marty, I'm being serious."

"So am I."

"My practice is here in Cartersburg," Suzanne argued. "I don't want to commute for an hour twice a day."

Marty smiled at her, his deep blue eyes exploring her face. "Believe me, sweetheart, I don't want you to. That's why I keep telling you about the veterinary clinics in Richmond—reasonable hours, no pigs rolling in the mud, weekends off."

"Marty—" Suzanne's voice was firm.

"We don't have to decide anything tonight," Marty interrupted, squeezing her hand. He stood up and walked behind her to rub her shoulders. "We've got until April third before we have to know absolutely for sure. Right now let's go into the living room for a little while."

His hands were warm and sensuous as he massaged her tired muscles. He leaned down and nuzzled her hair, but Suzanne's nagging feeling of discomfort lingered. She was more disturbed than she liked to admit about their discussion of where to live. Marty had glossed it over, put it off, but she knew all too well where he stood on the subject, and Marty was a man used to getting his way.

As they started into the living room, the phone rang, producing a round of barking from Lady.

"Shut up, dog," Marty ordered as Suzanne picked up the phone.

The voice on the other end brought an instant smile to her face. It was Jed. He asked about her day and she told him that it had been hectic but very productive, then added that Marty was still there. Jed apologized for interrupting them and explained that he'd called to ask what he could do to stop Lucky from chewing everything in sight, including Jed's favorite running shoes and the legs on the kitchen table. Laughing, Suzanne promised to get Lucky a rawhide bone like the ones she ordered for Lady. In the meantime, she suggested puppy chew toys in every room where Lucky was likely to go.

She was still chuckling when she hung up the phone, but when she turned to Marty, the sound died in her throat. His face was drawn tight into an expression she'd never seen before. The boyish twinkle was gone from his eyes, which had narrowed and become a flat, angry blue.

"Who was that?" he demanded.

"Jed Parker, Kacie's father." She took a step toward him. "Marty, what's the matter?"

He ignored her question. "What did he want?"

"He just—" She felt herself stammering as she searched for words. "He wanted to know how to get his puppy to stop chewing."

"At eight o'clock on a Saturday night? Not likely." Marty moved toward her and Suzanne backed away, frightened by the intensity of his anger. "He was checking to see whether I'd left yet, and you told him I hadn't." Marty took a quick step and grabbed both her arms. "What's going on between you and him?"

"Nothing, Marty," Suzanne protested. "He's just a friend."

His fingers pressed hard into her arms. "Just a friend, is he? Tell me the rest of it."

Suzanne tried unsuccessfully to pull away. "There's nothing, nothing else. Marty, stop! You're hurting me."

He pressed harder for an instant then let her go, but the pain stayed and Suzanne rubbed her upper arms. "You hurt me, Marty," she said again.

Suddenly he was solicitous. "Let me see," he said, pushing up her sleeve and examining the deep red marks on her upper arm. "It doesn't look too bad." He slipped his arm around her. "You have to understand, Suzanne, how much I love you. Like I told you this afternoon, you're a lovely woman. You have to watch out for other men."

"But, Marty—" She didn't finish. He'd never understand her friendship with Jed. Marty was so possessive and so jealous, even more so now that they were engaged. She knew he acted that way because he loved her, but she still found it disturbing. Maybe once they were married, things would be better.

SUZANNE WAS GLAD when Kacie arrived the next afternoon. She had been so preoccupied with Marty and his jealous outburst that nothing had gone right all day. She needed someone to take her mind off her problems, and she also needed some help. The German shepherd she was dipping in a medicated solution to get rid of a chronic flea infestation wasn't cooperating.

"Kacie, grab him right there behind his flank," she said as Kacie pulled off her coat.

"Does he bite?" Kacie asked skeptically as she approached the dog.

"He's as gentle as can be, but he sure loves to splash."

"I thought we were going to the movies," Kacie protested as they wrestled with the dog.

"Right." Suzanne had forgotten. "In just a few minutes, as soon as we dry him off." It took both of them and several large towels to subdue the dog and dry his thick coat.

When they were finally finished, Kacie looked at her soaked sweatshirt. "And I thought Lucky was bad."

Suzanne laughed. "I guess we are a little wet. I'll go to the house and get us both dry sweatshirts and we can check and see what movies are playing." She took off her soggy flannel shirt and hung it to dry, leaving only the blue T-shirt she wore underneath.

"What happened to you?" Kacie asked as Suzanne reached for her jacket.

Suzanne followed Kacie's gaze to the dark purple marks on her upper arms. She'd forgotten about them when she took off her shirt, and now that Kacie had seen them, she'd have to explain. But what could she say to a thirteen-year-old?

"Suzanne?" Kacie asked.

Seconds were ticking away. She had to answer. "I was mopping the floor yesterday and I slipped and fell against the desk."

Kacie watched Suzanne quickly put on her jacket then let herself be hustled to the house, where she changed her sweatshirt and they looked at movie listings. But all afternoon, through the movie and the ice cream afterward, Kacie kept thinking about those bruises. Suzanne hadn't fallen. She had spent all day Saturday in Richmond with Marty. The marks on her arms were exactly the shape of fingerprints. All the evidence added up to Marty, and that thought made Kacie feel sick to her stomach.

As soon as Suzanne dropped her off at home, Kacie went into Jed's studio where he was working at the drawing table. "Dad?"

"Mmm." Jed didn't look up.

Kacie knew he didn't like for her to bother him when he was working, but she wandered over to the drawing table and looked over his shoulder anyway. He was doing a sketch of Lucky up to his belly in cornflakes. "I like that," Kacie said, remembering the awful drawings of a girl buying a bra, which her father fortunately hadn't used—at least not yet. "Maybe you should concentrate on Lucky for a while," she suggested.

Jed nodded, a half smile on his face. "I get the message. Now, is there something particular on your mind?"

"Well—" Kacie shuffled from one foot to the other. "Do you think someone could get big bruises on the top of their arms from falling against a desk?"

Jed didn't miss the serious expression on Kacie's face. "I suppose so, depending on how they fell. But it would be kind of hard to bruise both arms that way."

"Yeah, that's what I thought, too." Kacie was pensive for a moment. "Well, thanks, Dad." She turned and headed for the door.

"Kacie!"

Jed's voice stopped her midway, and she looked over her shoulder. "What, Dad?"

"Is there any particular reason you wanted to know about bruises on someone's arms?"

Kacie shrugged. "No, not really."

"I see." He picked up his drawing pencil. "Do you have any more hypothetical questions, or can I go back to work?"

"No . . . well, I guess one more."

"What's that?"

"Do you like Marty, that guy Suzanne is going to marry?"

Jed began to sketch. "I don't know him."

"Me, neither," she answered. "I'm going over to Billy's now."

As Kacie disappeared through the doorway, Jed laid down his pencil. Her questions hadn't been hypothetical. He knew better than that. When she had asked about the bruises, he'd thought she might be reacting to a movie or a book or a story she'd heard, but she had followed up with that question about Marty. Jed sat for several minutes doodling on his sketch pad. Then he abruptly stood up, left a note for Kacie on the refrigerator and got his coat.

Suzanne was in the clinic when Jed arrived, sketch pad in hand. She looked both pleased and very surprised to see him.

"You promised I could sketch you, and I've been thinking about it so I thought I'd see whether I could hang around for a little while now."

Suzanne could have reached out and hugged him. After Kacie left, her thoughts had turned to Marty and she'd come back to the clinic not so much because she needed to work as because she felt unhappy. She'd resolved much of the night before in her mind, understanding how her side of the conversation with Jed could have given Marty the wrong idea. But she couldn't shake the memory of how frightened she'd been when Marty approached her in anger. Seeing Jed standing in her doorway made her whole world brighter. "Come in," she said with a smile. "You couldn't have picked a better time. I was just straightening up around here."

"Go right ahead," Jed told her as he leaned down to pat Lady. "I'll just sit over here in the corner."

"You don't want me to do anything special?"

He turned, and she saw the warmth and gentleness in his deep brown eyes. "Just be yourself," he told her, "just like always."

Suzanne went about her work, cleaning syringes and laundering towels and lab coats, but she found herself humming while she worked. The clinic was quiet except for the sound of the clock ticking and Jed's pencil moving across the paper. The late afternoon sun, deep orange as twilight approached, cast a mellow glow on Jed as he sat in front of the window. He was absorbed in his work, his face a study in concentration.

Suzanne felt better than she had all day. Even though they weren't talking or really even doing anything together, Jed's presence warmed her and made her feel peaceful inside. Lady obviously felt the same way, because she had settled down with her nose resting on one of Jed's shoes. Suzanne saw him lean over and absent-mindedly scratch the dog behind her ears. She glanced at him again and found him watching her, which of course he was supposed to be doing, and she smiled, not the least bit self-conscious.

"Suzanne, would you mind taking off your sweater?"

Startled, she looked at the bulky blue cotton-knit sweater with the sagging neck that she'd pulled on over a light yellow shirt.

"Not that I don't like it," Jed added quickly, "but I seem to be seeing mostly sweater and not enough of you."

"Actually, I don't like it, either." She stretched her arms over her head and wiggled out of her sweater, tossing it on her old metal desk. "I only wear it to work in."

Once the sweater was off, Suzanne's upper arms were partially bare, which was what Jed had in mind. "Kacie said you fell against the desk yesterday while you were mopping the clinic," he commented after a few moments. "Those are nasty-looking bruises."

Suzanne set to work rinsing the syringes that had been soaking in a basin and prepared to sterilize them in the autoclave. She had forgotten about the bruises again. "They don't hurt." Her voice was barely audible over the running water.

"I thought you were in Richmond with Marty yesterday." Jed's response was slow, casual.

Suzanne felt herself sinking deeper and deeper into the lie. "I was. I fell before we went."

"I see," Jed replied quietly.

Suzanne stood at the sink with her back toward Jed. She couldn't lie to him. It didn't feel right. It had been awful with Kacie, but this was even worse. She turned and waited till he looked up, her gray eyes meeting his gaze. "That's not true. It's what I told Kacie because I didn't know how to explain what really happened."

"Sometimes it's hard with kids." Jed laid his pencil down. "If there's something you need to talk about, try me. I'm a pretty good listener."

Suzanne hesitated for a moment, then pulled the desk chair near Jed and sat down. "I don't know how to begin," she admitted. "I'm not sure I completely understand what happened."

Jed reached over and took her hand, and at his touch she relaxed. Slowly at first, then more easily, the story spilled out. She told him about her day in Richmond with Marty and all they'd accomplished and how they had come home for dinner and how everything had been fine except for their discussion about where they would live.

"But when I hung up the phone after talking to you, he was different." Suzanne searched for words to describe the look on Marty's face and, finding none, she went on. "He's always been jealous and very possessive. That's just how he is. But this time..." She twisted the ring on her finger. "This time he was really angry. He grabbed my arms and shook me, and when I told him he was hurting me, he let go, but not right away."

His jaw set, Jed looked away, listening while she made excuses for Marty and explained how easy it must have been for him to misunderstand her end of the phone conversation. He spent several minutes controlling the rage that boiled up in him as he visualized the scene she described. No man ever had a right to hurt a woman, and to hurt a woman like Suzanne— "Why do you want to marry this guy?" he demanded.

"Why?" Suzanne looked at him in surprise. "For the same reasons everybody gets married. We've dated for a long time. We both want a home and children and..." Suzanne frowned. Why you were going to marry someone was a very hard thing to explain. She looked at the ring again. "He can be lots of fun and I know he loves me—"

"So much that he leaves nasty purple bruises on your arms?"

"Jed, that's not fair."

He looked at her for a long moment, then took both her hands in his. "Maybe not. Maybe I came on too strong. But he did hurt you, Suzanne. I'll be willing to bet that even before this you had some second thoughts about him."

Suzanne nodded and looked away. "Sometimes, but getting married is such a big step I'm sure everybody has second thoughts."

"Maybe." There was so much more Jed wanted to say, and yet he couldn't. Not then. Not yet. He leaned over and very gently kissed her forehead. It was all he could do to pull back without taking her in his arms.

CHAPTER SEVEN

JED CRUMPLED yet another sketch into a perfect ball and bounced it off an overflowing wastebasket. Every time he had sat down at the drawing table for the past week, he'd found himself sketching Suzanne. The pen, which was balanced lightly in his fingers, moved along the sketch pad as though it had a mind of its own. Effortlessly it fashioned the slender body of a woman running across a meadow, brushing back flowing hair with long, slender fingers, one adorned by a huge diamond ring. In a single motion he wadded up the sketch and tossed it toward the wastebasket.

He had to figure out some way to bring Suzanne to her senses. She had no business marrying a man who left bruises on her arms. Anyone could see that. Anyone except Suzanne. Jed stood up and walked to the window. The sky was December gray, very much like his mood. A light dusting of snow covered the lawn and clung to the bare oak branches. He looked at the low limb that had given his cartoon strip its name and he felt like he was climbing out on that limb again, getting too concerned about a woman who belonged to someone else. But she didn't belong to Marty, dammit. Not for another three and a half months. And not even then if he could help it.

Jed walked to the drawing table, but he had no desire to work. Instead he wandered out to the kitchen where Lucky was taking a nap. As soon as Jed climbed over the gate, the puppy was on his feet wagging his tail. "Sorry, fella, I don't feel much like playing today." Jed patted Lucky on the head and the puppy whimpered hopefully. "Oh, all right," Jed agreed, getting his jacket. "Maybe we'll take a run." He snapped on Lucky's leash and they walked out the back door together in what was becoming a daily ritual. The puppy, once he'd gotten the hang of it, had proved more than willing to lope along beside Jed for a mile or two, and Jed had found that when they got back he could sometimes get some work done.

As they ran along the uneven sidewalk on Cherry Street, past big old frame houses with evergreen wreaths on their doors, Jed drank in the fresh crisp air and began to relax. They turned the corner at Sixth Street, and even when a squirrel scampered across their path, Lucky stayed right at Jed's side without pulling at the leash. Maybe it was a good thing they'd kept the puppy, Jed thought, even though he was a lot of work. He could be a friend for Kacie like Lady was for Suzanne. Suzanne again. Gentle, thoughtful, lovely . . . if he could only convince her that Marty was no good for her.

Jed ran faster, and Lucky easily kept pace. The big picture was suddenly clear to Jed, and he didn't like it. He cared too much about Suzanne. And he might as well quit kidding himself. No matter what he said, she was going to marry that traveling salesman in April, and that was that. The only answer was to stay as far away from her as he possibly could. He circled around and headed toward the house. He might as well quit mooning about her and get to work.

SUZANNE LEANED over the steering wheel and rubbed at the frost on the windshield of the truck with her glove. It was dark and the snow was beginning to get heavier. She found herself thinking about Jed as she turned into the long gravel road leading to Al Kenner's farm. Jed had been on her mind often during the past two weeks, but she'd been so busy she hadn't had a chance to see him. She needed to straighten things out, because she knew she'd given him the wrong impression about Marty.

Jed didn't even know about the flowers, she realized as she wiped the fog off the windshield again. They'd arrived after he'd left that Sunday. A dozen long-stemmed roses and a card that simply said, "I love you, Marty." A few days later she and Marty had talked over dinner, and every day since then he had called with news of the wedding or his job. Suzanne was convinced that Marty's outburst had been a one-time thing. But the look in his eyes still bothered her.

The truck bumped over a rut in the road, and lights from the farmhouse came into view. Suzanne parked beside the barn.

"Glad you could get here, Doc." Al Kenner pulled open the door of the driver's side of the pickup. "I was worried with the snow and the dark you might not be able to make it, and Princess Margaret is real bad."

"I'd have been out sooner but it's been one of those days." Suzanne pulled the hood of her jacket over her head and stepped into the swirling snow. Al Kenner and his family had kept the cow since she was a calf, and

one of Al's daughters had decided she had a regal
bearing, so they'd named her Princess Margaret. Once
she had the name, she seemed to develop a matching
personality and they all pampered her. "What's the
matter with my favorite holstein?" she asked.

"It's that foot again, Doc. She's been limping
around for a couple of days now. Could barely walk
when I called you this morning."

Suzanne reached into the portable clinic unit in the
back of the truck where she kept the tools of her trade:
syringes, bandages, ropes, vaccines and drugs. She tied
on a leather ferrier's apron as she followed Al over to
Princess Margaret. "Do you think we can get her into
the barn?"

"She's been a little mean lately. Might not be too
cooperative." Giving the cow a wide berth, he looped
a rope around her neck and began to lead her through
the open door of the barn. Princess Margaret balked,
straining at the rope and digging her hoofs into the
muddy snow. "Come on, Princess," Al coaxed.

They spent almost twenty minutes subduing the cow
and getting her into the barn, where Suzanne could
examine the infected foot. Holding the cow's leg
against her thigh, which was protected by the leather
apron, she cleaned out the infected tissue and packed
the hoof with a medicated ointment. "You're going to
have to soak it and apply the dressing once a day," she
explained to Al as she finished. "I'll write it all down.
I'll want to see her again in about a week."

The farmer nodded. While Suzanne was gathering
her supplies, Al Kenner disappeared for a moment then
returned with a large rawhide bone. "Picked this up for

Lady,'' he said, handing it to Suzanne. ''Kind of an early Christmas present.''

With a warm thank-you, Suzanne accepted the bone and walked to her truck. The people around Cartersburg were some of the nicest people in the world, she decided, as she turned the truck around and headed toward home. Once Marty spent more time there, he'd see that, too.

Maybe they'd have a chance to talk about it over the holidays. She thought about the beautiful red poinsettia Marty had sent the day before, with a note attached inviting her to his mother's house in Richmond for Christmas dinner. Then, when they had talked on the phone, she had agreed to stay a few days after the holiday, visiting with him and his family. She had already arranged for the vet in Hillsboro to cover for her while she was gone. The only real problem with the visit was Lady. Maybe Jed and Kacie would keep her for a few days. Suzanne frowned. Lady was a problem, and not just for the holidays. For some reason Marty didn't like Lady, and Suzanne knew the feeling was mutual. That was something else she was going to have to work out, but she'd worry about it later.

As she rounded the curve on the highway and saw the lights of town ahead, she glanced down at the rawhide bone and thought about Lucky. Kacie had told her the day before that those bones had really worked for his chewing, but the hardware store was out of them. Lady would be glad to share. Suzanne glanced at her watch. Almost ten o'clock. Kacie would be in bed, but Jed might not, and she could talk to him about keeping Lady for her. She drove slowly past the house, and when she saw the lights on she pulled the truck into the driveway. She really would like to see Jed.

Kacie was still awake when the doorbell rang, and she tiptoed to the top of the stairs to see who was coming so late. She heard her father inviting the person in. From the sound of his voice, it was someone he was very happy to see. Then she recognized Suzanne's voice and hurried down the stairs with Lucky beside her.

"Kacie, I hope I didn't wake you. I brought a rawhide bone for Lucky," Suzanne told her.

"Great! We're completely out." Kacie took the bone and Lucky barked hopefully. "How about some hot chocolate?"

"Sorry, Kacie," Jed interrupted. "You've got school tomorrow."

"Aw, Dad..." But she could tell by his expression that there was no point in arguing. She started toward the stairs. "C'mon, Lucky. They're throwing us out."

"See you tomorrow, Kacie," Suzanne called after her.

Kacie lingered at the top of the stairs until she heard Suzanne and her father walk toward the kitchen, then she headed for the bathroom heat vent. "Lucky, you've got to be quiet," she whispered. Lucky barked enthusiastically. "No, Lucky, you don't understand. Here, chew on this." Lucky took the new toy and lay down to gnaw on it. Kacie hoped it would keep him quiet. The last time she'd listened at the heat vent the conversation had been very interesting.

"You don't need to apologize for coming at ten o'clock," Kacie heard her dad saying. "I'm a night owl. Always have been."

"Actually I did expect Kacie to be in bed," Suzanne replied.

"Normally she would be." Neither of them spoke for a moment, and Kacie leaned closer to the heat vent to make sure she wasn't missing anything.

"If you thought Kacie was asleep, then you must have come to see me," Jed observed.

He was right, Kacie realized. The thought gave her kind of a funny feeling inside. She liked the idea of Suzanne and her dad being friends, but she wasn't sure she liked the idea of Suzanne coming to see just her dad and not her.

"Well, actually, I guess maybe I did come to see you. I'm going to Richmond over the holidays and I wondered whether you and Kacie could keep Lady."

"Of course, Suzanne, you know we will."

"Thank you, Jed," Suzanne said. "There was one other thing," she added after a moment.

She hesitated. Obviously she was having difficulty with whatever she was going to say.

"Jed, I'd been thinking about what I said to you about Marty, and well, I just thought—" She hesitated again.

"You're embarrassed and you wish you hadn't talked to me, is that it?" Jed's voice was brusque.

"No, Jed, that isn't it at all." Suzanne paused. "I felt much better after talking to you, but I'm afraid I gave you the wrong impression. When I thought about what I'd said, it sounded so awful, like Marty attacked me or something, and it wasn't like that at all."

Kacie stifled a cough and pressed her ear hard against the heat vent. So it was Marty. He really was the one who left those bruises on Suzanne's arms. Kacie listened to see if she could find out how it happened.

"Suzanne, did you hear something?"

Kacie held her breath.

"A noise like a cough?"

"Exactly like a cough." Jed's chair scraped against the floor. "Maybe I ought to check on Kacie."

As quietly as possible Kacie tiptoed into her bedroom. Lucky scampered after her with a happy bark. Kacie crawled into bed, wishing the springs wouldn't squeak and Lucky would be quiet. The last thing she needed was for her father to find out she'd been listening at the heat vent.

In the kitchen, Jed put his hand on Suzanne's shoulder and gestured toward the upstairs. She smiled and nodded.

"Why don't we go out to my studio, as you call it," he suggested. "That might be more private. Sound carries through the heat vents in this house," he explained, as he walked beside her. "I don't know whether Kacie was listening or not, but out here we can be sure she won't hear us."

Suzanne frowned, suddenly concerned. "Oh, Jed, do you think she heard what I said to you about Marty? I lied to her about the bruises, and I felt terrible about it, but I didn't think she'd understand."

Jed hesitated. From the questions Kacie had asked him, he was sure she'd figured it out on her own. "Kacie is very perceptive. I think she already suspected."

"Should I talk to her about it?"

"At this point, it's probably better to leave it alone. Unless, of course, it happens again."

Suzanne leaned toward him. "It won't, Jed. I'm certain it won't. Marty and I talked about it, and I'm sure he didn't mean to hurt me."

Jet met her eyes, no more convinced than he had been before. "And are you also sure you want to marry him?"

She looked away and studied the diamond sparkling on her finger. It was a beautiful ring, a symbol of the promise she and Marty were going to make to love each other for a lifetime. She wanted to believe in that promise. She looked at Jed, her gray eyes unwavering. "You asked me that before. I guess all I can say is I think so."

Jed ran his fingers through his hair and stood up, walking to the window then pacing across the room. "I think so" wasn't enough for a lifetime commitment, but he didn't know how to persuade her. For a minute he continued to pace, his hands jammed into his jeans pockets. Then he turned to Suzanne. "I want you to be happy," he said in a husky voice. "I care about you. I care about you very much. I just want to be sure you know what you're doing." He sat beside her again and took her hand in his. "I don't want you to marry him because you feel obligated. You're special, Suzanne. You deserve a man who understands that, a man who loves you and cares for you—"

"How can you say Marty doesn't love me? He's bought me this beautiful ring and arranged a wonderful wedding. He takes me to romantic restaurants and phones at least twice a day when he can't see me. He sends flowers all the time. He's always concerned about what I'm doing and where I've been. He's insanely jealous if I even look at another man. Doesn't that sound like he loves me? What more could he do?''

"All right, all right, so he loves you. But do you love him? Love him enough to marry him?''

"Oh, Jed...." Suzanne gripped his hand tightly as she tried to find the words to explain how she felt. "All my life I've wanted to be married to a man who wanted the same things I do—a home, children, financial security. I didn't have any of those things when I was growing up. My mother was a single parent. My father walked out on her when I was only a baby. There was never enough money, even though my mother worked two jobs. I was a latchkey kid before I was seven years old. I don't want my children to live like that. I don't want them to cry alone in their beds at night because they're terrified there's no money to pay the rent and they're going to be evicted again—''

"You never told me all that." Jed looked at her with a new understanding and a deep compassion.

"I never tell anyone.''

Jed squeezed her hand. "Even Marty?''

Suzanne turned pale. "All I've ever told him is that my parents are dead, and that's mostly true. My mother died right after I graduated from high school, and my father might as well be dead. I haven't seen him since he walked out on us." She looked for understanding and found it in his eyes. "Marty's background is totally different," she continued. "He wouldn't understand.''

"I see." For a moment Jed sat quietly, remembering the first years when he and Elizabeth had been married. They had no money, but it didn't seem to matter. They had lived in a tiny apartment over a garage, eaten a lot of hot dogs and peanut butter, and made love endlessly on the lumpy old bed from his mother's attic. Kacie's arrival had been totally unplanned and wonderful. Most of her clothes and baby furnishings had come from the thrift shop. The crib had cost $3.50, and he had painted it bright red because he thought a kid would be happier looking at a red crib than a white one. They knew that some day there would be enough money. The hell of it was that hadn't happened until after Elizabeth had died and "Out on a Limb" had become successful. But those early years had been good anyway, probably the best of his life. How could he explain to Suzanne what a marriage should be like? Besides, maybe he was wrong. Maybe she really did love Marty.

Jed put his arm around Suzanne and gave her a gentle hug. "I guess you have to trust your own feelings."

She looked down again and studied the diamond ring on her finger. "I do," she whispered.

He didn't believe her, and he didn't know how to keep her from making a terrible mistake.

KACIE PEERED through the snow-covered branches enclosing the tree house and watched as Billy darted between the bushes and swung up the rope ladder to the platform. He was late as usual, but she'd waited because after what she'd heard the night before she knew for sure Marty had hurt Suzanne, and she had to talk to someone.

"Sorry," Billy apologized. "I had to deliver these stupid cookies for my mother. They were supposed to look like Santa Claus, but you'd never know it." He stopped talking for a minute to catch his breath and took a good look at Kacie. "Hey, what did you do to your hair?" He reached out and tugged on a strand that had escaped from Kacie's knit hat.

Embarrassed, Kacie jerked away and stuffed her hair under her hat. "I curled it. With my new curling iron."

"Oh."

"Does it look weird?"

"No, it's okay."

"I was practicing for Christmas Eve, when I have to sing in the choir."

"Oh." Billy stared at Kacie for a few more seconds then cleared his throat loudly. "Is that why you wanted to meet me here today, to look at your hair?"

"Don't be dumb." Kacie turned away from him and scraped at the snow with her boot. "I don't know what to do about Suzanne." She waited to see if he'd make some smart remark, but he didn't, so she went on. "A couple of weeks ago she had these big bruises on her arms just like fingerprints and she tried to cover them up. She said she fell against the desk in the clinic."

"So?"

"So, it was a lie. Marty did it to her."

"How do you know?"

Kacie looked him square in the eye. "I listened at the heat vent last night, and I heard Suzanne talking to my dad. I still don't know how it happened, because they moved to where I couldn't hear them before they got to that part."

Billy walked once around the tree house making a line of symmetrical footprints in the snow before he came back to face Kacie. "If Suzanne marries this Marty character, she could have a real problem."

Kacie nodded glumly. "I know."

"No," Billy continued, "I mean a real problem. Remember that book?"

"Book?"

"You know, the one by Allison Craig about the kid whose father was beating up on her mother."

Suddenly Kacie did remember. She'd read the book the year before and at the time it hadn't made much impression because she couldn't imagine anyone behaving like that. "Yeah, and didn't the mother keep lying about how she got the bruises and then she finally had to go to the hospital and the doctor figured the whole thing out?"

"Something like that." They stood silent for a moment, both tracing patterns in the snow with their feet, remembering the story and not liking it. Then Billy shrugged. "Maybe you ought to give Suzanne the book and let her see what she's getting into."

"Yeah." Kacie nodded. That was exactly what she'd do. "Thanks, Billy." She grabbed his hand with both of hers and noticed his whole face seemed very pink, probably from the cold. He muttered something she couldn't quite understand then put his arm around her and helped her down from the tree house. In all the years they'd gone up there, he'd never done that.

The following morning Kacie was in the school library before the first warning bell rang. Impatiently she leafed through a magazine until Margaret Henniker arrived carrying a cup of tea in one hand and a bulging folder in the other.

"You're in here early this morning, Kacie," Margaret observed. "Problem with an assignment?" She dumped the folder on her desk and prepared herself to hear a frantic plea for information on some obscure topic for a report due that day.

Kacie shook her head. "Not this time. I want that book by Allison Craig, *Life Isn't Always Like It Seems*, and I can't find it on the shelf."

"Let's check the returns," Margaret suggested, leading the way to the cart. "If we don't have that particular one, I know there were some other Allison Craigs that came back yesterday."

"No," Kacie told her, "I only want that one."

As she sorted through the books in the return cart, Margaret thought about Kacie's request. She was acting like a kid with a purpose, and the book she was so definite about wanting was about a man beating his wife. Margaret had learned over the years that requests like Kacie's usually reflected problems that were bothering students.

Within a few minutes, she located the book and handed it to Kacie. "Is there some special reason you wanted this book?" she asked casually.

"Huh? Oh, no." Kacie looked up from the first page, which she was already reading. "I just heard it's a good story."

The answer made Margaret more suspicious. "Don't I remember you participating in our discussion group on this book last spring?"

"Oh, yeah," Kacie said vaguely. "I guess I forgot." At the sound of the first bell she trailed out of the library, her eyes glued to the book.

Soon after the final bell had rung, the hall quieted and Margaret looked up to see Ed walking into the library. He visited almost every morning, always when they were alone so that no one would see the looks that passed between them.

On this particular morning, however, Margaret was still concerned about Kacie. "Ed, can you think of any particular reason why Kacie Parker would be anxious to read a book about wife beating?"

Ed laughed. "You mean that book she was reading when she almost ran over me in the hall?"

"She came to school twenty minutes early to get it. I can't figure it out unless one of her friends has a problem," Margaret mused.

"With anyone else, I'd tell them their imagination was overactive." Ed brushed his hand lightly across Margaret's back and smiled. "But, with you, I know how good your instincts are." His eyes twinkled as he added, "Along with a lot of other things."

"Ed!" Margaret looked at her desk, trying to hide the flush of pleasure she knew colored her cheeks. "I'm trying to figure out what to do about Kacie."

"You'll work that out," Ed said confidently. "I know you. But right now, I'm trying to figure out tonight." He grinned at her. "Are you free from, say, dinner to about 5:00 a.m.?"

Margaret looked up and smiled. "Only for you." She knew how much he wanted to kiss her and that he simply couldn't in the middle of the school library, and she enjoyed his dilemma.

"Just wait till tonight," he threatened.

Margaret laughed. She could hardly wait.

At lunchtime, Margaret was walking through the crowded, noisy cafeteria, hoping the strawberry yogurt wasn't sold out, when she spotted Kacie totally engrossed in *Life Isn't Always Like It Seems*. Something about that still bothered her, enough that she decided to give Jed Parker a call and ask him to stop by. If Kacie did have a friend with a problem, she needed some adult support.

CHAPTER EIGHT

JED WAS PRETTY SURE that Margaret Henniker had asked him to stop by the school library because she wanted to solicit his support for the book program. He was ready to give it. Since his conversation with Suzanne and Kacie at dinner several weeks before, he had changed his attitude about the Allison Craig books. Many of the issues the books dealt with weren't ones he'd have chosen, but if the kids were as interested as they seemed to be, the books must be on target.

As Jed walked into the library, dodging paper snowflakes suspended from the ceiling, Margaret appeared from behind some tall bookshelves. "It was so good of you to come, Mr. Parker."

"No problem." He decided to offer his support up front; that way she wouldn't have to give him a sales pitch and they'd both save time. "I wanted to talk to you anyway and let you know I've dropped my objections to the Allison Craig books. After reading a couple of them and talking to Kacie, I can see they have merit."

Margaret was surprised, but more than willing to have another supporter. There hadn't been many of late. "I'm certainly glad to hear that, Mr. Parker."

"Now you understand I'm not endorsing everything she writes," Jed added quickly. He wanted to make certain he wasn't getting in too deep.

Margaret nodded. "Neither am I, Mr. Parker. I'm simply in favor of the children having the opportunity to explore social issues that are important to them."

Jed extended his hand. "Let me know if I can be of any help to you," he offered and turned to go.

"Mr. Parker," Margaret said quickly, "as much as I appreciate your support, there was another reason I asked you to come."

Jed felt totally unprepared. "Is Kacie in some kind of trouble?"

"Oh, no, nothing like that," Margaret assured him. "Why don't you come over and sit down?"

Jed followed Margaret to one of the long library tables where he listened to her explain Kacie's book request. "It's been my experience that such an urgent request for a particular Allison Craig book usually reflects a specific personal need," she explained. "I wondered whether any of Kacie's friends might have problems at home."

How close she was, Jed thought. He looked at the librarian with renewed admiration. "I want to thank you for letting me know." Jed chose his words carefully. "Kacie is aware of a situation, which I've been watching closely. I'll talk to her." He wished he could say more so that Margaret could know just how intuitive she was.

Margaret didn't question him any further. "I'll leave it in your hands, Mr. Parker. Battering problems are so frightening that I thought she might need help."

Her words stayed with Jed as he drove home and they haunted him as he sat in his studio trying to concentrate on his work. Kacie wasn't the only one who needed help. So did Suzanne. Except... The doubt crept back. What if she was right and he was wrong? What if the bruises were indeed a one-time mistake by a man who was tired, distraught, got angry and pressed a little too hard, but had then felt great remorse and would never do it again? But what if he did do it again? Unable to work, Jed wandered into the kitchen. When Kacie came home from choir practice, he was at the stove stirring a pot of chili.

"Hi, Dad." Kacie's backpack landed on the floor as she leaned down to hug Lucky. The puppy yipped in delight and licked every inch of Kacie's face with his long, wet tongue.

"How was choir?"

"Okay. The same as usual, except the organist practiced with us today because the Christmas Eve performance is coming up." She walked to the stove and sniffed the chili. "When's dinner? I'm starved."

"Right now." Jed ladled the chili into two bowls and set them on the table along with some crackers and a bowl of grated Cheddar cheese. Kacie sat across from him and Lucky took his accustomed place at her feet. Jed decided dinner was a good time to talk to Kacie about Suzanne. "I noticed you're reading a new Allison Craig book," he ventured conversationally.

"Uh-huh."

"What's it about?"

Kacie blew on a spoonful of chili. "A girl whose father beats her mother, but the mother lies about it."

"Any particular reason you chose that book?"

Kacie's expression was guarded. She was staring at her chili. "I heard it was a good story."

Jed decided to change his approach. He never had been very good at the indirect method with Kacie. "Are you worried about Marty hurting Suzanne?" he asked bluntly.

Kacie crumbled crackers into her chili and added more cheese. A full minute passed before she answered. "Yeah. How did you know?"

"I guessed." He didn't see any need to add that the evidence had been overwhelming.

For the first time since she had sat down to dinner, Kacie looked at her father. "I know he made those bruises on her arms—I don't care what she said. It's just like the woman in the book. And do you know what happens at the end?"

Jed shook his head.

"The man hits his wife real hard and she falls down the stairs and almost dies."

They sat in silence as Jed absorbed what Kacie had told him and Kacie thought about it.

"Can't you tell Suzanne not to marry Marty?" Kacie asked finally. "She'd listen to you."

How Jed wished that were true. He had tried every way he could think of to raise questions in Suzanne's mind. "I can't tell her what to do, Kacie. She has to make her own decisions."

Kacie shot him an accusing look. "But what if he hurts her, really hurts her, I mean? How are you going to feel then?"

Jed looked at his daughter. That was the question he had asked himself a dozen times. Right along with, how could he stop Suzanne from going ahead with the wedding? And whether he had any right to try. "I'm doing my best, Kacie, okay?" He knew he sounded defensive, but it was all he could think of to say.

"I know you are, Dad," Kacie answered.

And for a moment Jed wondered who was supporting whom.

THE WEEK BEFORE CHRISTMAS flew by and almost before they knew it, it was Christmas Eve. The church was bathed in candlelight, the altar was laden with red poinsettias, and the rough wooden manger was waiting. Soon a small child would lay a doll wrapped in swaddling clothes in the manger, and for a moment everyone would once again be a part of the miracle of the Christmas birth.

Kacie sat in the choir loft trying to focus on what the minister was saying instead of on the pile of presents at home under the tree. She'd been happy all day wrapping packages and baking cookies, and when she and her dad had picked up Suzanne to come to church, her life seemed complete. Afterward they were all going back to the house to have eggnog and the Christmas cookies she'd baked. Then Suzanne was going to bring Lady, because she would be leaving early the next morning for Richmond.

Kacie's eyes wandered across the congregation, picking out the various people she knew well. Billy was in the third row with his family, wearing a suit and a red tie. He looked really nice except for the way he had his hair slicked down. She hoped he liked the ring puzzle she was giving him. Miss Henniker and Mr. Arnold were sitting together almost at the back of the church. They were together a lot. She wondered if other people noticed that, too, or if she and Billy were the only ones. Suzanne and her dad were about halfway back. Suzanne was right on the aisle in case she had to leave for an emergency. She was the vet on call so she had to wear her beeper on the belt of her red dress. She looked pretty. Her cheeks were pink and her eyes were all sparkly. Her hair was curled around her face like those pictures of women in shampoo advertisements in magazines. Kacie wished Suzanne wasn't going to spend Christmas with Marty.

The organist raised his hand and the choir stood up, quietly and all together just as they had practiced. Kacie could tell the choir director was pleased. They were halfway through the second verse of "Joy to the World" when Kacie saw Suzanne and her dad leave their pew and walk quickly up the aisle toward the back of the church. The beeper must have gone off. That meant Suzanne was going to the telephone.

The choir finished the last verse of "Joy to the World" and began "Silent Night." Kacie sang with one eye on the choir director and the other on the back of the church. If Suzanne and her dad didn't come back pretty soon, they weren't going to. That meant there was some exciting emergency, and she was being left behind. Halfway through "Silent Night" Kacie made her decision. Covering her mouth with her hand as if she might be going to throw up, she squeezed between two choir members and raced down the back stairway. Trading her robe for her coat, she ran for the parking lot, with the strains of "Silent Night" echoing behind her.

Jed and Suzanne were just getting into Jed's car as she caught up to them.

"Kacie!" Jed exclaimed. "What are you doing out here?"

"The choir is almost through and I saw you leave and I wanted to go with you." Her father looked none too happy, but she caught the hint of a smile on Suzanne's face.

"You need to be inside, Kacie," Jed said firmly.

"But I can't go back now. I'd be a disruption."

Jed sighed. "All right, get in the car."

"What's the emergency?" Kacie leaned over the front seat as Jed pulled the car out of the parking lot.

"I have a mare in trouble delivering her foal out at the Delaney farm," Suzanne answered. "Your dad is taking me home to get the truck. We don't have much time."

"Can I go with you?"

Suzanne glanced at Jed. "Maybe you'd both like to go with me. There's a lot of tradition behind spending Christmas Eve in a stable."

"Can we? Can we, Dad?"

Jed hesitated, feeling his irritation with Kacie drain away. He could think of nothing better than spending Christmas Eve watching the miracle of birth with the people he loved most. He smiled at Suzanne, realizing they were all about to share something very special. "Yes, Kacie. We'll spend this Christmas Eve in the Delaneys' stable."

Jed parked the car alongside Suzanne's pickup, and before they got in Suzanne pulled on a pair of olive drab twill coveralls to protect her dress and traded her pumps for a pair of well-worn sneakers. Then they all squeezed onto the seat, with Kacie in the middle, and headed out of town.

As they drove, Kacie pelted Suzanne with questions. "Why is this foal being born now instead of in the spring?"

"I don't know for sure because this mare is not my regular patient. I'd guess she got a little off schedule when she came into heat."

"Why is the foal being born at night? Are all foals born during the night?"

"Most of them," Suzanne answered. She turned on the radio so they could listen to Christmas carols as they rode. "It goes back to when horses ran in wild herds. Darkness provided extra safety for newborn animals because predators are less likely to find a baby at night. Domesticated animals are still controlled by their ancient instincts for survival."

"Does it take very long? For a foal to be born, I mean."

Suzanne slowed the truck, looking for the gravel road that led to the Delaneys' farm. "No, most foals are born in less than an hour, although the mare may pace around and be pretty uncomfortable for a couple of hours before that."

"And this mare has a problem?" Jed interjected.

Suzanne knew what he was thinking, and she knew she had to warn Kacie, and Jed, too, that the evening might not have a happy ending. "I don't know exactly what's wrong with her, Kacie. I'm hoping it's something I can help with. But there's always the possibility that the foal won't live."

For several moments Kacie was very quiet. Suzanne reached over and squeezed her hand. "I know that's hard," she said quietly.

"I don't want the baby to die." Kacie's voice quivered.

"Neither do I, Kacie. I'll do my best."

Fred Delaney was waiting for them when Suzanne parked the truck beside the barn.

"Merry Christmas, Fred," Suzanne said as she climbed out of the truck.

The old farmer nodded. "Sorry I had to get you out here on Christmas Eve, Doc, but Lulu doesn't look like she can drop this foal by herself."

"I'll see what I can do," Suzanne told him.

The sweet, musky scent of hay greeted them as they walked into the barn. A single light burned over a large stall where the gray mottled Appaloosa mare paced restlessly. As Suzanne approached her she pawed the floor with a front hoof, scraping through the hay to the wooden floor. Then she threw her head toward her hindquarters.

"This is how she's been, real agitated," the farmer told Suzanne. "Could hardly get the wife and kids to go to church with her like this. Lulu's the kids' horse, you know. They'd be heartbroken if anything happened."

Suzanne reached for her gloves. "Just hold on there, Lulu," she said in a soothing voice. "I'll see what's the matter here."

Kacie found an old wooden chair across from the mare's stall and settled herself on it to watch. Jed stood quietly near her, his eyes riveted not on the mare, but on Suzanne. Even wearing the baggy coveralls, her long hair pulled back into an elastic, she was beautiful. In the dimly lit barn, she was a study in light and shadow, moving with quiet confidence that calmed them all. Searching his pockets, Jed located a pencil, and after looking around for a moment found an empty paper sack. He sat on some hay bales and started to sketch, wanting to capture the night and the moment, but most of all the gentle beauty of the woman in front of him.

Suzanne pulled on long obstetrical gloves, which reached well above her elbows, and began murmuring to the mare in quiet tones, moving carefully as she stationed herself to the side of the horse's rear leg to avoid being kicked. Fred Delaney stood by the mare's head, holding her halter and talking to her. Suzanne lifted the tail and slowly reached beneath and worked her hand inside the birth canal to determine the position of the foal. "I found the problem," she told Fred softly. "All I can feel is the nose and one front foot."

"Not both front feet?" Fred asked. "They should be coming out first."

"It feels like the left foreleg is bent back. I'll have to try to work it around."

Jed's pencil made scratching sounds as it swept across the paper in the otherwise silent barn. He could see Suzanne's profile, her face intense as she worked. Her whole being was focused on helping the mare and her foal. Beads of perspiration stood out on her forehead as she braced herself against the back of the stall and pushed hard, trying to force the foal farther back in the birth canal so she could maneuver the bent leg into the correct position. Jed watched her manipulate the baby inside its mother, sometimes closing her eyes in concentration. He remembered what she had said about there not being much time, and he hoped there would be enough.

All at once the mare snorted and jerked away, and Suzanne jumped aside just in time to escape a gush of straw-colored fluid. The mare snorted again and lay down in the hay.

"What happened?" Kacie asked, wide-eyed.

"Her water broke, and I think we've made it," Suzanne answered. "Can you see her belly contracting, Kacie?"

Kacie came closer and peered into the stall for a better look.

"That's her uterus working to push the foal out," Suzanne explained. "Move around here and watch closely now and you'll see the front feet coming out."

An endless minute passed. Jed stopped sketching and leaned closer to see around Kacie. His fingers tightened around his pencil and he held his breath. Then the mare's belly heaved and he saw two tiny feet appear, then the head resting between the legs.

"It's coming! The baby's coming! I see it!" Kacie cried excitedly.

"You got it, Doc," Fred Delaney announced, and went to his mare's head to urge her on.

Jed said nothing but breathed a huge sigh of relief. His pencil began to move again and in a few minutes he was working to capture Suzanne bending over the foal, which was lying in the hay.

"Is it a filly or a colt?" Fred asked.

Suzanne finished wiping the wet foal's nose and mouth then inspected it. "You've got a colt, Fred," she told the farmer, "a Christmas colt."

"Good work, Lulu." Fred stroked the mare's neck, which glistened with sweat. "We'll name him Noel.

The kids will think this is the best Christmas present they ever had.''

For a few moments they all watched the newborn colt thrash in the hay. ''Shouldn't you help him?'' Kacie asked Suzanne in a worried voice.

Suzanne peeled off her long gloves. ''Not any more. He needs to struggle like this so he can establish his breathing outside his mother.''

Soon the exhausted mare was on her feet, nuzzling and licking her colt. ''Lulu loves her baby already, doesn't she?'' Kacie asked in awe.

''Yes, Kacie,'' Suzanne told her, ''from the very beginning. The love of a mother for her newborn is one of the strongest instincts there is. Right now they're learning each other's scent. It's what we call bonding.''

Jed sat back watching the scene before him, laughing with the rest of them at the colt's awkward efforts to stand and cheering with the others when it finally got its footing. But his thoughts were with Suzanne. While Kacie petted the colt and Fred Delaney tended to his mare, Suzanne walked over and sat down beside Jed. He could see the joy in her face, and he shared it. He slipped his arm around her waist.

Suzanne looked at him and smiled. ''I was afraid I might lose him there for a minute,'' she confided. ''I couldn't get that left leg free.''

''You were wonderful,'' he whispered, ''and you must be exhausted.''

''Sort of.'' She let her head rest on his shoulder. ''I'm glad you and Kacie came.''

''Me, too.'' He held her against him and tried to pretend they were friends sharing a special victory. But there was more, and he knew it, and if they had been alone he might have told her. His heart ached at the thought that this night was only a moment snatched out of their lives. Tomorrow she would be off to Richmond to spend Christmas with another man. She lifted her head from his shoulder and he fought the urge to hold her there. They fit together exactly the way a man and woman should.

"I'm not needed here any more," she said. "I'll gather up my things and we can go."

"Suzanne—" She turned to him and he wasn't sure what to say. He wanted to touch her cheek, smooth the lock of hair that had escaped from the elastic, lean over and kiss her lips, which were so terribly inviting. But he couldn't do any of those things. "I . . . I just wanted to tell you," he began haltingly, "this has been a wonderful Christmas Eve. Thank you."

"I feel the same way," she told him softly. "Thank you, Jed."

He savored her words, but more than that, he wondered at the light in her eyes as she said them. It had been a very special night for all of them.

The colt had moved up against his mother by the time they left, nuzzling her belly looking for milk. The mare gave him a gentle nudge toward her udder, and he began sucking contentedly. Together, with Kacie behind them, Suzanne and Jed walked out of the barn into the cold, star-filled night. Kacie climbed into the truck as Jed helped Suzanne put away her supplies in the back. When they were finished and she turned to thank him, he put his hands on her shoulders and looked into her eyes. "Do you have to go to Richmond tomorrow?" He knew he shouldn't ask, but he had to. He saw a flicker of surprise then understanding.

Suzanne lowered her eyes. "I need to go, Jed."

For one brief moment he held her, then he bent and kissed her cheek. "Merry Christmas, Suzanne," he whispered.

"Merry Christmas," she answered.

They got into the truck with Kacie between them and were very quiet all the way home.

CHAPTER NINE

CHRISTMAS IN RICHMOND seemed so unreal afterward that Suzanne could hardly believe any of it had happened. She tried to remember it in detail as she paced restlessly around the clinic waiting for Jed. He'd be there any minute to bring Lady home. Strange, she thought, how all the parties and the Christmas festivities with Marty and his family blurred together, but how clear her memory was of Christmas Eve with Jed and Kacie.

She heard Jed's car tires crunching on the gravel in her driveway and the engine shut off and the car door slam. She hurried to the reception room and was there when he arrived. Lady came in first, scampering across the waiting room and straight into Suzanne's arms as she knelt to greet her dog. Lady whimpered with excitement as her tongue licked a path of love across Suzanne's face.

"I missed you, Lady." She gave the dog a big hug. "I'm so glad to see you." She looked up to find Jed's brown eyes filled with laughter as he watched them. He was fresh as morning, clean-shaven, with his sandy brown hair combed back. He wore jeans and a sweatshirt and a pair of work boots. His red plaid jacket was unzipped, but the collar was still turned up around his ears. "I missed you, too, Jed," she said almost shyly.

She didn't tell him how often he had crept into her thoughts while she'd been away or how many times she'd relived their Christmas Eve. "Come on in and tell me about your holiday," she said, standing up. "I've got some fresh coffee made."

While she poured their coffee, he told her about opening presents with Kacie and eating frozen pizza for Christmas dinner after their attempt to cook the turkey turned into a fiasco, and about going sledding two days later after a three-inch snowfall. Suzanne listened wistfully. He made it all sound like such fun.

They sat in the chairs next to Suzanne's desk with Lady stationed next to Suzanne looking up expectantly. "She was a real doll," Jed said, nodding at Lady, "but I know she missed you."

"Thanks for keeping her." Suzanne leaned down to pat the dog. "I don't leave her often."

"Tell me about Richmond," Jed said, stirring his coffee. "How was your trip?"

"Well—" Lady nudged her knee and Suzanne walked over to the cabinet where she kept the dog biscuits. "Marty's mother had an enormous party on New Year's eve so that all of their friends could meet me." She turned and handed the dog her treat.

"I assume everyone thought you were wonderful."

"Yes.... Everything seemed to go very well." A shadow crossed her face and she turned away from Jed to put the box of dog biscuits in the cabinet. "Marty's family lives in a huge house, you know. It's impeccably decorated and there's a magnificent curved staircase going from the foyer up to the second floor." She returned to her chair and sat down. For a minute she was silent, gazing through the window toward the woods in back of the clinic.

Jed gathered from her hesitation that there was more to tell. He glanced at her hand, but the engagement ring was still on her finger. He had let himself hope that maybe, after Christmas Eve, she'd have had second thoughts. The phone rang, and Suzanne reached for it, automatically pushing the hair back on one side of her face so she could settle the receiver over her ear. Jed stared at her then looked away, fighting the anger that flashed through him. Nearly hidden in her hair was a laceration, probably two inches long, with several black sutures holding the raw edges together.

Suzanne laughed as she hung up the phone. "Amazing what some people consider an emergency. This puppy—"

"Suzanne, what really happened in Richmond?" His tone was brusque.

"But, Jed, I was just telling you—"

"Your head, Suzanne. What happened?"

Suzanne reached up, covering the injury with her hand. "Nothing, really," she stammered. "Marty and I were standing at the top of that long staircase I was telling you about, and somehow I lost my balance. When I fell I must have hit my head on the railing."

Jed slammed his coffee mug down on the desk. All he could think about was Kacie's book and the woman who had been pushed down the stairs. "I don't believe you," he said roughly.

"What do you mean you don't believe me?" Suzanne's voice rose. "You don't have any right to question me like this."

"What the hell are you doing, Suzanne?" Jed exploded. All the anger at Marty, pent up since he bruised Suzanne's arms, poured out. "Why are you covering up for this guy?"

"I'm not covering for anyone." Suzanne stood so abruptly that Lady whimpered in surprise. "You are being absolutely ridiculous. I hit my head on the stair rail. That's all. I had a few stitches and everything is just fine."

"Is it, Suzanne? Is everything fine?" Jed stood up and laid his hands on Suzanne's arms, willing her to look into his eyes. "I don't think so."

"Don't touch me like that." Her voice was barely above a whisper.

"Why? This is how Marty bruised you that night, isn't it? He was angry and he grabbed you. And now you think I'm angry and you're frightened I'm going to hurt you, too, aren't you?"

Suzanne yanked away from him. "No, that's not true. I'm not afraid of you. And I'm not afraid of Marty, either. He doesn't mean to hurt me. And if I just thought a little more carefully before I opened my mouth, he wouldn't have any reason to be angry with me."

Jed couldn't believe she'd said that. If he'd understood her correctly, she was saying what Marty had done was her fault. "Are you trying to tell me you're responsible for him hurting you? That's crazy, Suzanne. You've got it all twisted up."

"Stop this right now." Suzanne's voice was shaking. "You don't know what you're talking about."

"Suzanne! What's the matter with you? Where is that brain that got you through vet school? Has it stopped working since you got engaged to Marty?" He was shouting. He knew he was. But he was so damn angry. How could a woman, any woman, let a man treat her like that?

"There's nothing wrong with my logic, or my brain, either, for that matter," Suzanne shouted back. "I'm engaged and I'm going to be married in April. And that's the way it is, whether you like it or not, Jed Parker!"

"And do you love this man with your entire being? Would you lose part of yourself if you lost him? And do you trust him? Trust him totally and absolutely, even beyond reason?" He heard the words spilling out, all the things he had thought but hadn't said. Somehow he had to get through to her. He had to make her understand before it was too late. His eyes bored into hers. "If you can't answer yes to those questions, you sure as hell shouldn't be marrying him. And if you do marry him, I don't want to be the guy who has to identify your battered body at the morgue."

"Stop it, Jed! I don't want to hear any more." Suzanne grabbed his jacket from the back of his chair and thrust it at him. "Get out. Get out of my life. I don't want to see you again."

"That suits me just fine." Jed snatched his jacket and stalked out of her office, slamming the door behind him.

SUZANNE BURST INTO TEARS and stared at the closed door, a blast of cold air enveloping her and penetrating deep inside. Why had she done that? Jed was the one person she had thought she could talk to. He was a friend, a good friend when there was no one else.

Suddenly her anger was gone and in its place was a dark void. She felt terribly alone.

Lady nuzzled her leg and she knelt and hugged the old dog, wiping her tears against Lady's soft coat. If only Jed hadn't been so unreasonable, she could have told him how she felt. But not after what he'd said. Of course she was uneasy about Marty. He'd seemed very different since they got engaged. Not that he wasn't still as solicitous as ever. He called, he sent flowers, he bought expensive presents like the diamond heart on a fine gold chain he'd given her for Christmas. But the way he did it was different, almost as though she was a possession to be displayed for his pleasure. Suzanne shivered and stood up, giving Lady a gentle pat. Her thoughts trailed back to Richmond. She and Marty had been standing at the top of the stairs in his parents' house on the day of the big party in her honor. When she thought about it now, the whole thing seemed so foolish, but at the time...

"You're not going to wear your hair like that," Marty had said.

"What's the matter with it?" she'd countered, touching the ribbon that pulled her thick brown locks together at the nape of her neck.

"You know I like it down." He reached for the ribbon, probably playfully, Suzanne thought, looking back. But it hadn't seemed playful at the time.

"Stop that." She pulled away. "If you hadn't insisted on my coming with you this morning to pick up the flowers for the party, I'd have had time to shampoo it."

"If you hadn't slept so late—"

"Marty, I was up by eight o'clock and we were out last night till almost one."

"Stop making excuses." He reached for the ribbon again and she tried to stop him.

She couldn't remember exactly what had happened next. At the time she thought he had pushed her, but now that didn't seem reasonable. She remembered pitching down the stairs, pain shooting through her head when she struck the rail, then Marty's arms around her to break her fall. She had protested that she wasn't hurt while his mother fluttered around and his father brought the ice bag. All the time Marty was there, cradling her in his arms. He insisted on taking her to the emergency room to have the cut looked at and held her hand while the doctor sutured it. For the rest of the day, he'd been so concerned and so caring. All through the party he had stayed at her side and, although he was the perfect host, his attention was focused solely on her. He hadn't said it in so many words, but she knew he felt very bad about what had happened.

Suzanne sighed and sat at her desk, gingerly touching the gash on her head then pulling her hair across it so it didn't show. Whatever had happened surely had been an accident. She wouldn't even question it at all if there hadn't been the time when Marty had made bruises on her arms. She understood Jed's problem. He'd seen the bruises on her arms and now the cut on her head, and he'd blown everything out of proportion.

But he didn't have to get so angry. His anger was very different from Marty's, not less intense, exactly, but different. He didn't get that look in his eyes that frightened her. What did bother her was what he'd said. He'd managed to zero in on all the doubts she had. But she and Marty were so far along with the wedding plans now that it would be hard to turn back, and besides, she was almost certain there was no real problem.

Enough! She couldn't spend all day worrying. Resolutely she opened her account book and took two sharp pencils out of her desk drawer. The neat columns of figures blurred before her as she bent to work on closing her books for the year.

Suzanne was still there several hours later when Kacie burst through the door of the clinic with Lucky at her side.

"We missed you on Christmas," Kacie said in greeting. "How was your trip?"

Suzanne closed her account book, relieved at the interruption. "My trip was just fine." She didn't add that she'd missed them, too, and that for some reason Christmas Eve had been the high point of the holidays.

Kacie showed Suzanne Lucky's red Christmas collar and described the presents she'd received. As Kacie talked, Suzanne thought about Jed. She didn't want her argument with him to change her relationship with Kacie. Actually, she didn't want it to change her relationship with Jed, either, which was no doubt why she felt such an emptiness whenever she thought about him.

"Look at what he's learned," Kacie said proudly, grabbing Lucky's collar. "Sit," she said in a firm tone.

Lucky looked up at her and barked twice.

"No, dummy, sit." She pushed on his rump. He wagged his tail and wiggled playfully.

After several more tries, Kacie got the puppy into something resembling a sitting position and looked at Suzanne. "He did it for me right away at home."

"How many times did you try it?"

"Two."

Suzanne laughed. "Repetition, Kacie. Just keep at it. After two hundred times, you may start getting the idea across."

"I suppose. It's just that nothing is going very well today. Well, except this." She fished a paper out of her backpack and handed it to Suzanne. "I got the notice about the Big Sister ice skating party. It sounds neat."

Suzanne studied the bright red and white flyer inviting them to the ice rink with other Big and Little Sisters from around the area. She glanced at the calendar on the wall. The first weekend in February. That was the Saturday Marty was getting back from his trip, and he'd said he wanted to go shopping. Suzanne hesitated, then she saw the look of anticipation on Kacie's face. Marty would have to understand. They could shop any time, but there would be only one ice skating party.

"We can go, can't we?" Kacie asked.

"Of course we can go," Suzanne reassured her. "I wouldn't miss it."

Looking relieved, Kacie took off her coat. "At least that's one good thing."

"I take it you've had a rotten day," Suzanne said sympathetically.

"Yeah. Ever since I found out what they're doing to Miss Henniker." She took another sheet of paper out of her backpack and handed it to Suzanne. "Look at this."

Suzanne frowned as Kacie handed her what appeared to be a petition. She scanned it quickly, her frown deepening as she got to the bottom line. "And because she refuses to remove these offensive books, we the undersigned believe that the best course for the welfare of our children is to terminate the employment of the librarian."

"They want to fire Margaret Henniker?" Suzanne read it again.

Kacie nodded glumly. "It isn't fair. Just because they don't agree with her, they want to get rid of her."

"They'll never do it, Kacie. People aren't going to sign this petition. It's censorship, pure and simple."

"Don't bet on it." Kacie slouched down in an old wooden chair across from Suzanne's desk. "Billy says his mother already has more than fifty signatures and they've just started. They're aiming for three hundred, then they're going to present them to the principal. They figure with that much support he'll have to get rid of the books or Miss Henniker or both."

Suzanne stared at the blank lines marching down the legal-size piece of paper. She thought about the years Margaret had given to the children in Cartersburg. Someone who cared less would have simply removed the Allison Craig books long ago, but not Margaret. The town owed her a debt, and this was how she would be repaid.

"What are we going to do, Suzanne?" Kacie pulled Lucky away from the supply cabinet and pushed a chair in front of it to make sure he couldn't get the door open.

"I don't know, Kacie."

"But it isn't fair."

No, it wasn't fair. Life wasn't fair, sometimes, but that was a tough lesson for a thirteen-year-old. "Have you considered a counter petition?" Suzanne asked slowly.

"What's that?"

"A petition saying Miss Henniker should keep her job."

Kacie looked at her thoughtfully. "You mean we print up some forms and try to get more signatures than they do."

"Something like that."

Kacie shook her head. "The people behind this are all big shots in the PTA. Nobody would sign our petition except kids, and they don't count."

"Maybe they do, Kacie. With enough of the kids backing you, at least it's worth a try."

Kacie put her coat on. "I'll talk to Billy. C'mon, Lucky."

Suzanne followed her to the door and watched her run down the gravel driveway with Lucky racing alongside. She wished she'd been able to come up with a better solution, because she was afraid Kacie was right. With few adult signatures, a counter petition probably wouldn't work. The irony of it was that the kids were the ones who had read the books. She'd be willing to bet that ninety percent of the adults who signed that petition had no idea what the stories were really about.

Turning to her desk, Suzanne noticed a worn paperback lying on a stack of papers. She picked it up, seeing Allison Craig's name along the spine. Kacie must have put it down when she was getting the petition out of her backpack and then forgotten it. *Life Isn't Always Like It Seems,* it was titled. That was certainly a truism. She leafed through the book, then turned it over and read the blurb on the back: "Michelle's mother seemed to fall a lot and once she even had a black eye. Michelle was worried about her, but when she woke up late one night and saw what was really going on, she realized the problem was far more serious than even she had imagined."

Suzanne flipped through the pages again. The book was about a girl whose father beat her mother. She turned to the beginning and began to read, interested initially in the author's treatment of the subject. Not till she reached chapter three did it occur to her that Kacie might not have left the book by mistake.

KACIE PULLED HER COLLAR tight around her neck and turned her back to the wind that swept through the tree house. Below her Lucky whimpered and tugged at his leash, which she had looped around a tree. Billy was late again. Sometimes it seemed to her all she did was wait for him, especially this week when they'd been working so hard on their petition. Lucky's whimper changed to a sharp bark and moments later Kacie heard ice crunching down the path, then she heard the familiar whistle. He was coming, but his footsteps were slow and heavy and long minutes seemed to pass before she caught sight of his blue jacket.

"Sorry," he said, as he swung up to the platform.

"Your mother again?"

Billy shrugged. "She's been on the phone all afternoon. They've got over two hundred signatures on the petition to fire Miss Henniker and it's been less than two weeks. They figure two more weeks and they'll be ready to go."

"But we've got signatures, too. Not that many, but we'll get more."

Billy kicked at an icy patch on the tree-house platform then sat with his back against the tree trunk. "It's no good. They know about our petition. My mother called it 'amusing.'"

"Amusing. That's really wonderful." Kacie sank down beside him, grateful for the warmth as his body broke the wind. "They're not even a little bit worried?"

"Nope." Billy pushed back the shock of red hair that had escaped from his knit cap. "My mother talked about it being a 'cute' thing for us to do and said it showed how much children imitate adults and that was just one more reason someone like Margaret Henniker was a bad role model."

"Oh." Kacie felt betrayed. They'd worked so hard all week to gather almost a hundred signatures, and none of it was going to matter. Billy slid a little closer to her until their shoulders were touching. Apparently he was cold, too.

He picked up a stray acorn and pitched it to the ground, sending Lucky into a frenzy of barking. "Shut up, Lucky," he called to the dog.

"This whole thing is so stupid," Kacie said, feeling better with Billy's shoulder against hers but still very angry inside. "There must be something we can do."

Suddenly Billy turned to look at her, squinting in the late afternoon sun. "Maybe there is. There are these stink bombs that smell really awful. This kid at school has a catalog where you can order them. We could put them in all those old biddies' cars."

"Including yours?" Kacie asked pointedly. "After all, your mother—"

"Yeah, I know." He slouched against the tree. "So maybe we could spread garbage on their front lawns."

"It would serve them right," Kacie agreed. "At least they'd know how we feel about their dumb petition. I'm sick of following their rules and having them say it's cute."

They sat silent for several moments, considering the logistics of hauling enough garbage to do the job. The wind whistled around them, shaking the bare tree branches, but Kacie didn't feel cold any more. She liked having a friend like Billy, somebody who really understood. She liked everything about him but his mother, and his mother wasn't really his fault.

"Maybe we could get enough garbage out of that dumpster behind the school and haul it in wagons," he suggested.

"Good idea. Except what if it's frozen? It gets pretty cold at night."

Billy sat forward with a start. "I know. Let's TP their trees."

Kacie looked at him dubiously. "Did you ever put toilet paper in anybody's tree?"

"No, but the high school kids do it when they're mad at somebody. They really get attention."

Kacie nodded. "Then everybody in town would know exactly who the targets are."

"At least it will show them a thing or two."

Billy was grinning at her, and Kacie grinned back. He had really good ideas sometimes and he wasn't afraid to go through with them. That was part of what she liked about him. He had lots of imagination and he had courage.

They agreed to buy the toilet paper a few rolls at a time and stash it in plastic bags in the tree house. By the following Monday, they decided, they should be ready. They would start at exactly midnight and hit all five houses belonging to members of the PTA board, including one tree in Billy's yard, just to make sure no one would figure out who did it. They took off their gloves and shook on it, and Kacie found Billy's hand warm and strong. She was excited about their plan, especially because she'd be doing it with Billy.

SUZANNE MADE A FIRE in the fireplace and snuggled in front of it with a yellow legal-size pad and a mug of hot chocolate. The wedding was only two months away, and she needed to make a list. The primary things were taken care of—the church, the flowers, the invitations, the caterers, her dress. Marty had seen to all that. But there were other personal things, like the clothes she would take on the honeymoon and the arrangements for her veterinary practice while she was gone.

She laid down the yellow pad, realizing she hadn't written a word, and stared at the fire. The doubts that so often lingered around the edges of her thoughts crept in again. Ever since her argument with Jed, she hadn't been able to push them away. Marty could be so charming and so much fun, but then there was the other side of him—angry, suspicious, domineering. She glanced at Kacie's book, which lay open on the table. Was it possible he would be abusive? The idea was so foreign to her that she could hardly imagine it. But Kacie obviously was worried about it, and so was Jed.

Idly Suzanne stood up and went to the kitchen to get water for the flowers Marty had sent the day before. Daisies . . . daisies in February, so thoughtful and impulsive, so very much like Marty, or at least like the part of him that had drawn her at the beginning. She was sure he loved her and he made her feel special like no man ever had before. But did she love him? That question haunted her most.

The phone rang and Lady looked up from her place in front of the fire as if to make sure Suzanne was going to answer it. The voice on the other end was resonant and deep. "Hi, little dove, how are you tonight?"

Suzanne felt a wave of uneasiness, guilt, she decided, for ever having doubted him. "Hi, Marty," she answered in a cheerful voice. "I'm just fine. I was waiting for your call."

They talked for several minutes about his trip and the sales he had made, and he assured her again that he'd be home the following weekend. Suzanne swallowed hard. "Marty, I'm afraid I can't go shopping on Saturday."

"Why not?"

Only two words, but his voice seemed completely changed. "There's an ice skating party for Big and Little Sisters and Kacie is very anxious to go." Marty didn't answer. "I was sure you'd understand," Suzanne said quickly.

"Does everything else come first? Your office hours, your big-time emergencies, some kid, even your damn dog seems to be more important to you than I am."

Suzanne flinched. Marty's anger was swift and overwhelming. "That's not true, Marty, and besides, what does Lady have to do with this?"

He ignored her question. "We're about to be married, Suzanne. I expect a little consideration."

"Marty, that's not fair."

"I'll call you tomorrow, assuming you're home."

"But Marty, I—" She heard the click at the end of the line, and slowly replaced the receiver. Lady whimpered then stood and walked slowly to Suzanne. Suzanne knelt beside the dog. "What am I doing, old girl?" she whispered. Lady licked her cheek. Jed's words came back to her, converging with all her own doubts. One minute Marty was charming and the next he was jealous and domineering and angry. She felt like a yo-yo with him holding the string. She'd heard from so many people that the months before the wedding could be awful, and so maybe after they were married everything would settle down. She had to talk to Marty, really talk to him. Maybe if they postponed the wedding so they had more time, or maybe—

She thought about Jed again, how patient and gentle he was, how much fun they had together, how they liked all the same things. For the first time she realized it was Jed, not Marty, who occupied her thoughts when she was alone. It was Jed who sent chills through her when he lightly touched her arm, not Marty. She hugged Lady tight. "I'm awfully far into this to get out now, old girl, but, you know, I think I've been making a big mistake."

CHAPTER TEN

SUZANNE HADN'T BEEN ice skating since she was Kacie's age and she hadn't been very good then.

"C'mon," Kacie said, tugging impatiently at her arm.

Suzanne grabbed the top of the low circular wall for support as she teetered on the thin silver blades. "Just a minute." Pulling on a pair of Kacie's red and white striped mittens that matched her red sweater, she looked out over the slick ice. The rink was crowded with Big and Little Sisters, skating, laughing, falling. Some of the women were obviously quite a bit older than she was, and many of the girls were much younger than Kacie, and yet they all seemed to be having a wonderful time.

A woman about sixty and a little girl no more than six zipped by, holding hands and skating in time to the loud, fast-paced music, an unlikely blend of holiday songs and popular rock. A skate guard in a neon orange vest glided across the ice backward on one skate. Suzanne shuddered and pulled on her second mitten.

"You're not going to chicken out on me now, not after I got you here and we're all ready to go." Hands on her hips, Kacie stood as solidly as if she was wearing hiking boots instead of ice skates.

Suzanne glanced at the ice apprehensively. She knew she had stalled about as long as she could. Kacie had already skated with her caseworker and with some of the other Little Sisters. Now she was looking expectantly at Suzanne.

"I warned you, Kacie, that I haven't skated in years and I never was very good." Tentatively Suzanne shifted her weight to one foot and slid a few inches across the ice. Her legs felt like rubber. She held tightly to Kacie's hand as she shifted her weight and went a little farther forward.

"Great!" Kacie said as she glided alongside Suzanne without ever lifting her skates.

"How do you do that?" Suzanne asked her. Kacie didn't answer, but Suzanne felt herself being propelled along faster and faster until they were swept up by the momentum of the skaters, and she found herself circling the rink with Kacie.

"See, I told you it would be all right." Kacie grinned. Her eyes sparkled and her cheeks were red from the cold. "Now let's skate backward."

"Absolutely not!" Having found something she could do, Suzanne wasn't about to give it up. "You go backward and I'll push you, or guide you, or whatever you call it."

Kacie turned smoothly to face Suzanne and took her Big Sister's hands. Suzanne was sure they were both going to spill over momentarily, or worse yet, crash into other skaters. Kacie couldn't possibly have any idea where she was going with nothing but an occasional glance over her shoulder. Nevertheless, after two turns around the rink, they were both still upright and they hadn't run over anyone. Even more astonishing, the whole time they skated, Kacie never stopped talking. Suzanne, using all her energy to maintain her balance, was barely listening to her Little Sister.

"Did you hear me, Suzanne?" Kacie stopped skating backward and glided beside Suzanne.

"No, I'm sorry, I really didn't." Suzanne dodged a small wobbly child, bundled in a green snowsuit.

"I asked you if you read that book I left for you. *Life Isn't Always Like It Seems.*"

Suzanne nodded, hoping Kacie wouldn't pursue the subject. Yes, she had read the book and it had made her even more uncomfortable than going ice skating. As much as she'd wanted to stop reading it, she hadn't been able to put it down. She had felt very drawn to the woman who was being battered, and had found herself in tears when the woman nearly died after she was pushed down the stairs. Even though the man in the book had been nothing like Marty, the story stirred all her doubts. The thought that Kacie might have given her the book for a reason made her even more uneasy.

"Didn't you think that husband had a terrible temper?" Kacie persisted.

"Yes, he did." Suzanne agreed, searching for something else to discuss.

"Why do you suppose some men are like that? And why do some women stay with men who hurt them?"

"I don't know, Kacie. I don't have any answers." Suzanne gazed across the ice, not really seeing all the swirling skaters. "I guess the women love the men."

"But how can you love somebody who is hurting you and making you so unhappy?"

Suzanne felt trapped. She didn't know the answer, and in her case, she didn't know if the question applied. She wasn't sure any more if she loved Marty or truly ever had. "Some things are really puzzling, aren't they?" she answered, and before Kacie could say anything else, she added quickly, "Actually, I could use some time out. I think I'll go sit on the bleachers for a little while." She could see the disappointment in Kacie's eyes and didn't know whether it was because she'd ended the discussion or she wanted to take a break.

"I'll come sit with you," Kacie volunteered.

Suzanne gave her an affectionate squeeze. "No, you go ahead and skate and let me watch you." To her relief Kacie spotted some girls she knew and glided onto the ice to join two other Little Sisters about her age.

Feeling awkward, Suzanne made her way to an empty section of bleachers and worked hard to concentrate on the skaters and to not let herself think about Marty. Absently she twisted the diamond engagement ring on her finger.

"Thinking about your wedding?" Janet Sawyer sat next to her. "Refresh my memory. When is the big day?"

"April third." Suzanne answered automatically. She kept her eyes on Kacie as she glided around the rink.

"Getting close. Less than two months away. When my wedding was that close, I was a basket case. One minute I was so ecstatic I could hardly contain myself, and the next minute I was a quivering mass of terror." Janet laughed at the memory.

Her response piqued Suzanne's interest. "Really? Sometimes you were terrified?" Maybe she wasn't alone with her feelings.

"Absolutely. I was sure I would trip going down the aisle, or the flowers wouldn't be delivered to the church, or the London broil we had ordered for dinner would be overcooked. If anything could go wrong, believe me, I thought of it, and I worried."

"How about actually getting married?" Suzanne asked the question as casually as she could. "Were you ever worried that Ron wasn't the right man?"

Janet shook her head vehemently. "Absolutely not. I was so in love with him—and I still am—that I knew I couldn't live without him. Don't you feel like that about Marty?"

"Yes. Oh, yes. Of course I do." Suzanne felt like she was stumbling over the words as they fell out of her mouth. And she was growing more and more sure that what she'd said wasn't true.

"And is Kacie going to be a bridesmaid?" Janet waved as Kacie and her friends zipped in front of them in a lively game of ice tag.

"No, we're just having Marty's two sisters."

"Probably better that way. Actually, Kacie still doesn't seem too happy about you getting married. I skated with her for a little bit, and she sure sounded less than enthusiastic about your wedding plans."

"I think you were right, Janet. She's jealous of Marty and afraid that once I'm married I'll have less time for her." Suzanne spoke with far more conviction than she felt. She knew that Kacie had an intense dislike for Marty that escalated as the wedding drew closer.

"You are going to continue as her Big Sister, aren't you?" Janet asked with a worried tone in her voice.

Suzanne was taken aback by the question. She couldn't imagine not having Kacie as part of her life. Kacie had wound her way into Suzanne's heart and tied the knot so tight that nothing could sever it. Kacie and Jed—Suzanne swallowed hard when she thought of Jed—were becoming the family that Suzanne had never had. "I will definitely continue as Kacie's Big Sister," Suzanne said firmly. "She's terribly important to me."

Janet laughed. "You sound very sure of yourself in that department."

"I am."

"Well, then, since you're such a dedicated Big Sister, I'm going to put you to work. As of this moment you're in charge of the hot dogs and cocoa we're going to have when this skating session ends. All the supplies, including the marshmallows and the potato chips, are in the back party room."

With a laugh Suzanne stood up. "Frankly, I welcome any excuse to get out of these ice skates and into my comfortable old sneakers. I'll just tell Kacie where I'm going—I'm sure she won't object since my mission involves food."

Within a few minutes, Kacie joined them in the party room, chattering constantly and, to Suzanne's relief, not mentioning the book again. While they ate hot dogs, they talked with other Big and Little Sisters, and they both were genuinely sorry when the party was over.

"That was great fun," Suzanne said, giving Kacie a hug as she dropped her off at home.

"Even the skating?" Kacie asked with a mischievous glint in her eye.

Suzanne laughed. "Even the skating." She glanced at the house and found herself wondering if Jed was home and what he was doing.

Kacie interrupted her thoughts. "Well, I'd better be going." She opened the door of the truck.

"You know, Kacie, I was thinking—" She stopped. What had she been thinking? That she'd like to see Jed, but she couldn't say that. "I was thinking we might order a pizza or something," she finished lamely.

"We just ate hot dogs," Kacie reminded her.

"Oh, yes." Suzanne searched for another approach. "Well, if you're not busy, maybe I'll come in and say hello to Lucky."

Kacie fidgeted. "Actually, I can't." She looked very uneasy. "I've got this thing I have to do with Billy and we can't put it off, I mean—"

Kacie's discomfort made only a fleeting impression on Suzanne because she was so caught up with her own disappointment. "That's okay, Kacie," she answered lightly. "We'll do it another time."

"Thanks again," Kacie called over her shoulder as she hopped out of the truck and raced toward the house. Suzanne watched her go inside then sat in the driveway for a few seconds more, but Jed didn't appear. Reluctantly she pulled the truck into the street and drove home, wishing her life wasn't such a mess and wishing she could talk to Jed, the one person who really understood her.

Listening to Janet describe how she felt about her husband had been the final straw. She didn't feel that way about Marty. She wasn't sure she ever had. As terrible as she felt about breaking the engagement, marrying the wrong man would be far worse. She had to tell Marty it was over, and she had to do it as soon as she could.

Suzanne hadn't been home more than a few minutes when the phone rang. She heard Marty's voice and a shiver ran through her. But before she could say anything, Marty launched into a long explanation about how he wouldn't be home on Sunday because of a new account and about how much more money he was going to make from it.

"It's really good to hear your voice," he said after a few minutes. "I've missed you, and you're so often not there when I call."

"I'm sorry," Suzanne apologized automatically. "I do want to talk to you—"

"Tomorrow. Getting this account sewed up means I can be home tomorrow night. How about dinner at eight?"

"That will be fine." She didn't particularly want to go to dinner, but a restaurant might be a good place to talk to him. She didn't know how Marty would react to what she was about to tell him, and she didn't want to be alone when she found out. After she hung up the phone, she leaned down to pat Lady, who was sitting at her feet. She tried to summon some sense of regret for what she was about to do, but the feeling wasn't there. She had felt no delight at hearing Marty on the telephone, no elation at seeing him sooner than expected. "I made a mistake, old girl," she said as she rubbed the dog's neck, "a really big one, but not as big as it might have been." Lady whimpered and nuzzled her leg. "One more day, old girl, one more day and it will all be over."

SUNDAY NIGHT didn't go as Suzanne had planned. As she backed the truck out of Martha Gresham's driveway, she checked her watch. Almost one in the morning. By then she'd expected to have finished her dinner with Marty, to have broken her engagement and to be in bed sound asleep. Instead, she had spent the evening playing midwife to a three-year-old dachshund named Greta.

Under other circumstances, Suzanne wouldn't have gone to Mrs. Gresham's at all, because Greta could have handled everything just fine. But Mrs. Gresham couldn't. She was a widow whose son had promised to be there for the big event, but his plans had changed at the last minute. Mrs. Gresham had been terribly upset, and by her third phone call, Suzanne had decided the only solution was to keep her company until the puppies were born. This was what she'd done for the past several hours. She now knew all about Mrs. Gresham's three children and nine grandchildren, including all their dogs, cats and hamsters. Maybe if she hurried home, she could still get some sleep.

As Suzanne turned the truck onto Tenth Street, she was thinking about Marty. She'd phoned him a dozen times, but got no answer. He'd have found her note on the front door hours ago, and he was probably furious, which was one more reason the marriage wouldn't work out. He didn't understand that being a vet with a practice like hers was a twenty-four-hour job.

Suzanne sighed and looked out the window. The town was totally deserted as she drove along the quiet residential streets. So unlike a city, she thought, where life slows in the early morning but never quite stops. So unlike Richmond, where Marty had wanted her to live. She was rounding the corner onto Poplar when her lights caught a flash of movement. She jammed on her brakes as a familiar figure froze in the beam of light. Forgetting about Marty and Richmond and everything else, Suzanne was out of the truck and running as soon as the vehicle screeched to a halt. "Kacie," she called. "Kacie, what are you doing?"

Suzanne waited, scanning the area, until Kacie slowly emerged from behind a large evergreen in the corner yard. She didn't look hurt or frightened, which meant she probably wasn't in any danger. Then Suzanne caught sight of the sheets of toilet paper trailing from the branches of a large tree across the street. With difficulty she suppressed a smile. This wasn't a crisis after all.

"Aren't you out a little bit late?" she asked as her Little Sister approached.

"Please turn off your lights and don't make so much noise," Kacie pleaded. "You'll wake everyone up."

Returning to the truck, Suzanne turned off the headlights and the engine as Kacie had requested. Obviously she had encountered her Little Sister at a very awkward moment. "Now, Kacie," she said as firmly as she could manage, "suppose you tell me exactly what you're up to."

"It's pretty obvious, isn't it?" Kacie gestured toward the tree. "I think we did a real good job."

Suzanne gazed at the toilet papering job, which was one of the most thorough she'd ever seen. "Do you realize what a mess that's going to be if it rains tomorrow like it's supposed to?"

"Yep," Kacie answered with pride. "The toilet paper will stick on those trees for weeks, and it serves those people right."

"Kacie!"

"Well, it does. They have no right to go after Miss Henniker and try to get her fired."

So that was it. Suzanne looked around but saw no one else. "Are you doing this alone?"

Kacie started to say yes, then looked away. "No, Billy's with me," she mumbled.

"And the two of you decided this was the way to respond to the movement to fire Margaret Henniker. What happened to the counter petition?"

"Oh, we did that, too. They found out about it and said it was 'cute.'"

Suzanne was beginning to understand. The kids had tried to play by the rules and they were laughed at, so in frustration they struck back at the system. At least they hadn't resorted to destroying property, like so many kids would have done. "How do you think your dad would feel about this, Kacie?"

Kacie's eyes widened, and for the first time she looked scared. "You're not going to tell him, are you?" she asked in a tiny voice. "He'd kill me."

"I doubt that."

"No, he would. Please don't tell him," Kacie pleaded. "If he found out we went out at night—you know how he is about me doing things like that. Please don't tell him."

Kacie was probably right. Her father would be very angry. Suzanne considered her dilemma. She really should tell Jed, but on the other hand, that would cast her as an adult in Kacie's eyes instead of a friend. Of course, having two thirteen-year-olds running around the streets at one o'clock in the morning covering people's trees with toilet paper wasn't desirable, either, but it wasn't exactly a capital offense. Besides, she hadn't talked to Jed for more than two weeks, ever since she'd told him she didn't ever want to see him again. She wished she hadn't said that.

"Tell you what, Kacie. I'll take you and Billy home and for right now, at least, we won't mention this to anyone else. But I don't want any recurrences. A deal?"

"Thanks, Suzanne," Kacie said gratefully. Then she grinned. "When we bought the toilet paper last night, we got extra. Do you suppose we could finish just one more tree?"

"Absolutely not. You and Billy get into the truck right now." So that was why Kacie had been in such a hurry after the skating party. Suzanne realized she should have been more alert.

Apparently Kacie had assured Billy that their secret was safe, because on the way home they talked excitedly about their exploits. Suzanne hoped she'd made the right decision about keeping their secret for them. She decided to discuss it with the caseworker as soon as possible. Janet had proven to be a good person to talk over ideas with. She never pushed, but she usually had very good suggestions. Suzanne smiled. The Big Sister agency was really helpful.

Suzanne turned off the headlights before she pulled into Kacie's driveway, and as Billy and Kacie lifted their wagons out of the back of the truck, she spoke to them very firmly. "You understand that your part of the bargain is not to TP any more trees—or do anything else like that."

They both nodded.

"And I really am sorry about Margaret Henniker. I wish I had some answers."

"Yeah," said Kacie. "Me, too." She hesitated for a moment then added, "You don't have to wait for me to go inside."

"I certainly do."

"Well, um . . ."

Billy snickered.

"Actually I go up the tree over there and into my bedroom window. It's quieter that way."

Suzanne knew she probably should reprimand Kacie, but she didn't. "I'll wait anyway. And I think this should be the last of the midnight outings, okay?"

"I guess."

Suzanne didn't miss the fact that Kacie had stopped short of a promise.

MARTY'S FIREBIRD was waiting in the driveway when Suzanne got home. Her mouth went dry. She didn't want to talk to him, not when she was so tired and he was angry. But as he opened his car door and emerged, she knew she would have no choice.

She got out of the truck as he approached her. "Marty, I tried to call you . . ."

"So what's your story this time?" he demanded in a coarse voice that didn't sound like his.

Suzanne took a step backward. "Didn't you find my note? I had an emergency over in Smithton, a widow who needed help."

"Yeah, right, tell me another one."

He was still approaching her, his eyes narrowed. Suddenly Suzanne realized that she was terribly afraid. He was angry and he obviously didn't believe her. "Marty, I went out to Mrs. Gresham's about seven o'clock. I tried to call but you weren't home."

He took two quick steps forward and grabbed her arms. "Dammit, I know where you've been. Now tell me the truth." His fingers pressed hard into her upper arms, compressing the flesh into deep throbbing pain.

"Marty, stop, you're hurting me—" She tried to pull away but his grip was relentless. He pressed harder.

"Tell me the truth," he demanded again.

The pain was so intense that Suzanne could barely talk. "Marty, I am telling you the truth. I was at Mrs. Gresham's—"

"Don't give me that. You were with him."

At first Suzanne didn't understand. Then she remembered how Marty had warned her to stay away from Jed, and she knew that's who Marty was talking about. "You mean with Jed?"

As soon as she said Jed's name, Marty's hand came down hard in a brutal smash across the side of her face and Suzanne sank to her knees. He stood over her, his lips twisted into a perverse smile. "I suppose you think I'm going to apologize, but this time you're wrong. You deserved that. Now get up and we'll go in the house. And don't ever let this happen again."

Suzanne stood up shakily, her head spinning with pain. Marty put his arm around her waist and walked beside her toward the porch. She could feel the anger draining out of him, and he gave her a familiar squeeze as though nothing had happened. Apprehensively she touched the rising welt on her cheek, relieved to find it wasn't bleeding.

"I'll fix you some ice to stop the swelling," he said as they walked up the porch steps.

Suzanne unlocked the front door and opened it a crack, but instead of going inside she turned to face

Marty. Her head was clear now, although a knifelike pain shot downward in front of her right ear. She looked at the man standing before her, his body relaxed, his wavy hair slightly rumpled, his eyes a clear startling blue. At that moment she saw why she'd been attracted to him, and she knew she'd been wrong. "It's over, Marty," she said softly.

"What did you say?"

She raised her voice, unsure whether he really hadn't heard or whether he simply couldn't accept what she'd said. "I said it's over. I can't marry you." Her right hand moved toward her left and she slipped off the ring.

Marty frowned, seeming almost puzzled. "You don't mean that. You're just having bride's jitters."

"No, Marty. It simply wouldn't work." She held out the ring but he ignored her.

"Come on, little dove, let's go in the house and have a good long talk." He stepped toward her, gently grasping her elbow. "Think about the wedding. Everything's ready to go. We've got the church and the dress, and the invitations should arrive any day. I even ordered the cake yesterday. You can't back out now."

"Marty, I'm sorry, but—"

He didn't let her finish. "If that doesn't move you, then think about how much I love you. I don't get to tell you as often as I'd like...I've been traveling so much lately. But it won't always be like that. You'll see." He smiled at her, his eyes almost pleading. "Let's go in and talk about it."

He was at his most charming, but Suzanne felt no hesitation. She leaned heavily against the doorframe, her cheek throbbing as it swelled. "We have nothing to talk about, Marty. I've had enough of your jealous rages. Take the ring and leave, and please never come back."

Marty's hand closed on her elbow like a vice, and in the shaft of light from the inside hall his eyes turned cold and nasty. "It is him, isn't it, just like I thought."

As his voice rose, Suzanne heard a menacing growl on the other side of the door. She tried to back up but she couldn't move.

"You been out whoring around and then you come crawling back here lying to me." His hands moved toward her throat. "I'll teach you a thing or two!"

"Marty, no—" As his fingers tightened, the growl from inside the house got louder, but Marty seemed not to hear it at all. Suzanne lurched backward just far enough to shove the door ajar and Lady bolted through the opening, throwing herself between Suzanne and Marty and sinking her teeth deep into his arm. Marty's hands fell away from Suzanne's neck as he staggered and fell. He pounded at Lady, but the dog hung on, tearing at his flesh.

"Lady, no." Suzanne's command sliced the air. She grabbed the dog's collar and pulled her until Lady stood quivering, teeth bared, a growl rumbling low in her throat. "Good girl," Suzanne whispered softly, patting the dog's neck. She stared at Marty. He was like a stranger, a man she'd never known. "The ring is there on the floor. Pick it up and go and don't ever come back here."

Clutching his arm, which hung limp with blood oozing from the teeth wounds, Marty stood up. He grabbed the ring and stuffed it in his pocket. "You haven't heard the last of this," he muttered.

Lady growled and pulled against Suzanne's grip on her collar. Suzanne's back stiffened and with effort she restrained the dog. "I meant what I said, Marty," she warned him. "I stopped Lady this time. I might not be able to again."

She turned toward the door but Lady's feet were planted solidly and she didn't budge. They stood there together, with Suzanne's hand wrapped firmly around Lady's collar, until Marty's car roared down the driveway and his headlights disappeared in the distance. Only then did they relax. Suzanne released her grip, and she and Lady walked into the house together.

Suzanne's whole body was shaking and her cheek throbbed unmercifully. She dropped to her knees beside Lady, and the dog nuzzled her and licked her cheeks. Only then did she realize that Lady was shaking, too. "You saved me, old girl." Tears welled up in Suzanne's eyes as she stroked Lady's neck. "God knows what he might have done if you hadn't been there." She sat alone in the silent hallway, her mind and body numb, her arms wrapped around Lady, until the throbbing in her cheek forced her to get up and go to the kitchen for ice. She wanted nothing but to go to bed and sleep and forget.

Lady followed her into the bedroom and watched while she stripped off her clothes and pulled on an old flannel nightgown. When she collapsed on the bed with the ice bag, Lady stretched out on the braided rug beside the bed. Suzanne slept fitfully during the few hours before dawn, awakening intermittently to reach for Lady, who nuzzled her hand. "Go to sleep, old girl.

It's all over now,'' she murmured once, but Lady only whimpered softly.

When she awoke the next morning, Suzanne wondered whether she'd had a nightmare, but the pain in her cheek told her the memories were only too real. Aching with fatigue, she took a long shower then scrutinized herself in the mirror, gasping at what she saw. The side of her face was swollen and discolored where Marty had hit her. He had left his fingerprints in purple bruises on her neck and arms. She still couldn't understand how a man who said he loved her could do that to her. She didn't hate him. She wasn't even angry with him. She simply felt an enormous sense of relief that it was over.

She pulled on a cotton turtleneck and used makeup to cover the marks on her face as best she could. Then she went to the kitchen with Lady at her heels and fixed them both breakfast. She remembered Jed's warnings about Marty and the book of Kacie's she'd read. How could they have seen what was happening when she didn't? Without Jed and Kacie she might have gone ahead with the wedding, still believing that somehow she'd work things out. Her stomach lurched as she realized how close she'd come to making a horrible mistake. She considered calling Jed, but she didn't want to see him, or Kacie, or anyone just yet. She needed time alone for her mind and her body to heal. After that, she would think about the rest of her life.

For the next several days, Suzanne kept appointments and made several calls in the country but avoided seeing anyone she knew well. She called Kacie and said she had a virus and, while she wasn't very sick, she didn't want Kacie to come because she might catch it.

She hated the lie, which she had to repeat daily when Kacie called, but she wasn't ready to talk to her Little Sister about what had happened, and she knew Kacie would spot the marks on her face immediately.

At first Suzanne found herself looking up nervously when someone came into the clinic and hesitating when she answered the phone in case it might be Marty. But as the days passed and he made no attempt to contact her, she began to relax. At least he had the good grace to accept the fact that their relationship had ended. Lady was her constant companion, following her everywhere, not letting Suzanne out of her sight for even a few moments. By Friday, Suzanne was beginning to look and feel a little more like herself, and when Janet walked into the clinic late that afternoon, she was happy to see the caseworker's familiar face.

"I was in the neighborhood and I thought I'd stop by and find out how you are," Janet explained.

Suzanne put down the surgical instruments she'd been about to sterilize. "Just fine," she answered with a smile.

"Really?" Janet frowned. "Kacie said you'd been sick all week and wouldn't let her come over. She's worried about you."

"Oh, that." Suzanne took a deep breath. She'd forgotten. "Well, I . . . I feel much better."

Without taking off her jacket, Janet sat in the straight chair near Suzanne's desk. "Is something wrong, Suzanne?"

"No, I just—" She was tired of lying and she knew she didn't do it well. "Last Sunday night I broke my engagement. I was pretty upset and I just needed some time."

Janet nodded sympathetically. "I'm sorry."

"No, it was for the best." Suzanne didn't go any further. Janet apparently hadn't noticed the bruise on her cheek, which was now almost completely hidden by makeup, or if she had she wasn't going to mention it.

"Sometimes those things are for the best." Janet hesitated before continuing. "Kacie talked to me about Marty more than once. For some reason she really didn't like him."

Suzanne wandered over to her desk and sat down, wondering how a thirteen-year-old's instincts could have been so much better than her own. "I know. I'll call her tomorrow. I think I'm ready to see her now." She looked up at Janet and suddenly remembered her manners. "Won't you take off your jacket? Could I get you coffee or a soda?"

Janet shook her head. "Thank you, but I really was just passing by and I have to get back to the office." She stood up, still looking at Suzanne. "Just one other thing. Kacie said her father has been upset lately— crabby and impossible was how she put it. She seems to trace it to one day when she came back from seeing you."

"Really?" Suzanne was outwardly casual but inside she felt very different. That would have been the day after she came home from Richmond when they argued about Marty. Jed had respected her wishes and stayed away, but apparently he hadn't liked it.

"I just wondered if there was some problem that might affect Kacie," Janet continued.

Suzanne wasn't sure how to answer. "We did argue," she admitted, speaking slowly and carefully, "but it was basically a difference of opinion. I realize now that I was wrong. I just haven't told Jed yet."

"Maybe you should," Janet advised, as she opened the door to leave. "Kacie says he's pretty unhappy."

Suzanne stood up. "Thanks for letting me know."

To Suzanne's relief, Janet left quickly, not expecting her to explain further. The door had barely closed when Suzanne picked up the phone. She was finally ready to tell Jed what had happened, and to talk to Kacie. She was ready to close a chapter and get on with her life.

The phone rang ten times before Suzanne accepted the fact that no one was home. "Well, old girl," she said to Lady who was sitting expectantly beside her, "maybe they'll be back later. Right now I'm going to have to go to the grocery store, or we'll neither one have any dinner."

When Suzanne left, Lady stood by the door barking, and Suzanne realized it was the first time all week she'd gone anywhere without her dog. She made a mental note to get Lady another box of dog biscuits.

The grocery store was crowded with Friday afternoon shoppers, and Suzanne spent well over an hour selecting food then waiting in line. She was hungry as she hurried up the porch steps with an armload of groceries, and she knew Lady would be, as well. They'd have dinner, she decided, then take a run before dark or play Frisbee in back of the house. She hadn't felt much like playing for some time, and she knew Lady missed it.

"Here, Lady, come on, girl," she called as she set her purse and the bag of groceries on the hall table while she hung up her jacket.

There was no answer, no welcoming bark, no sound
of Lady's claws clicking on the wooden floor as she
scampered down the hall from the back of the house.
Puzzled, Suzanne walked toward the kitchen to inves-
tigate. Lady hadn't been out of her sight for nearly a
week. This wasn't like her. "Here, Lady," she called
again, more loudly this time. Maybe she was so sound
asleep she hadn't heard the front door open. As Suzanne went by the living room, she glanced in. Lady
often napped in front of the fireplace. But she wasn't
there. Then Suzanne heard a muffled whimper coming from the kitchen, and a sudden terror struck her
heart. She broke into a run, heading in the direction of
the sound. "No," she whispered as she reached the
doorway.

The black lab staggered to the center of the kitchen,
struggling to reach Suzanne. Her legs trembled, and
saliva ran from the sides of her mouth. "Dear God,
no!" Suzanne reached Lady just as the dog collapsed
in a heap on the floor. Lady's chest heaved with the
effort to breathe. Her deep brown eyes were fixed on
Suzanne, pleading for help. Frantically Suzanne
checked Lady's gums, which had lost all their pink
color and turned a dull gray. Her heart rate was very
slow and wildly irregular, her eyes glazed. *Get her to
the clinic...oxygen...fluids...* Suzanne's thoughts
swirled wildly. But as she gathered Lady in her arms,
the dog took a deep, shuddering breath and then was
still.

Suzanne fell to her knees, her arms still around Lady,
her head buried in the dog's soft fur. "No," she
moaned. "No, no, no..." Sobs wracked her body and
Lady's soft coat soaked up her tears.

CHAPTER ELEVEN

THE BARREN TREES cast stark shadows in the moonlight as Suzanne and Jed walked slowly toward a low, sandy hill along the edge of the woods, each of them clutching one end of the soft blanket that held Lady's body. Suzanne's steps were heavy. Jed had been her strength since she had called him a few hours earlier, just after Lady died, and she was relying on him now.

They paused at the edge of the opening in the earth and laid the blanket on the ground. Jed turned toward Suzanne. "Is there anything you'd like to say before we . . . before we finish?"

Her eyes sought his with a deep sadness. She looked very small and very much alone, standing there in an old canvas jacket she'd pulled on over her sweater and slacks. Her brown hair hung loose to her shoulders, framing her face, which was pale in the moonlight. Jed wanted to help her but he knew that the next few moments, the final goodbye, were hers alone.

She knelt beside the dog who had been her friend and companion for thirteen years and stroked Lady's soft fur. There would be no whimper of welcome now, no wag of the tail, no familiar pressure as Lady rested her head on Suzanne's knee. They'd never run together again in these woods. Lady would chase no more rabbits. "Goodbye, old girl," Suzanne whispered softly. "I'll miss you." She covered Lady's body with the old towel she had slept on every night, then slowly stood up. Her eyes met Jed's. "I'm ready," she said quietly.

He nodded, and together they lowered Lady's body gently into the shallow grave. Their breath showed white as they mounded dirt over the hole in the earth. The only sounds in the quiet night were the rhythmic scraping of their shovels and the call of a hoot owl somewhere off in the trees.

When they finished, Suzanne stood silent, gazing at the fresh grave. It seemed impossible that Lady was there, and yet she knew it was true. Something in the ritual of burial had forced acceptance. "I wish I had some flowers to leave," she finally said.

Jed put his arms around her. "I'll help you plant some in the spring."

Suzanne's eyes filled, and tears began slipping down her cheeks. "Violets. From the woods. Lady always managed to find the first ones blooming every year."

"Come on," Jed said as he picked up the shovels. "Let's go into the house. It's cold out here." Without looking back, they walked hand in hand across the yard, their shoes crunching on the frosty grass.

Jed hung his jacket on the hook inside the kitchen door and reached for Suzanne's jacket before he realized she hadn't taken it off. She was standing in the center of the room staring at Lady's food and water bowls. The water bowl was filled, as always, but the food bowl was empty.

"Should I get rid of these?" she asked helplessly.

"Not tonight. I'll take care of them for you." Jed unzipped her jacket and helped her take it off.

"When?"

"Before I go. I'll take them with me." He hung her jacket next to his. When he turned she was still standing in the center of the kitchen.

"I don't know what to do," she continued in a small voice. "It's time to feed Lady, but she isn't here."

He saw the tears well up in her eyes and put his arm around her to comfort her. Confronting the finality of death was the loneliest task in the world. Jed knew that he could offer warmth and friendship and that would help, but there was nothing he could do to heal the wound left from losing Lady. Only time would do that. "Let's go into the living room," he suggested gently. "I'll build a fire and we'll just sit for a while."

She nodded agreement. "Thank you, Jed." Her eyes met his with a sadness that almost broke his heart. "I don't know what I'd do if you weren't here. Lady was with me for so long. She was always there, waiting. I loved her, Jed. I feel so all alone."

He hugged her, but he didn't answer because there wasn't any answer. They went into the living room, and after he built a fire he sat next to her on the sofa.

"I guess a lot of people wouldn't understand how I could feel this way about a dog." Suzanne stared into space. She was cold, a kind of pervasive inner cold that not even the crackling fire or the warmth of Jed's body close to her could change. Slowly she continued talking, sensing Jed's empathy. "I mean, after all, Lady wasn't a person. But, in a way, she was to me. She seemed to understand my moods better than I did, and whenever I was unhappy or frightened she was right there. Some people would say dogs can't love, but Lady did. I know she did."

Jed slipped his arm around her shoulders. "She was a once in a lifetime friend, Suzanne."

He did understand. She'd known he would. "I wanted to take her out and run with her this afternoon. We hadn't done that for a while. I'd been so busy. And then when I got home and I called her and she didn't come, I knew something was wrong. I heard her whimper and went into the kitchen. She used all the energy she had left to stand up and stagger across the room toward me, and she died. She died in my arms before I could do anything at all."

The tears in Suzanne's eyes spilled over and Jed held her tighter, cradling her head against his chest. He ached inside, wanting somehow to make it easier for her. But he knew he couldn't. She had to grieve before she could accept what had happened and go on. Suzanne's body shook against him, and she cried as if she would never stop. As he held her, he felt her anguish as if it was his own. A fierce desire to protect her from anything that might hurt her surged through him. When she shivered, he pulled a knit afghan around her, then he sat quietly holding her until her sobs subsided. Tenderly he smoothed some hair from her wet face, and she shuddered in his arms.

"I didn't mean to cry," she whispered in a shaky voice.

"It's all right," he told her.

"I'm glad you're here, Jed."

With her head resting against his soft flannel shirt, he continued to stroke her hair. Her eyes closed and her breathing became slower. After a few minutes Jed realized she had fallen into a deep, exhausted sleep. He held her close and watched the fire until it had burned

down to embers, thinking about how hard it must have
been for her to watch her beloved friend die. He
frowned as he pictured the scene she had described to
him. She had said Lady used all her energy to stagger
across the kitchen and then had collapsed and died in
Suzanne's arms. He had never seen an animal die, but
that somehow wasn't quite how he'd pictured it. He
wondered about the cause of death. A heart attack,
maybe? Lady was getting up in years, but she'd seemed
so healthy and Suzanne had never mentioned any
problems.

Jed let his thoughts wander, but always they returned to Suzanne. He remembered the times they'd
spent doing simple things like building the doghouse or
eating pizza together. He loved her spontaneity and her
common sense and the laughter they so often shared.
He wondered whether he should tell her all that, or
whether it would make things more difficult between
them. His gaze strayed to her left hand. She wasn't
wearing the engagement ring, but sometimes she
didn't. More than an hour passed before Suzanne
stirred in his arms.

"Jed?" she asked. "Was I asleep?"

"For quite a while. You were exhausted."

She raised her head to look around then rested it
against him. "You've been here a long time. You must
need to go home. Where's Kacie?"

Jed smiled. She was beginning to think of things
outside of herself, and that was good. "After you
phoned me I sent her over to Billy's for dinner. I hope
by now she's at home in bed fast asleep."

"Did you tell her about Lady?"

"Yes, I did. Was that all right?"

Suzanne nodded.

"Are you hungry?" Jed asked her.

"No, I'm just tired, very tired."

"Maybe you need to go to bed," he suggested, not wanting her to go yet realizing that a good night's sleep would be the best thing for her.

Suzanne sat up and brushed the hair out of her face. "I think you're right. I feel numb all over."

Jed was struck by her pallor and the overwhelming sadness he saw in her eyes. He knew she would come back to being herself and she'd laugh again and life would go on. It always did. But he also knew she'd feel an emptiness for a very long time. "Why don't you get ready for bed? I'll wait till you're settled before I go."

After she left, Jed paced across the living room, fighting the desire to ask her if he could sleep there tonight. The thought was foolish, totally out of the question. He knew that. And yet he was struggling with an emptiness of his own. From the moment Suzanne had moved out of his arms, he'd wanted her back. He wanted to lie in bed with her and hold her until they both fell asleep. And then he wanted to awaken with her and in the gentle light of morning.... "Damn," he muttered softly, and walked resolutely toward the kitchen. He was upset that he was soon going to lose her to another man. He recognized the feeling, and yet he couldn't understand it. How could he lose something he'd never had?

He walked into the kitchen, and as he bent down and picked up Lady's dishes, he noticed a steak bone almost hidden under the edge of the kitchen cabinets. He picked it up and turned it over in his hands curiously, then dropped it into the trash. He didn't know Suzanne let Lady have bones. She had told Kacie not to give them to Lucky. He emptied Lady's water into the sink and, as he put her bowls beside his jacket so he wouldn't forget them, the act of taking them away seemed very final. He would keep the bowls, he decided, at least for a while, just in case Suzanne asked about them. They were among the only things that had belonged uniquely to Lady.

Suzanne called to him, and taking a deep breath, Jed walked down the hall to her bedroom. He resolved to keep a firm grip on his emotions. The bedroom door was open and the room was dark except for the glow from a small night-light. As he sat on the edge of the bed, Suzanne moved over to make room for him. The cotton lace of her pink flannel nightgown was barely visible above the soft white quilt that covered her bed.

"I'm still so cold," she told him. "I guess it's from being outside all that time while we— From being outside all that time," she repeated.

The moment was even harder for Jed than he'd feared. He wanted to wrap her up and hold her and warm her through and through. Instead he sat very stiffly on the edge of the bed and said nothing.

"Thank you for coming when I needed you."

"You know I'll always come." She looked very vulnerable.

"Yes." Her voice faltered slightly. "I know."

Jed bent down, meaning to kiss her cheek, but somehow his mouth found hers, and then her arms were wrapped around his neck, and she was pulling him close. Her body was warm and soft against him. He could hardly let her go.

"I'm sorry, Jed. I didn't mean to do that," she whispered.

"Didn't you?"

"I—I don't know." Her voice was so quiet he could barely hear her.

"I don't know, either." He wanted to say more but he couldn't. Not then. She'd gone through too much already. "Good night, Suzanne, I'll see you in the morning."

"Good night, Jed."

He leaned down again, this time very carefully kissing her on the cheek.

As he drove home, Jed's emotions soared when he thought about Suzanne in his arms, her soft warmth against him as he kissed her. He brushed aside all other thoughts. For tonight, he would have his fantasy. Knowing he would never sleep, he decided to go to his studio and sketch for a while. The house would be quiet, and he would be alone with his thoughts. But the moment he opened his front door, his plans changed.

Kacie came flying down the stairs with Lucky on her heels. "Is Suzanne all right?" she asked. "What happened?"

As much as Jed loved his daughter, he didn't want to see her right then. She and Lucky followed him into the kitchen. "Suzanne is as all right as somebody can be when her best friend has died," Jed replied carefully. He stirred up two cups of hot chocolate and put them in the microwave to heat. "Aren't you supposed to be in bed?"

"Tomorrow is Saturday. I don't have school and I can sleep late." Kacie flopped down on a kitchen chair. "What did you do with Lady?"

Jed sat at the table and set one cup of hot chocolate in front of Kacie. He was going to have to talk to her about this, and as long as she was awake anyway, it might as well be now as any other time. "Suzanne and I buried Lady behind the house, near the woods."

"Oh." Kacie was silent for a moment. "Did Suzanne cry?"

The memory of Suzanne sobbing against his chest nearly tore Jed apart. He took a slow sip of his hot chocolate before he answered. "Yes, she cried."

"A lot?" Kacie continued. "Remember how much I cried when Mom died? You cried, too," she added hesitantly.

"You remember me crying?" Kacie had been just six years old when Elizabeth died.

"When you told me Mom was dead—in the hospital waiting room—you were crying. I remember it," Kacie said quietly. "I just wasn't sure if someone cried when their dog died."

"Lady was Suzanne's family, all she has," Jed reminded his daughter. "It's going to be very hard for her now."

"She has us," Kacie pointed out. "And I guess she's supposed to have Marty—"

"Yeah," Jed answered. That was the last thing he wanted to think about. "I think you had better get to bed, Kacie."

Kacie reached down to pat Lucky who was lying at her feet. She had finished her hot chocolate, but she was obviously not ready to end their discussion. "Why did Lady die?"

"Old age, I guess."

Kacie sat thoughtfully for a moment. "But she wasn't that old. She was only thirteen, and Suzanne said a dog that's in good health can live a long time. I know Lady was healthy because Suzanne gave her a real thorough checkup a couple of weeks ago."

Jed didn't know what to tell her. He found the subject unsettling for some reason he couldn't quite figure out. "I guess it's like people, honey," he said finally. "Sometimes they die before it seems time, and we don't know why."

Kacie sat quietly for a moment, still petting Lucky. "Can I go see Suzanne tomorrow and take her a card or some flowers or something?"

"I think she'd like that," Jed answered, "but right now you need to get to bed."

"I guess." Reluctantly Kacie took Lucky upstairs and left Jed alone in the kitchen with his thoughts. Hungry now, realizing he hadn't eaten dinner, Jed fixed himself a bologna sandwich and paced in the kitchen while he ate it. Something was disturbing him, and he couldn't pinpoint what it was. Maybe it was just everything that had happened that night, but somehow he didn't think so.

Jed slept restlessly, tossing and turning until dawn when he finally got out of bed, showered and dressed. He left Kacie a note on the refrigerator and drove out to Suzanne's house. When he saw that her kitchen light was on, he knocked on the back door, standing directly in front of the window so she could see easily who was on the porch.

She opened the door immediately. "Jed! I'm so glad you came back."

She looked better than when he had left her the night before. She was still pale, with dark circles under her eyes, but the glazed, vacant look was gone. Apparently she was fresh from the shower because her hair was still damp where it curled around her face. Jed noticed a fading bruise on her cheek but decided not to mention it. Instead he took off his jacket and hung it on the hook. "I just came by to see how you were doing." He had an overwhelming desire to take her in his arms.

"I'm lonely, Jed." Suzanne wrapped her arms around the thick folds of her sweater and walked to the window to stare at the gray light of dawn. "Lady has always been there. She's shared all my secrets since I was fifteen years old. It's like I've lost a part of me."

Jed sat at the table watching her. "Lady had a good life, Suzanne, a perfect life, actually. She had a friend who loved her and appreciated her absolute loyalty. And then when she got old, she died without suffering."

Suzanne stared out the window for several moments, willing the tears not to come again and fighting against the emptiness. Then she turned to Jed. "What did you do with Lady's dishes?"

He tried to remember. "I think they're still in the car. But I wasn't going to throw them away," he added quickly. "I thought I'd keep them for you in case ... well, I don't know, just in case." He thought back to the night before. "The only thing I did throw away was that steak bone I picked up."

"What steak bone?"

He gestured toward the cabinets. "The one that was on the floor over there by the sink."

"You must be mistaken, Jed. I never gave Lady bones."

Jed shrugged. "Well, there was one there."

"There couldn't have been."

Jed met her eyes. She was tired and upset and probably had forgotten. "It's right here in the trash," he said quietly.

Jed got the bone and set it on the kitchen table. Suzanne stared at it for several moments then looked at Jed. "I didn't give Lady that bone."

"But you must have," he argued. "How else would it get here?"

"I have no idea," she said firmly, "but I don't give dogs bones." She picked up the bone and looked at it more carefully. It appeared to be fresh, although it had been well chewed. The events of the day before unfolded slowly in her mind. She'd been gone for quite a while at the grocery. When she'd left, Lady had been absolutely fine. And then when she'd come home... Again she reviewed all Lady's symptoms in those moments before she died, the gum color, the wild heart rate, the staggering, the saliva running from her mouth. A cold, sickening fear welled up in her. "Oh, my God, Jed—"

He reached for her hand. "Suzanne, what's the matter?"

Suzanne kept staring at the bone. "Lady. The way she died. I've seen it before. I just didn't think—"

Jed frowned, not sure what she was getting at.

"The signs of toxicity were all there. I don't know why I didn't see them."

"You mean you think Lady was poisoned?"

Suzanne looked up at Jed with anguish in her eyes. "Oh, Jed, she must have been."

Jed watched her turn the bone over, examining it as though it might supply the missing pieces of the puzzle. "But who?" he asked her. "Who could have poisoned Lady?"

For a long time Suzanne turned the bone over and over in her hands. Then she met Jed's eyes. "It had to be Marty. He's the only one who would have wanted her dead."

Jed stared at her. "Marty? You're going to marry this man and you think he killed your dog?"

Suzanne nodded miserably. "His family business is a pharmaceutical company. He has access to any drugs he wants, and he knows how to use them." She looked past Jed, toward the window. "Besides, I'm not going to marry him. I broke the engagement Sunday night." She stopped, swallowing hard. "He was angry and vicious. He was trying to hurt me and Lady attacked him. She saved my life, Jed. I should have known then..."

He reached across the table and took her hand again, holding it in both of his. "Suzanne, why didn't you tell me?"

She turned to him, her eyes pleading for understanding. "I don't know, Jed. I didn't tell anyone. I just needed time alone. It was all so awful—"

He went to her and took her in his arms, stroking her hair as she leaned her head against him. He loved her. After so long pretending, he knew now. He would never let anyone hurt her again. His thoughts raced ahead. A man who would poison a dog was sick, deranged, capable of anything. He couldn't let Marty get near her. "Suzanne, I don't think you should be here alone. Why don't you come and stay with Kacie and me for a while?"

"Why?" She looked at him.

"Because you're not safe here."

"Oh, Jed, you don't think—"

"Suzanne, if you're right about what he did to Lady, Marty's really sick. God knows what else he might do."

"I think he's already done it, Jed."

"Suzanne, please come stay with us," Jed pleaded.

Suzanne hesitated, then shook her head. "I can't run away and hide from Marty. That's no kind of life. Besides, I have two dogs out in the kennel and some difficult surgeries scheduled this week. I really need to be here."

"But what if he comes back, Suzanne? You don't have Lady to protect you now."

She closed her eyes as she forced herself to face what had happened. No, she didn't have Lady and never would have again. But still it was hard to believe that she might be in danger. Again she shook her head. "No, Jed, I'm going to stay here. I'll be all right."

He looked away, his jaw set. She was stubborn and independent, and there was no way he could make her change her mind. He stepped away from her, his body tense. "If you insist on staying here, we need to check the locks and find out how he got in."

Suzanne nodded, and they walked together through the house, checking the front door and all the windows. "I don't see how he did it," Suzanne mused. "I don't think Lady would have let him in anyway."

"Maybe she didn't need to." Jed was standing by the kitchen window that opened onto the porch. "Remember that lock you bought at the hardware store last fall?''

''The burglar lock so I could leave the window partway open.''

Jed raised the window until the lock caught. ''Just wide enough to let Marty reach in and toss a hunk of steak over by Lady's bowl.''

Suzanne almost cried as she imagined the scene. Marty had known about the window. He had raised it for her once. She thought about him there, with Lady barking, unable to get to him and about him tempting her with a juicy piece of sirloin. She buried her head in her hands. ''How could he do it, Jed? How could he kill Lady?''

Jed took her in his arms again, almost unable to believe that any human being could be so cruel. ''He's sick, Suzanne. He'd have to be.''

''And I was going to marry him. I was actually going to marry him.'' She couldn't make any sense of what had happened. ''I don't understand how I could have been so wrong.''

''Didn't you say he'd changed, that he was different since you got engaged?''

Suzanne nodded. ''He'd been so charming and so nice, but then he started to be jealous of anything that didn't include him. I kept thinking it would get better, that there were just these isolated incidents...except it kept getting worse. But I kept hoping—''

''You believe in people, Suzanne,'' Jed told her gently. ''There's nothing wrong with that.''

''Except this time.''

''Except this time,'' Jed echoed.

Suzanne felt herself fighting back tears, over-whelmed by what Marty had done and frightened when she realized how close she'd come to marrying him. She looked at Jed, her eyes about to overflow. "Do you realize that if it hadn't been for you—and Kacie—I might have gone ahead with the wedding?"

Jed frowned. "What do you mean?"

She pressed her cheek against his shoulder. "I kept thinking about all the things you said that day we ar-gued. And then Kacie left a book, one by Allison Craig about abuse—"

"I know which one you mean. It scared me, too." He leaned down and pressed his cheek against hers. "But that part of it's over, Suzanne. Now you need to put Marty behind you. Forget he ever existed."

"That's exactly what I'm going to do." She hugged Jed hard.

He slipped his hand under her hair and stroked the soft skin on the back of her neck, letting his fingers slide beneath her shirt collar. There were so many things he wanted to say to her, but they would have to wait. She needed time to pick up the pieces and re-sume her life before she was ready to make another commitment. He could only hope that Marty wouldn't show up. "Suzanne, are you sure you won't stay with Kacie and me just for a while?"

She was tempted. Standing there, encircled by his arms, she felt more whole and complete than she ever had with Marty. But she shook her head. "I can't run away, Jed."

He held her away from him and looked into her eyes. "If Marty comes back, call me, or call the police. Don't wait."

"He won't be back, Jed. He's had his revenge."

"God, I hope so." He leaned down and touched her lips with his in a whisper of a kiss that was magic for both of them. Its memory stayed with Suzanne, tempering her sadness long after he had gone.

Later in the day, when Kacie rode out on her bike with a bouquet of mixed flowers from the glass case in the supermarket, she found Suzanne smiling as she worked in the clinic.

"The flowers are beautiful," Suzanne told her. "Do you mind if I lay them on Lady's grave? Yesterday, when your dad and I buried her, I felt badly because I didn't have any flowers to leave with her."

"I hoped that was what you would do with them," Kacie said solemnly. "And I'm sorry about Lady," she added. "Do you know what happened to her?"

"We think she might have been poisoned."

Kacie's eyes widened. "Really? How?"

Suzanne explained briefly about the steak bone and the open window, but when Kacie asked who did it, Suzanne hedged and said she wasn't sure. Some part of her wanted to deny that Marty was capable of such an awful thing. She took Kacie's hand and together they went to Lady's grave and laid the flowers on the freshly turned earth.

"You're really going to miss Lady, aren't you, Suzanne?" Kacie asked.

Suzanne swallowed hard, fighting back her tears. "Yes, I'm going to miss her terribly."

Kacie gave her Big Sister's hand a squeeze. "You can come and play with Lucky any time you want. I could even bring him out here for visits."

Then Suzanne's tears did spill over. So much love. First Jed, now Kacie. Even without Lady, maybe she wasn't totally alone after all. "I'd like that, Kacie. I'd like that very much."

CHAPTER TWELVE

KACIE HAD BEEN UNHAPPY all week. She had cried about Lady's death and again when she thought about how bad Suzanne felt. But she hadn't cried about the toilet paper escapade. That just made her angry. Now a week had passed and she was still angry.

As she had predicted, an early morning drizzle had turned the toilet papered trees into a soggy mess. But she and Billy didn't get the reaction they'd hoped for. Instead, there had been a general uproar about vandalism, which was practically nonexistent in Cartersburg. A picture of one decorated front yard had made it to the local afternoon newspaper the next day, along with a story linking all the victims to the committee trying to have the school librarian dismissed. Quotes from some of the controversial books were reprinted. Read out of context, there seemed to be no doubt that the subject matter was inappropriate for impressionable adolescents.

Kacie sat unhappily on her front porch. She had failed. Instead of generating support for Miss Henniker, the publicity had convinced even neutral parents that the librarian's stand on the Allison Craig books was a real threat to traditional values. Maybe the toilet paper idea hadn't been so good after all.

There was nothing she could do about Lady dying, but she did have one more idea that might help Miss Henniker. The only problem was getting Billy to go along.

From inside the house Lucky barked and jumped at the storm door, wanting to be outside with Kacie. In spite of her unhappiness, Lucky's antics made Kacie smile. Lucky was one of the best things that had ever happened to her, almost as good as having Suzanne for a Big Sister. Kacie got up and went inside to tell her father she was taking Lucky for a walk. Maybe they'd head out to Suzanne's and play Frisbee until dinnertime.

Kacie was nearly halfway to the clinic, trying in vain to get Lucky to heel, when Billy screeched up behind them on his bicycle.

"Wait up!" he shouted. He jumped off his bike and wheeled it along. "Your dad told me you were going to Suzanne's—"

"Billy," Kacie interrupted. "I was going to come over later. There's something I want to ask you."

Billy shifted his weight uncomfortably. "Well, I wanted to ask you something, too."

"Me first," Kacie insisted. "Will you help me write a letter to the newspaper telling them why we toilet papered all those trees?"

"Are you crazy? My mom would kill me if she found out."

"We wouldn't sign the letter," Kacie retorted. "I'm not stupid. We'd just explain why Miss Henniker shouldn't be fired and say how good the books are and sign it Concerned Students."

"Oh." Billy scuffed the gravel along the edge of the highway with the toe of his high-top sneaker.

"We could use your computer so no one would recognize the handwriting," Kacie continued.

Billy concentrated on balancing his bike with one finger. "I don't know if a letter to the newspaper would do any good. When I left, my mom was on the phone talking about giving the petition to fire Miss Henniker to the school board."

"We have to try," Kacie insisted. "Those books are important. After I read *Life Isn't Always Like It Seems,* I left the book for Suzanne, then she broke up with Marty."

"You don't know if that's why," Billy interjected.

"Even if it wasn't, those books are important. And it's not fair to fire Miss Henniker."

"Okay, I'll help," Billy said grudgingly.

"On your computer?"

"Yeah, on my computer."

"When?"

Billy pondered for a minute. "Monday after school. My dad will still be at work and my mom has a meeting."

"Great." Kacie grinned happily. Maybe there was still a chance to help Miss Henniker, after all. If they wrote a good enough letter and a lot of people read it, maybe some of them would change their minds and try to help. She and Billy walked along silently until they turned onto Suzanne's road.

"Kacie?" Billy seemed nervous.

"What?"

"About what I wanted to ask you—"

Before he could finish, a red car streaked toward them, swerving so close that they both jumped down the grassy incline beside the road, pulling Lucky with them. "Boy, that was close," Billy said as he rolled away from Lucky's flailing legs.

Still holding tight to the leash, Kacie sat up. "Are you okay?" she asked Billy.

"Yeah, no thanks to that jerk showing off in his Firebird."

Lucky barked loudly and tugged at the leash as Kacie tried to hug him. "Are you sure it was a Firebird?"

"Of course I'm sure," Billy answered smugly. "I can identify every car on the road. Make, model and year."

"Marty drives a red Firebird." Kacie swallowed hard. Her mouth had suddenly turned dry.

"Come on." Billy grabbed her hand and pulled her to her feet. "We've got to see if Suzanne's all right."

Billy leaped on his bike, and Lucky and Kacie pounded down the road behind him. "She's not here," he yelled at Kacie from the front porch.

"Try the clinic," Kacie shouted.

But Suzanne wasn't there, either. They found a note stuck to the door that read, "Out on call. Back by five."

"Then Suzanne must be all right. She wasn't here when Marty came." Kacie sank to the ground and Lucky, panting heavily, flopped next to her with all four legs spread in different directions. "He needs a drink of water," Kacie said.

"Man, so do I." Billy mopped sweat from his forehead with the back of his hand. "Let's see if we can get in that back window to the kennel like we did the other time."

"Well..." Kacie hesitated.

"It's not like we're trespassing or anything. We know Suzanne wouldn't want Lucky to get dehydrated."

With a little trouble, they managed to raise the clinic window, and Billy wiggled inside. After getting a drink himself, he handed out a paper cup of water for Kacie then filled it three more times for Lucky. "Suzanne really ought to keep this window locked," Billy remarked as he squirmed outside.

"I'll tell her," Kacie said, "and I'll tell her about the Firebird. I'd really like to know if that was Marty."

Kacie and Billy threw the Frisbee with Lucky for a few minutes then started home. Kacie thought Billy was awfully quiet. Two or three times he appeared to be going to say something to her, then seemed to change his mind. When they reached her front porch, she started inside.

"Wait a minute."

"What?" Kacie tugged at Lucky, who was clearly ready to go in.

Billy shuffled from foot to foot a few times and finally blurted out, "Do-you-want-to-go-to-the-spring-dance-with-me?" The entire question sounded like one long word.

Startled, Kacie blinked hard and stared at Billy. "You mean the formal dance, in March, where girls have to wear dresses and boys have to wear suits?"

Billy nodded, his ears turning red.

"Oh."

"Well, do you?" he prodded.

Kacie studied the worn porch boards for a long minute before she answered. "Okay." She didn't look at him. "I'll go." Then she turned and fled into the house, pulling Lucky behind her.

"Dad," she shouted. "Where are you? I have something important to tell you." Everything else that had happened that day was suddenly forgotten as she ran into Jed's studio with her news.

"What is this important thing?" Jed leaned back in his chair, trying to suppress a grin. Kacie's cheeks were flushed and her hair hung in tangles below her shoulders. As usual, her jeans and shirt were baggy and torn, and her sneakers were full of holes and had no laces.

"I need a new dress for the spring dance."

"You do? I thought you said it was dumb and you weren't going."

Kacie smiled, a different smile than Jed had ever seen before. "I'm going with Billy."

While he was still registering that bit of information, Kacie raced ahead.

"But you don't have to go shopping with me. I'll ask Suzanne. You just have to give me the money."

"Sure thing," he answered. "Just let me know when." It wasn't until Kacie had disappeared into the kitchen that he allowed himself a grin. Her first date. And with Billy. Somehow, that was appropriate.

ED HAD BEEN QUIET all evening. Still wearing her apron, Margaret walked behind him and gently massaged his shoulders. They had just finished the dishes— she washed and he dried as had become their custom—and they'd discussed the weather and the sewer repair down at the corner and the danger of a late freeze killing the blossoms on the forsythia behind her house. But they hadn't really talked.

"What's the matter, Ed?" She moved her fingers rhythmically across the solid muscle of his shoulders. "You've been distracted ever since you got here. And don't say it's nothing. I know you too well for that."

Ed's shoulders heaved as he took a deep breath, then he turned and pulled Margaret down on the chair beside him. He sat facing her, holding both her hands, and she knew that whatever he was about to say was going to be something she didn't want to hear.

"I don't know what to do, Margaret." He squeezed her hands and let his eyes drop from hers. "Five women from the PTA showed up in my office this morning with a stack of petitions. They want you dismissed immediately."

The word hung ominously between them, and the look of pain that passed fleetingly across Margaret's face wasn't lost on Ed. "I tried to reason with them but they were spilling over with moral outrage and didn't hear a word I said. If we could just make them understand—"

"They aren't going to understand," Margaret interrupted. "I've tried. Their minds are closed. They aren't willing to even acknowledge their children's concerns, let alone help them deal with the world like it is today." Margaret stared at their hands twined together. She felt very old and very tired and very discouraged. During all these months of controversy she'd thought that somehow they could work things out. She'd be able to make these people understand that their kids were scared and often angry and needed to talk out their problems. But she had run out of time.

"You know I agree with what you're trying to do." Ed patted her hand. "I'm sorry, Margaret."

"No, I'm the one who's sorry." Margaret's eyes were gentle as they met his. "My poor Ed. I wanted to spare you this. I never thought they'd carry it this far. But now that they have, it's time to do something."

His chin firmly set, Ed's expression hardened. "I'm sure as hell not going to fire you, if that's what you have in mind. I'd quit first."

Margaret shook her head. "With five years until your retirement? That's foolish. Besides, it wouldn't matter. If you won't fire me, they'll take the issue to the school board and after a big, messy scene I'd be fired anyway. That isn't going to help the kids. I can't do that."

"So what are we going to do?"

Margaret looked directly at Ed. "I'm going to do the only thing I can do. I'm going to resign immediately."

"Margaret, I can't let you do that."

"What choice do I have?"

"But then they've won, and I know how much this means to you."

"No, Ed, they haven't won. Not really. If I take the books off the shelves, they win. If I leave, well, then everyone knows where I stand. I haven't compromised my beliefs. At least I can leave the children with that."

Ed reached out and stroked her cheek. "You've given all the children something very special. Did you see the letter the kids wrote about you in the afternoon newspaper?"

"No, I didn't get a paper this afternoon."

"The kids who put toilet paper on the trees wrote a letter—anonymously, of course—and tried to explain why they did it. It was quite a tribute of respect and love for you, Margaret."

"Oh, Ed, they actually took the time to write a letter?" Margaret was deeply touched that there were children who cared enough to follow through and try to make a difference.

"Do you know who did it?"

Margaret smiled. "Not really, but if I were guessing, I'd say Kacie Parker and Billy Hankins. They were very frustrated by the response to their petition."

"The kids love you, Margaret," Ed said, taking her hands again, "and they're not the only ones."

She felt herself blushing and looked away. He was so dear and she loved him so much.

"I love you, too, Margaret, and if you're really determined to resign, there's something I want to ask you."

She looked at him through misty eyes. "What's that, Ed?"

"Margaret, will you marry me?"

Margaret's eyes widened. All those times he'd broached the subject of marriage, she'd refused to discuss it because school board policy prevented a husband and wife from working in the same school. That wouldn't be an issue any longer. She looked at him and thought again that he was the most earnest, sincere, wonderful man she'd ever known. At fifty-five, after all these years of being alone, her life was about to begin anew with someone she truly loved. She answered him, her eyes gleaming, her voice shaking with emotion. "Oh, yes, Ed, yes, I will."

He gathered her in his arms and whirled her around the kitchen. "You just made me the happiest man in all of Cartersburg, in all of Virginia, hell, in the whole wide world. My God, how I love you."

"Oh, Ed, I love you, too. I should never have made us wait so long." Margaret laughed and wrapped her arms around his neck.

He touched her cheeks lovingly then reached around to begin pulling the hairpins out of her hair. "You did what you had to do, Margaret. That's how you are, and I wouldn't change you for the world. Besides, now we're not going to wait a minute longer than we have to. Let's elope over spring break."

"But, Ed, that's less than two weeks away."

"Exactly my point. You can announce your resignation the last day of school and that night we'll take off."

"But Ed—" Suddenly Margaret grinned. "Why not? Let's do it."

He took out the last pin, and her hair fell free. "And right now, my darling," he whispered close to her ear, "what do you say we go upstairs?"

"Oh, Ed." Margaret pressed tight against him. "I thought you'd never ask."

SATURDAY MORNING, early spring. Jed woke at dawn, his sleep interrupted by the chirping of the birds. He lay quietly for a few minutes, thinking of how much he'd missed their song over the winter. Then he decided he might as well get up. Like it or not, the day had begun.

Yawning, he pulled on a worn gray sweat suit and laced up his running shoes. As soon as he hit the stairs Lucky was right behind him, wagging his tail in anticipation of a good run. Happily he followed Jed into the kitchen. "You know, fella, you're a real pest. I was going to sneak out the back door and have a long run all by myself. Alone. Solo. Do you understand?''

Lucky's tail wagged even harder, and Jed couldn't help grinning as he snapped the leash onto the dog's collar. "Keep this up, mutt, and I may even learn to like you—but not unless you stop chewing up my drawing pencils.'' Lucky surged ahead of him, out the back door and across the porch, straining the leash to its limits before Jed broke into a run. With Lucky still in the lead they headed down the block, past the Methodist church and around the corner to Third Street.

The air was chilly and still, and the sun had just begun to push its way into the gray sky. Tall maple trees that lined the street were bare of leaves, but their buds were fat and bursting with promise. For the first half mile or so, Jed let his mind go blank. He wanted to do nothing more than savor the beginning of a new day. And maybe even the beginning of a new life. He had a sense of being complete, of being in harmony with himself, which he hadn't really felt since Elizabeth died. It was a good feeling.

He ran past Kacie's school and admired the brilliant yellow stand of forsythia bushes in front of the office window. This was going to be a very good day. As he began searching for the very best way to spend it, his first thought was of Suzanne. One thing he was sure of—his perfect day would include her, just as almost every day had in the past three weeks since she had broken her engagement.

Sometimes they had done no more than share a coffee break in the middle of the morning. Other times they had gone out together—once to a movie, another time to a Chinese restaurant for dinner. One night he and Kacie and Suzanne had made spaghetti. Kacie and Suzanne had rolled dozens of meatballs while he stirred the tomato sauce and ran the dough through the pasta machine. They had talked and laughed and eaten long into the night. Suzanne's bruises were gone, and she had finally lost the pallor that had haunted her since Lady died. She was relaxed and happy and becoming more and more a part of Jed's life. And that was exactly what he wanted.

Lucky yanked on the leash, pulling Jed toward the dirt path that ran through the town park. Jed's running shoes made dull thuds on the ground as he let Lucky lead him into the woods. Abruptly the puppy veered to the edge of the path and squatted. Jed waited, chuckling and wondering when Lucky would realize he was male and begin to lift his leg properly against a tree instead of squatting down next to a clump of violets. Violets. Jed leaned over and inspected the wildflowers more carefully. Dozens of tiny purple blossoms poked their heads up among the clusters of green heart-shaped leaves. He remembered Suzanne telling him that Lady always found the first violets in the spring. Lady was gone now, but Lucky had found the violets for her. All at once Jed knew how he was going to spend his day.

SUZANNE HEARD THE BANGING on her front door through the hazy mist of sleep. Opening one eye, she focused on the clock radio. Seven thirty-seven. She groaned and closed her eyes again, but the banging didn't stop. Probably someone bringing in an emergency, she decided, as she shoved back the covers and pulled an old terry-cloth robe around her on the way to the door.

"Who's there?" she asked sleepily.

"It's me, Jed. Open up."

Suzanne was instantly wide awake. Quickly she threw the dead bolt and opened the door, expecting the worst. "What's wrong?" But he didn't look as though anything was wrong. He leaned against the door frame, wearing jeans and a faded green sweatshirt and sporting a broad grin. He was clean-shaven and smelled faintly of after-shave lotion. In one hand he held a bag from a fast-food restaurant, and in the other he had a brown cardboard carton with a thermos and two trowels inside. "Aren't you going to invite me in?"

Of course she was going to invite him in. He was all she thought about these days, all she wanted. He looked so good standing on her doorstep. No man had the right to be so, well, so sexy at such an ungodly hour of the morning. Yet she hesitated. Why, oh why, wasn't she one of these women who wore silk nighties to bed and tossed on a matching peignoir in the morning? Why didn't she have beautiful blond hair that, even unbrushed, tousled into soft waves? Why hadn't she worn slippers? Well, none of that could be helped now. "Please come in, Jed. It will just take me a minute to get dressed."

For a moment Jed didn't move. He had never seen another woman look so delectable in the morning. Her thick brown hair tumbled on the shoulders of a white robe that gently followed her curves. Her cheeks were blushed pink with sleep, and her big gray eyes were shimmering like the moon on a foggy night. Misty. Soft. Wonderful. He wanted to pull her close, feel her breasts pressing against him. Kiss her. Run his fingers through her hair. Then he caught a glimpse of her bare toes poking out from under her nightgown, and he laughed instead. "Where we're going, you'll have to put on shoes," he teased.

She took hold of the sleeve of his sweatshirt and propelled him inside so she could shut the door. "I always wear shoes—almost always." She looked into his dark brown eyes that were so full of laughter and happiness, and she wished he would take her in his arms right then and hold her forever. They had been good friends, and now she was beginning to have such intense feelings about him. She clutched her robe tight around her to suppress a trembling deep inside. "This may seem like a silly question," she began, "but what are you doing here? The sun is barely up. And what do you have in that sack?"

"Breakfast," he answered. "Omelets on English muffins and orange juice." He paused and nodded at the cardboard carton. "And I've also brought our activity for the day, or at least the morning. Now hurry up and get dressed."

Suzanne laughed. "Give me ten minutes."

She disappeared down the hall, and before Jed had even reached the kitchen he heard the water running in the shower. By the time she reappeared, in exactly eleven minutes if his watch was correct, he had filled the thermos with hot coffee and was sitting at the table waiting. She was worth waiting for. Her freshly scrubbed face glowed. Her eyes sparkled with anticipation. Her damp hair curled around her face.

"Am I dressed properly for this event?" She looked at her sweatshirt and jeans. "I copied you, since I don't know where we're going."

"Well, I'm not absolutely sure, either. I thought we'd have a breakfast picnic."

The delight in her eyes told Jed he'd chosen well. "I've never done that," she exclaimed, "and I know just the place."

Jed grinned. He loved seeing her so open and spontaneous. He let her lead him into the woods, striding broadly to keep up with her. The trees towered above them, their branches barely beginning to bud. Damp brown leaves, which had fallen to the ground the previous autumn, cushioned their feet as they walked. Suzanne jumped across a narrow stream and pointed to an immense fallen tree just ahead of them. "How do you feel about an oak table?"

"Exactly what I had in mind," Jed replied. He crossed the stream in one smooth movement and set the bag of food and the carton on a flat part of the fallen tree. Just above him, in a tall evergreen, a bright red cardinal chirped lustily to his rose-gray mate.

"I think they have a nest up there." Suzanne settled herself on the log and arched her head, trying to get a better view of the birds. "Did you know that cardinals mate for life?"

"That's how it ought to be." He took a sip of coffee from the single thermos cup and offered it to Suzanne.

"Yes, I think so, too," she answered quietly. They both knew they weren't talking about cardinals. She took a drink of coffee and reached for the English muffin sandwich Jed held out to her. "Mmm, my favorite. Cold omelet muffin.'' Then she looked at Jed nervously. Marty would have been very angry if she'd made a crack like that.

Jed simply laughed. "The question is, does cold omelet muffin in the woods beat hot omelet muffin in the kitchen?''

"Hands down,'' Suzanne answered. They finished their breakfast while watching a rabbit that scampered alongside the fallen tree and sat up curiously to see what they were doing. After they had gathered up the remains of their meal and stuffed them into the sack, Suzanne wrapped her arms around Jed and hugged him. "Thank you,'' she whispered. "Thank you for a wonderful breakfast.''

"Thank you,'' he answered, "for making it wonderful.''

His arms tightened around her and she felt his chest hard and strong against her cheek. She could hear the soft, steady thud of his heart beating, a sound that was somehow reassuring and made her feel safe. Her feelings for Jed were so much more than those of friendship. True, they had started as friends, but somehow they had arrived here. And where was here? Suzanne didn't have any idea. She only hoped it was a beginning. Jed's breath was warm against her hair. She shivered and lifted her face, waiting expectantly.

Jed gazed into her eyes and smiled as he brushed a strand of hair from her face. She shivered more as his fingers touched her cheek. From deep in the evergreen tree the cardinal called to his mate again. Suzanne smiled at Jed and tentatively touched his cheek. Then he tightened his arms around her and bent his head. As she closed her eyes, she could feel his warm breath trailing across her forehead, her cheek, her mouth. Finally, his lips covered hers.

At first the kiss was light and cautious, little more than a whisper, as they explored each other. She wrapped her arms around his neck, and his mouth opened slightly. Her lips softened, inviting more. She wondered at the throbbing deep inside her. He shuddered and pulled her tightly against him as the kiss deepened, and she felt the warmth of his hands against her back.

"Oh, I like this very much," Suzanne murmured.

His response came not in words, but in sensations as his tongue traced a tender path across her lips, first on the bottom then on the top. Then she did the same to him and laughed aloud with delight when he shuddered.

He pulled away slightly and struggled to suppress a grin. "There's nothing funny about kissing," he said sternly. "It's serious business."

"No, it isn't. It's play. Wonderful, wonderful play." As if to prove her point Suzanne pressed her mouth on his, teased him with the very tip of her tongue and turned her face aside quickly just as he began to respond to her.

"Hey, that's not fair," he protested. He drew her back, and this time he teased her with his tongue, finding each tiny sensitive place on her lips until she trembled beneath him and couldn't have pulled away even if she had wanted to.

"Do you have any idea how that makes me feel?" she whispered.

"Like more than my friend, I bet." Jed chuckled and kissed her again, then cradled her head against his chest. For a long minute they held each other quietly, watching a squirrel scamper through the leaves while they waited for their hearts to stop pounding.

"I really don't want to stop," Suzanne ventured.

"Neither do I," Jed replied. He squeezed her gently and kissed her softly on her forehead. "But this is only the beginning, and I'm trying to convince myself that anticipation is half the fun."

Suzanne looked at him. "Do you really believe that?"

Jed paused thoughtfully for a few seconds before answering. "Yes. I think we have a long journey ahead of us, Suzanne, and I'm not in any hurry. I want us to enjoy every step along the way."

Suzanne found herself fighting back tears, and she lowered her eyes.

"Don't hide your feelings," Jed told her. "It's all right. Really."

"I know," she replied in a tremulous voice. "But so much has happened in the last few weeks. I never expected to feel this way about you. Never in my wildest dreams, and it's happened so fast."

"No, our feelings for each other haven't happened that fast. They've been growing since the first time we met."

"But I thought the closeness I felt for you was friendship—"

"It was friendship, but now it's more." Very soon, he suspected, she would be ready for the absolute joy that love brings, but he didn't want to push her too fast. He handed her the cardboard carton and the two trowels. "Come on," he said. "I have more planned for us this morning." He picked up the food bag and the thermos.

"Where are we going?" Suzanne asked curiously.

Jed smiled. "Again, I'm not sure, but I happen to know the violets are in bloom, and I remembered you wanted to plant some on Lady's grave. I thought if we walked through the woods we'd probably come across some we could dig up."

"Oh, Jed..." Suzanne didn't know what to say. She reached up and touched his cheek. "Thank you."

He stuffed the paper bag in his jeans pocket and took her hand. Together they started down the path, looking carefully on either side for a cluster of the shy purple flowers. Neither spoke, sensing that idle chatter wasn't necessary. They were totally comfortable with each other and with the peaceful silence. The sun had risen and was filtering through the limbs of the trees high above them. The day was going to be warm. "I've found some violets," Jed announced, bending down. "Hand me a trowel."

Suzanne knelt in the leaves and helped him dig up the wildflowers, taking care to keep their roots packed in dirt. They set each plant gently in the cardboard carton, and soon it was full. Jed handed her his trowel and the thermos and picked up the box. "Now, let's go plant these before they dry out."

Suzanne nodded in agreement and followed him down the path to the edge of the woods where Lady was buried. "I really miss her," she said, looking at the fresh earth mounded over the grave.

"I know you do." Jed gave her a reassuring hug and set the carton of violets on the ground between them. Using his trowel Jed began to loosen the dirt, and after he dug out a small section of sweet-smelling earth, Suzanne set a cluster of violets in and he scooped dirt over the roots. They continued planting, matching each other in a rhythm that felt easy and natural.

"These are going to be beautiful next spring," Suzanne said after the bare ground was completely covered and they stood back admiring their work. "The whole area will be thick with violets. Lady would have loved them." She paused, remembering. Jed waited silently, giving her time to be alone with her thoughts. Finally she turned to him. "I feel better. Somehow, this part of my life seems finished now, and I'm ready to go on."

"So am I," Jed replied. He took her in his arms and held her in the warm sun for a very long time.

CHAPTER THIRTEEN

THE NIGHT of the spring dance Suzanne went to Jed and Kacie's to help Kacie finish dressing, much as any Big Sister would. But she arrived with more than Kacie on her mind.

"Jed, what's going on with 'Out on a Limb'?" She waved the cartoon strip she had torn out of the morning newspaper. "All these years your hero has been a single father and now you've brought a woman into his life."

Jed grinned. "Maybe he was due for a change."

"That's all?"

Jed didn't answer.

Suzanne thought the new woman in "Out on a Limb" bore an uncanny resemblance to herself, especially her hair and the expressions on her face. And she had a dog that looked a lot like the sketches Jed had done of Lady. At first Suzanne had assumed it was just a coincidence, but she didn't see how it could be.

"How does it feel to see yourself in print?" Kacie asked on her way through the living room. "I've been dealing with it ever since I was a little kid." She peered through the front door window, looking for Billy, who was to arrive momentarily. "A few weeks from now I'll probably be in the strip wearing my new dress, going out on my first date, and you'll probably be making out with the hero. Nothing is sacred in this house.''

Suzanne blanched and stuffed the comic strip in her pocket. She looked directly at Jed. ''See, I'm not the only one who thought this new 'significant other' of yours looked very familiar.''

Jed didn't answer, and seemed suddenly absorbed with some adjustments on his camera. Suzanne wondered if the strip had bothered Kacie, too, maybe as much as the ones about herself. Not only was her father obviously showing romantic interest in a woman—her own Big Sister—but he was also highlighting the story for the entire country to read and chuckle over.

The doorbell rang and Kacie turned white. ''Billy's here,'' she whispered.

''Don't just stand there,'' Jed told her. ''Let him in.''

''Yeah. Okay.'' Kacie gulped audibly. She wobbled unsteadily in her first pair of high heels as she pulled open the door.

Looking strangely unfamiliar in a blue suit and a red tie with his hair slicked down, Billy held out a small box tied with a narrow white ribbon. ''Here, this is for you.''

''For me?'' Kacie accepted the box hesitantly. ''Why did you bring me a present? It's not my birthday or anything.''

''Open it,'' Billy said.

She untied the ribbon, carefully opened the box and peeked inside. ''A corsage!'' she squealed. ''Little pink roses with a pin and everything!'' She lifted the flowers from the tissue paper and looked helplessly at Suzanne. ''How do I put it on?''

"Wait. Don't do anything yet," Jed directed. "I want to take a picture. Billy, you get the corsage and pin it on Kacie's dress." Poised and waiting, Jed focused the camera.

"Oh, no. Not me." His face ashen, Billy backed as far away from Kacie as he could in the narrow hallway.

Trying not to smile, Suzanne took the rose corsage and pinned it carefully to the shoulder of Kacie's white eyelet dress. Then she stepped back to admire her Little Sister while Jed snapped pictures. Kacie's long dark hair curled softly around her face, and her cheeks were blushed pink with excitement. She was the classic image of a young girl going to her first dance.

Jed set the camera on the hall table. "Now, are you two checked out on the transportation plans for tonight?"

"Daddy!" Kacie rolled her eyes and edged toward the door.

"Hold on. This is important. Billy's mother will drop you off at the dance, and Suzanne is going to pick you up when it's over because I'll still be at my Chamber of Commerce meeting. Eleven o'clock sharp, in front of the gym, right?"

"Right." Kacie pulled open the door and pushed Billy out.

"Have a good time!" Jed called after them. Then he turned to Suzanne. "Are you sure it's not a problem to pick up the kids tonight? Normally I'd do it myself, but this awards banquet is something I can't get out of."

"You know I don't mind." She smiled as he gathered her into his arms. His touch, his smell, the sound of his voice, everything about him made her want to be closer to him. She felt his hands moving up and down her back and pressed against him, murmuring softly.

"I really wish I didn't have this meeting," he said as he held her.

"And I wish I didn't have to go out to Pickett's dairy farm." His breath was warm as he nestled against her hair, and his arms were strong around her. Could it be possible that only a few weeks ago she thought he was just a friend? She tipped her head back and looked up at him. She'd been so naive, she realized. She hadn't acknowledged her feelings because they hadn't been appropriate, and he hadn't pushed her because she belonged to someone else. She shivered when she realized again what a terrible mistake she'd almost made.

"Are you all right?" he asked as he felt the tremor move through her.

"As long as I'm here with you, Jed, I'm just fine." His head lowered and his mouth found hers, gently at first, then with a longing that had been buried deep inside them both. She wanted him, genuinely wanted him as she never had another man. She pressed her body against his until they were melded together as one and she knew the sensations she felt coursed through him, too. When their mouths parted and she leaned against his chest, she shivered again but this time he didn't ask her why because he already knew. "Jed," she said reluctantly, "you have a meeting tonight." She looked over his shoulder at the clock in the hall. "In fifteen minutes."

"Damn the meeting." He buried his head in her hair, searching with his lips until he found her earlobe and touched it gently with his tongue.

She braced her hands against his chest. "Jed, you can't do that."

"I can't?" He spoke softly, his breath a whisper against her ear.

"No." She pushed harder. "Not if you're going to the Chamber of Commerce awards banquet and I'm going to get out to Pickett's so I'll be through in time to pick up Kacie." She looked up. His eyes were dark and intense. His arms were still locked around her, and his heart was pounding against her breast. He didn't want to stop any more than she did.

"Do you promise we can pick up right here where we left off?" he asked with an urgency that touched her heart.

"I promise."

"When?"

"Tomorrow night, the next night, as soon as we can," she answered.

"Or maybe all of the above." He kissed her hard on the mouth then let her go. She hurried to the pickup truck and hopped in. She knew that if she stayed a moment longer she might not leave at all.

THE MUSIC in the middle school gym was blasting at a hundred decibels. The pink and white crepe-paper streamers were sagging, and the punch was warm and insipid. But Kacie didn't notice. She was having a fantastic time. Ever since she had discarded her new high heels on the growing pile of shoes at one end of the bleachers, she hadn't stopped dancing. She had been worried about not knowing how, but that didn't matter. Mostly she just moved in time to the fast music, sometimes with Billy, sometimes with a group of kids.

When there was a slow song, she and Billy sort of clung to each other and swayed. That's what all the other couples were doing, too. It was great.

"Not exactly how we used to dance, is it?" Margaret remarked to Ed. They had stationed themselves near the back door of the gym where they could head off any couples who wanted to sneak out to the dark stadium behind the school.

"What do you mean 'used to'? I don't know about you, but I haven't quit dancing." He took her in his arms, pulled her close and began a reasonable two-step to an updated version of an old, familiar tune.

"Ed!" Margaret protested weakly. "We're in the gym where everybody in the world can see us, especially some of the mothers who have gone to the school board about firing me—"

"So? What difference does that make? You're going to beat them at their own game by resigning anyway. Before you know it we'll be honeymooning on a cruise ship and all this will be behind us. You'll be a free woman, Margaret, a lady of leisure with nothing to do but love me for the rest of your life."

Margaret laughed lightly as Ed whirled her in a circle. "The spinster is going to become a bride," she quipped. "It's terribly exciting." Then she grew sober. "But, even so. I'm going to miss all this, Ed, especially the children. For years teaching and books have been my whole life. They will be very hard to give up."

"Maybe you don't have to give up everything," Ed replied thoughtfully.

"What do you mean?"

"Well, have you ever considered combining your two loves—children and books? With your years of experience I bet you have all kinds of stories to tell. And you know even better than I do that there's a need for good children's literature.''

"Real stories, about real kids," Margaret mused. "I have to admit that once in a while I've dreamed about writing books like the Allison Craig stories. Do you truly think I could?''

Ed laughed. "You can do anything you set your mind to. And leave it to you to pick a hot, controversial kind of book to cut your teeth on. No cute little stories about fuzzy ducks and baby bunnies.''

"Of course not!" Margaret shuddered. "There are plenty of those already. But stories with a message . . .'' Her voice trailed off.

"Which is only one of the many reasons I love you." Ed brushed her forehead with a kiss and twirled her around like an aspiring Fred Astaire. "I'll tell you what," he continued. "Since you refused to accept a diamond ring as a token of my love, how about a computer with a word processing program instead?''

Margaret's whole face lit up. "Oh, Ed! Do you mean that? I'd love to have a computer to write on. I've wanted one forever! You're wonderful, absolutely wonderful." Impulsively she reached up and kissed him on the mouth. "I love you so much," she whispered. Her eyes shone with unshed tears of happiness.

Across the room, Kacie pulled abruptly away from Billy. "Did you see that?''

"See what?''

"Mr. Arnold and Miss Henniker. They're dancing and she kissed him. Right on the mouth! Right in the middle of the gym where everybody could see them.'' Kacie's voice was filled with horror.

Billy glanced over at them. "She's really asking for trouble. The whole PTA board is chaperoning tonight and they probably all saw it. Miss Henniker is gonna get fired for sure."

Kacie gulped. "Why would she do a thing like that? Kiss him right in public, I mean."

Billy shrugged and wiped his sweaty hands on his pants. "I don't know. I guess she loves him or something. Don't Suzanne and your father ever kiss?"

"I—I don't know," Kacie stammered in confusion. "I suppose so, but not in public, at least not where I've ever seen them."

"Yeah, I suppose kissing in public is kind of—well, public. Or something." Billy looked into Kacie's eyes for a brief moment and quickly looked away.

"Kissing should be done in private, in the dark," Kacie stated emphatically.

"Yeah. Like on your front porch late at night," Billy muttered.

Kacie wasn't sure she had heard him correctly. "What did you say?" she demanded.

"Nothing."

Billy's ears turned beet red, and Kacie knew she had heard him. Billy was going to kiss her. Tonight on the front porch in the dark when he took her home. Her heart gave a tiny little flip-flop inside her chest. She'd never actually thought about kissing Billy before. But suddenly the idea seemed quite nice. Then another thought struck her. How was he going to manage it with Suzanne driving them home? What if they dropped Billy off first? She had some things to figure out before Suzanne came to get them.

SUZANNE GLANCED at the clock on the dashboard of her pickup. Ten forty-five. She had fifteen minutes to get to the school. A fine drizzle was falling, and she turned on the windshield wipers. They beat a staccato rhythm across the glass. Lub-dub. Lub-dub. Lub-dub. Over and over, like Jed's heartbeat against her breast when he held her. Suzanne smiled when she thought of Jed. She had been thinking of him all evening while she worked. Actually, he was on her mind nearly all the time. She wished he was going to be home when she arrived with Kacie, but she knew he wouldn't be. The Chamber of Commerce awards banquet would run until at least midnight.

Carefully she guided her pickup around a sharp curve. The rain was getting heavier and the visibility was bad. She lifted her foot from the accelerator, but as she reached the next curve she was still going too fast, and the truck skidded on the wet asphalt. She pressed lightly on the brake pedal and the truck slowed, but only slightly. Suzanne frowned. She pressed harder on the brake pedal, pumping rhythmically with her foot. The pickup skidded again. She hit the brake pedal hard and clutched the steering wheel to regain control, but the truck didn't slow down.

Panic swept through her. She was approaching Miller's Hill, and if she hit the curve at the bottom too fast— She jammed the brake pedal into the floorboard as hard as she could. Nothing. She had no brakes at all. She came out of the curve too fast and the truck veered onto the shoulder, skidding nearly out of control in the loose gravel.

Suzanne looked up at the road. Her headlights reflected off the crest of Miller's Hill and disappeared into the darkness where the road dropped away. She had to stop before she got there. Gripping the steering wheel hard, she purposefully turned the truck toward the shoulder. Again she hit the gravel and nearly lost control. She was almost at the crest of the hill. Knowing it was her last chance, she turned sharply toward the edge of the road until her wheels struck the mud beyond the gravel. The truck rocked hard to the right, lurched wildly, then hit the far side of the drainage ditch and stopped with a jolt.

Shaking all over, Suzanne rested her head against the steering wheel and closed her eyes. Everything was quiet except for the rhythmic pulse of the windshield wipers. She tried to move, first her arms and then her legs. Nothing hurt. Slowly she raised her head. Her muscles ached from the tension, but that was all, except she couldn't stop herself from shaking.

The truck was pitched forward at an angle, its front wheels buried to the bumper in heavy Virginia clay. The headlights blazed across the unplowed rows of a farmer's field until they were lost in the darkness. Suzanne realized she was stuck, and she was alone. Hours could pass before anyone came along the deserted country road. But at least she was alive. Still trembling, she pushed the truck door open, climbed out into the mud and started walking.

JED GLANCED AT HIS WATCH as he turned into the driveway at the side of his darkened house. Eleven-fifteen. He was home almost an hour earlier than he had expected, but Suzanne should have dropped Kacie off by now. He climbed out of his car. Puzzled because there were no lights in the house, he went upstairs to check on Kacie. Her bed was empty. Immediately he picked up the phone and called Billy's house, only to discover that Billy wasn't home, either. Jed was in his car in an instant and at Cartersburg Intermediate in record time. He spotted Billy and Kacie immediately, standing alone except for a single chaperon.

"Get in," he called to them. And to the chaperon, he added, "Sorry. There was a mix-up in our transportation plans."

"Where's Suzanne?" Kacie asked as she and Billy leaned over the backseat. "We phoned the clinic and her house, but nobody answered. We kept thinking she'd come."

"I guess she got delayed at Pickett's farm, or maybe she had an emergency." Jed's voice was controlled, but his stomach was in a knot. Suzanne never, under any circumstances, would forget to pick up Kacie. Something was the matter. He pulled up in front of the house and turned around. "I'm just going to drop you two off so I can go check on Suzanne. Billy, you go straight home. Your mother is expecting you. And Kacie, you get right into bed—after you hang up your new dress. Don't dump it on the floor, okay?"

Kacie barely heard her father. All she could think about was the kiss. It was going to work. She and Billy would be alone on the dark porch with no one to bother them. This would be a night to remember.

They walked slowly toward the porch, waiting, Kacie decided, until the headlights of her father's car disappeared down the block. They were completely alone, and fortunately the bulb in the porch light was still

burned out. Kacie slowed down more to let Billy catch
up with her.

"You having trouble walking in those shoes?" he
asked.

"No." Kacie looked self-consciously at her high
heels. She had already figured out that Billy didn't like
the shoes much because they made her almost as tall as
he was. She took them off when she got to the porch
steps. At the door she turned and found Billy behind
her, looking much taller again. She wasn't sure exactly
how the kiss was supposed to happen and she had a
feeling he wasn't, either. "I had a really good time tonight," she told him. "And I like my corsage."

"Yeah, me, too." Billy shifted his weight from one
foot to the other. He didn't say anything else and he
didn't move.

"Well, I guess I should go in," Kacie said after a
long silence. She didn't want to go in, but they couldn't
just stand and stare at each other all night.

"Yeah."

Bitterly disappointed, she opened the screen door.
She heard his feet shuffle behind her. She took hold of
the door knob. Then she felt his hand on her arm.
"Kacie?"

He was going to do it. She knew, without any doubt
at all. She turned toward him slowly, like she'd read
about people doing it in books and said very softly,
"Yes, Billy?"

She couldn't see his face very well in the darkness,
but she could feel him coming closer. She tipped her
head back and closed her eyes, waiting expectantly. His
mouth barely touched hers at first and then pressed
down a little more. His lips moved and hers moved

with them and a warm, feathery sensation rippled all through her and then, when she was really starting to like it, the kiss was over.

She opened her eyes. For a moment Billy stood very still, staring at her. Then he mumbled, "Good night, Kacie," and disappeared into the darkness beyond the porch. Kacie stood by the door looking after him, a huge smile on her face. They'd done it, really done it, and she felt good all over.

JED TURNED onto Main Street, heading across town toward Suzanne's. The rain was coming down steadily now. He drove slowly, scanning the road on both sides, not really sure what he was looking for. When he reached Suzanne's and found the truck gone and no lights, he headed immediately for Pickett's dairy farm.

Jed gripped the steering wheel as a dozen scenarios raced through his mind, each one more ominous than the last. He rounded a curve and was momentarily blinded by the glare of headlights bearing down on him. The night was too dark and the car was going too fast for him to get a look at it, but all he could think of was Marty. Jed had grown complacent. Suzanne had assured him Marty was gone for good, and he'd believed her because he wanted to believe. He'd never forgive himself if anything had happened to her.

As he approached the hairpin turn at the base of Miller's Hill, he slowed down, his eyes searching the darkness beyond the curtain of rain. He was just starting up the hill when he saw her, a solitary figure walking along the shoulder of the road. He hit the brakes so hard he skidded onto the opposite shoulder. He jammed the car into park and jumped out. Moments later she was in his arms.

"Suzanne, Suzanne." His voice was a hoarse whisper.

"Oh, Jed, I'm so glad you're here." She collapsed against him, shaking as she stopped fighting the fear.

They stood in the rain holding each other like they might never let go. "Oh, Jed," Suzanne murmured again as she wrapped her arms tighter around him.

"Suzanne, are you all right?" he whispered.

She nodded.

"Come on," he said, one arm still close around her, "let's get out of the rain."

They were in the shelter of his car with Suzanne wrapped in a blanket before he asked her what happened.

"It was awful, Jed," she answered. "I tried to stop and the brakes didn't work at all and the truck skidded out of control." The scene came back almost like it was happening again, and she pulled the blanket tight around her, trembling from fear and cold. Jed wrapped her in his arms, rocking her gently. "I could see Miller's Hill ahead and I knew if I started down, I'd pick up so much speed that I'd never make the curve so I went off in the ditch."

"You're sure you're not hurt?"

"I don't think so. I don't even think there's any damage to the truck, except maybe the supplies inside. But Jed, I was so scared." She buried her head in his shoulder again.

As she talked, Jed remembered the car that raced past him on the darkened road and he thought about Marty. His stomach knotted again. As soon as he got

Suzanne home, he'd get the truck towed in and tomorrow they'd try to find out what had happened. He pressed his cheek against Suzanne's wet hair and wrapped the blanket tighter around her. Tonight all that mattered was that she was safe.

CHAPTER FOURTEEN

KACIE RACED OUT the front door of Cartersburg Intermediate without even bothering to go to her classroom to be dismissed. She'd been so excited about spring break but that was before she saw Miss Henniker's announcement on the bulletin board outside the library. Miss Henniker was resigning effective immediately. There had been an explanation following, but Kacie hadn't bothered to read it. She felt empty inside, overwhelmed by a sense of injustice. She should have fought harder; all of them should have. Making Miss Henniker leave was wrong. There should have been some way to stop it. She ran fast at first, then slowed to an angry walk, kicking at rocks and sticks on the sidewalk.

When she burst into the clinic where Suzanne was stocking the shelves, she didn't bother to say hello. "They won," she announced sullenly. "They made her resign."

"Margaret Henniker resigned?"

Kacie nodded.

"You're sure?"

"She put up an announcement on the bulletin board. I guess she didn't want to wait for them to fire her."

Suzanne paced across the clinic. "When we hadn't heard much about this in the past few weeks, I hoped maybe some kind of compromise was in the works."

Kacie's mouth dropped open. "You think she should have taken away the books?"

"Well, no—"

"Then what kind of compromise could there be?"

Suzanne thought about that for a moment. "I guess you're right, Kacie. There isn't much middle ground. Did she say what she's going to do now?"

Kacie shook her head. "Nope."

"I'll call her later today. Wait a minute." Suzanne flipped through her appointment book. "Margaret has something planned. She's due any minute to bring Othello in to board for a week. I assumed she was going on a trip over spring break."

"She can stay as long as she wants now." Kacie pulled off her jacket and threw it on a chair. "What reason does she have to come back?"

Suzanne wasn't sure how to answer Kacie. Before she had the opportunity, the bell on the door jangled and Margaret Henniker and Ed Arnold walked in carrying Othello. Suzanne and Kacie stared. Margaret was dressed in a cream-colored silk suit with matching pumps and a silky peach-colored blouse. Her hair was pulled up under a broad-brimmed hat decorated with a flat bow that matched her blouse. She looked radiant.

"Hello, Kacie," Margaret said, spotting her student.

"Hello, Miss Henniker." Kacie's eyes were still wide. "You look really pretty."

"She certainly does," Ed chimed in, slipping his arm around her waist.

Suzanne wasn't sure, but she thought Margaret blushed.

"We've brought Othello," Margaret told Suzanne as Ed set down the carrier with the big cat cowering in the corner. "I hope he won't be too unhappy."

"We'll do the best for him we can," Suzanne promised. "Is there somewhere I can reach you in case of any emergency?"

Margaret and Ed looked at one another. Suddenly Suzanne knew. She glanced at Kacie, who was raptly watching the principal and the former librarian.

"I'm afraid not," Margaret said. "Actually, shall we tell them, Ed?"

His smile broadened. "We can tell the whole world, as far as I'm concerned."

"Now, Ed," Margaret admonished. "It's a secret until we get back."

Kacie couldn't contain herself any longer. "Are you two going to get married?"

They both grinned at her.

"You are, aren't you?"

It was Margaret who answered. "Yes, Kacie, and you and Suzanne are the only ones who know. We're on our way to the airport to fly to Miami, where we're going to leave on a cruise. We'll be married aboard ship."

Suzanne stood up and hurried around the desk to hug Margaret. "Oh, that's wonderful," she said, feeling as though she might cry. "Congratulations, Ed," she added, reaching around Margaret and squeezing his hand. He looked so proud that Suzanne thought he would burst. That was the way it was supposed to be, two people so much in love that the whole world could see it. "Why have you kept this a secret?" Suzanne asked them.

"It seemed best," Margaret explained. "We couldn't both stay at the same school once we were married, and I wasn't ready to resign until now."

"So you don't mind resigning?" Kacie felt betrayed.

"It was the hardest thing I ever did, Kacie." Margaret stepped toward her. "I wanted to finish what I'd started and leave the book program intact. I never thought it would come to this."

Ed put his arm around Margaret's shoulders. "I've been trying to get Margaret to marry me for almost a year. She's a very committed woman."

Kacie looked from one to the other. "But what are you going to do now, Miss Henniker? I mean, except be Mrs. Arnold."

Margaret glanced at Ed and he smiled reassuringly. "Well, Kacie, I thought I might try writing books for students your age."

"Really? You're going to be another Allison Craig?"

Margaret looked embarrassed. "Well, I don't know about that."

"She'll be even better," Ed said proudly, as he checked his watch. "We have to be on our way. We have a plane to catch." He gave Margaret a hug. "Don't we, dear?" he added.

She looked at him. "We certainly do."

This time, Suzanne was absolutely certain Margaret blushed.

Suzanne and Kacie walked with them to their car and waved until they were out of sight. "This calls for a celebration." Suzanne put her arm around her Little Sister's shoulders. "I'm through with my appointments for the day. How about going down to the ice-cream shop?"

"Great," Kacie agreed. "I'm starved."

They got Othello settled, then locked up in record time and headed downtown in the car Suzanne had rented while her truck was in the shop. As they ate strawberry sundaes loaded with whipped cream, Suzanne found herself thinking about Margaret and Ed. "Were you surprised about Miss Henniker and Mr. Arnold getting married?"

"Well, sort of, I guess," Kacie admitted.

"What do you mean sort of? That was the best-kept secret in town."

"Well . . ."

Suzanne stopped eating and looked curiously at Kacie. "What do you know that I don't?"

"Well, one night when Billy and I were—I mean—Anyway we were walking past Miss Henniker's house one night kind of late and we saw Mr. Arnold kissing her."

"And you didn't tell anyone?"

Kacie shrugged and concentrated on finishing her ice cream.

Suzanne smiled. Obviously another midnight outing. They'd had to keep the secret or reveal that they had sneaked out. Someday she was going to have a discussion with Kacie about sneaking out at night, but that could wait. Enough had happened for one day.

Back at Suzanne's house, Kacie explained that she needed to leave because she was going to Billy's for dinner. Suzanne handed her the keys to the clinic and watched her run across the yard to get her backpack, which she'd left inside. As long as Kacie wasn't going to be home, she thought she might call Jed and see if he would like to have dinner with her. She had two steaks in the freezer and a clean linen tablecloth and some candles, and afterward—

She heard a shriek and saw Kacie come flying out of the clinic. "Suzanne, there's something awful in there. It's dead."

Suzanne ran toward the clinic. Pushing Kacie aside, she got as far as the doorway where she stopped and stared. On the floor in front of her, a bird was lying on its back, its wings twisted and its breast sticky with blood. It appeared to be a small gray dove. As she knelt and picked it up, its head flopped over her fingers.

"What happened? How did it get here?" Kacie stood quivering against the door frame.

Suzanne felt her heart beating faster and faster. She had left the clinic locked. There was no way for a bird to get in, unless it had been there before they left and she hadn't noticed. But how had it died? She examined the bloody stain on its breast, pulling aside the feathers. The body was still soft and supple. The bird hadn't been dead long. As she palpated the breast with her fingers, she felt a lump. When she examined it closely, she felt sick at her stomach. "My God," she gasped softly.

"What is it, Suzanne? What did you find?" Kacie's voice was a frightened whisper.

Still holding the bird, Suzanne stood up. "I'm not sure, but we're about to find out." She walked to the surgery table, selected a pair of forceps from her surgical instruments and went to work. Moments later, she extracted a small, hard object from the bird's breast and laid it on the table.

"What is it?" Kacie asked.

Suzanne looked directly at her Little Sister. "It's a bullet, Kacie. The bird was shot."

"Shot?" Kacie gasped. "But why? And how did it get into the clinic?"

Suzanne shook her head silently. All she could think of was Marty. Nausea seeped through her and she thought she might throw up. The memory of him stroking her hair and calling her "my little dove" engulfed her, and she tried to push it away. Surely he hadn't done this sick, cruel thing. But if he hadn't, who else would have? She walked slowly to her desk and sank down on the chair. Without any doubt, Marty had poisoned Lady. A part of her had denied it, but now she knew for sure. Involuntarily, she trembled. She thought about her accident the weekend before when her brakes had failed and the truck had gone into the ditch. She'd never really questioned that it was an accident, but now... Frightened and helpless, Suzanne buried her head in her arms.

"How did the bird get in? Suzanne, answer me," Kacie demanded. "Suzanne are you all right?"

Suzanne nodded, unable to speak.

"You are not," Kacie told her. "I'm going to call my dad."

Suzanne's thoughts whirled as she tried to get a grip on herself. The image of the bloody dove, indelible on her mind, had done its work, and a cold blanket of fear settled around her. Time was lost as she sat there, remembering and trying not to remember. Then she heard Jed's voice. She raised her head and he was beside her, his hand on her shoulder.

"Suzanne, are you all right?"

She was all right now that he was there, and she tried to tell him so. As she started to stand up, he lifted her from the chair and wrapped her in his arms with his head pressed against her hair. She felt an enormous sense of relief. She wanted him to keep holding her, except they weren't alone, or at least she didn't think they were. "Where's Kacie?" she whispered.

"I sent her home to take care of Lucky."

She rested her head on his shoulder, her arms still around him. She'd never known anyone like Jed, not until now. He understood her in a way no one else ever had. If she had met him first, Marty would never have happened. "I'm still a little shaky," she admitted as she leaned against him. "Let's go sit down."

He led her to the couch in the waiting room and sat beside her, quietly holding her hand. "Tell me what happened, Suzanne."

"Kacie and I came in from having ice cream and we found the dove—oh, Jed, it had been shot and Marty did it—this time I'm sure."

Her voice trembled, and Jed put his arm around her shoulders. "But why? Why would he shoot a bird and leave it in the clinic?"

Suzanne swallowed hard and looked away. "It wasn't just a bird. It was a dove. Marty used to call me his little dove."

Jed felt sick. "You think it was a symbol—a threat?"

"I don't know, but I'm absolutely sure now that he poisoned Lady. And I've been thinking about how the brakes failed on the truck." Suzanne spoke slowly. "Do you think it's possible Marty was responsible for that, too?"

Jed's expression was grim. "When Kacie called I was on my way over anyway. I went down to the service station this morning to talk to the mechanic who is working on the truck. He said two or three times he'd never seen a brake line fail like that."

"Then it wasn't an accident?"

Jed shook his head. "I asked the same thing and apparently it's not that simple. The line was worn and it could have sprung a leak. The mechanic didn't think so, but he said there was no way to be sure."

Suzanne stared at the floor. "He may not be sure, but I am." Her voice was almost inaudible. The last few weeks had been the happiest of her life, and she had managed to convince herself that Marty was gone forever. Now she couldn't pretend any longer. He was there, lurking in the shadows of her life, and she had no way of knowing what he might do next. "Jed, I'm scared," she admitted. Her eyes searched his. "What am I going to do?"

"For starters, you're going to stay with Kacie and me for a while. I'll fix up the spare bedroom for you."

"But, Jed—"

"No arguments this time." He put one finger gently on her lips. "You can't stay here alone. That man is dangerous, Suzanne. Anyone who would do this kind of thing is sick."

She nodded, knowing he was right. "But I still have my veterinary practice. I have to go on with my life."

Jed wished he had more answers. All he knew for the moment was that he had to keep Marty away from her. "Right now, let's go over to the house and you can pack some things. We'll take this one step at a time."

Suzanne spent only a few minutes packing a small suitcase with a nightgown and a robe, a few changes of clothes and a zipper case filled with toiletries. She wouldn't need much because she'd be back every day when she came to the clinic. Her anger at being forced out of her house was muted by a sense of anticipation about staying with Jed. She realized she'd need to call Janet Sawyer and let her know what had happened, but she knew Janet would be supportive.

When Suzanne came out of the bedroom, suitcase in hand, she found Jed hanging up the kitchen phone with a scowl on his face. "What's the matter?" she asked, almost afraid to imagine.

"I called both the Cartersburg police and the county sheriff, and got essentially the same answer from both of them."

"You called the police?"

Jed ran his hands through his hair. "Look, Suzanne, we need all the help we can get, although it doesn't look like it's going to be much."

Suzanne didn't like the idea of involving the police. It made the entire situation seem even more sordid than it already was. But she could see his point. "What did they say?"

"Basically that they'd drive by on a regular basis, and come out and talk to us if we wanted, but that unless we could at least prove that a crime had been committed, there wasn't much they could do."

"But what about Lady? And the brakes on the truck?"

Jed shook his head. "We don't know where Lady got the poison. There was no sign of anyone breaking in. And I told you what the mechanic said about the brakes."

Suzanne suddenly felt very vulnerable. "What am I going to do if he comes back?"

Jed took her in his arms and held her for a long time. "We're going to call the police. And beyond that . . ." He swallowed hard. "Beyond that, I don't know."

CHAPTER FIFTEEN

MARTY DIDN'T COME BACK, not that day or the next or in the weeks that followed. Margaret and Ed returned from their honeymoon, relaxed and radiant and started the entire town buzzing about their romance. Billy Hankins was grounded for a week after his mother caught him sneaking out at midnight. Suzanne got her truck back, completely fixed except for a small dent in the front fender, and she cleaned up the breakage in the portable clinic unit and restocked it. School resumed after spring break, and Suzanne, Jed and Kacie fell into a comfortable routine, fitting together as though the new living arrangement was the most natural thing in the world.

But Jed never let Suzanne out of his sight. When she went to the clinic, he went along, sketch pad in hand. He worked while she worked, and then often late into the night doing his final pen-and-ink drawings. Jane, the significant other, was playing a greater and greater role in his comic strips.

One Friday morning, two weeks after she had moved in with Jed and Kacie, Suzanne glanced at Jed across the breakfast table and realized how tired he looked. She decided his double life had to stop. "How late did you work last night?" she asked him.

Jed shrugged. "I don't know exactly what time it was, but I got the strip done. That's the important part."

"It was 2:00 a.m.," Kacie volunteered with her mouth full of scrambled eggs. "Lucky barked and woke me up."

That settled things as far as Suzanne was concerned. "Today you get to stay home and catch up on your life," she announced to Jed. "I'm going to the clinic alone."

"No way," Jed answered.

"Oh, yes, I am," Suzanne insisted. "Because if you don't agree, I'm going to move back home."

Jed put down the newspaper and glared at her across the table. Kacie stopped chewing and looked from one to the other. She had never heard them argue, or even mildly disagree. And she didn't want Suzanne to leave. Having her there had been like a dream come true for Kacie. Her dad was in a better mood than he'd been for a long time, and everything seemed to go right. The meals got cooked, the laundry got done, the trash got out on time and nobody yelled at anybody. They all pitched in together, and even the dumb jobs that Kacie hated were sort of fun. She and Suzanne had spent several evenings talking and had gone shopping twice for new spring clothes. She still wore the baggy shirts and torn jeans, but not all the time.

She had watched Suzanne and her dad carefully and listened at the heat vent at night when they thought she was asleep. Lots of times there were long pauses in their conversations, and sometimes she heard the springs on the sofa squeaking and then they would talk so softly that she couldn't hear what they said. She suspected they were kissing and that meant they might be falling in love. She wasn't absolutely sure that was a good idea, but so far it hadn't seemed to change her relationship with either one of them, which was what concerned her most. But now Suzanne was threatening to leave and that could spoil everything.

"Suzanne, you can't move back home." Jed's voice was firm. "It isn't safe."

"And it isn't sensible for you to stay up till all hours working because you're spending your days with me. Besides, I'll have to start living my own life again."

Jed glanced at Kacie. "Do you think we could discuss this later?" he asked Suzanne.

Suzanne stood and picked up her plate. "No, because I have an early surgery this morning, and I'm on my way."

"And I'm coming with you."

Suzanne's eyes were flashing. "Jed, I mean it. Either I go alone or I move back home."

They were both standing now, neither of them willing to give an inch. Something had to be done, but Kacie wasn't sure what. She remembered Miss Henniker talking in the book discussions about finding a middle ground so that both sides would give a little but neither had to back down. She cleared her throat. "How about if Suzanne takes Lucky with her to the clinic to protect her, like Lady did, and if you call her real often, Dad, just to make sure she's all right?"

Jed and Suzanne stared at Kacie. "I don't know what good Lucky is going to do—" Jed began.

"I think he might be a big help," Suzanne interrupted. As she said it, she wondered what she was doing. Lucky was a big, undisciplined puppy who was going to be lots of trouble and probably useless in a crisis. But, at the same time, she had to somehow persuade Jed that she would be all right without him because she couldn't have him watching over her indefinitely. Besides, she wasn't all that worried about Marty any more. At first she'd believed he'd meant the dove as a threat, but now, after thinking about it, she'd decided that the dove was his way of saying that she no longer existed for him. That was fine with her.

Jed hesitated. "I don't know..."

Kacie could see her dad relenting. "Lucky would be a help," she chimed in. "He would never let anyone hurt Suzanne."

"Really, Jed, I'll be fine." Suzanne's expression had softened and she smiled at him.

Reluctantly, Jed sat down. "I don't like it. I want you to call me if you notice anything even slightly unusual. And make sure you keep the truck locked."

"I promise." She let her hand slide gently across his shoulders as she walked past him to take her plate to the sink. The gesture didn't escape Kacie, nor did the half smile it brought to her father's face.

Once Suzanne had left with Lucky, Kacie made herself another piece of toast. She wasn't really hungry, but she had a few minutes before she had to leave for school and sitting there eating would be a good way to talk to her father. "I guess you like having Suzanne live here," she began.

Jed murmured assent but didn't look up from the newspaper. Kacie decided she'd have to be more blunt. "I suppose you're planning to marry her."

"Mmm," Jed said.

Kacie counted silently. She reached five when her father's head jerked back and he dropped the paper on the table.

"What did you say?"

"I was trying to get your attention," Kacie told him smugly. "Looks like I succeeded."

"You certainly did." Jed studied his daughter carefully. She'd be fourteen in a few months and she was growing up fast. She was becoming more intuitive every day. "What would make you ask if I was planning to marry Suzanne?"

Kacie slathered strawberry jam on her toast. "I live here, too, you know."

"And what's that supposed to mean?"

"Just what I said. I can see how you look at each other."

Jed sat back in his chair. He wasn't quite ready to discuss his plans with Kacie, but since she obviously was two steps ahead of him, he didn't have much choice. "Suppose—and I do mean just suppose—you were right. How would you feel about it?"

Kacie shrugged and took a large bite of toast. "I don't know."

"Of course you do, or you wouldn't have brought it up."

Kacie squirmed uncomfortably. This wasn't the direction the conversation had been supposed to take. "If you got married, that would make Suzanne my stepmother, right?"

Jed frowned. "Technically, I suppose."

"So, I don't want a stepmother. I like having her as my Big Sister."

"I see." Jed was treading on uncertain ground. He knew how important the relationship with Suzanne was to Kacie. Now he was in effect asking her to share Suzanne with him. His situation was even more awkward, because he hadn't talked to Suzanne yet. He'd come so close one night the week before when he had held her and stroked her and felt the wonderful softness of her body melting against him. He had wanted to take her to bed with him and love her till morning came, but she'd moved away and whispered that she thought she heard Kacie upstairs. They had gone to bed separately, and he'd lain awake most of the night thinking about her. He wanted to marry her. He had never been so certain of anything in his life. But he also wanted everything to work out for all three of them.

"Couldn't Suzanne just live with us and everything else stay like it is?" Kacie asked.

Jed smiled at his daughter. One moment she could be all grown up and the next a little girl again. "I don't know that anything ever just stays like it is, Kacie. We grow, we change, and sometimes things just keep getting better."

"I don't know if it can get better, Dad. It's pretty good right now." Kacie glanced up at the clock and stuffed the rest of the toast in her mouth. "Gotta go." She leaped from her chair and grabbed her books. "I'm gonna be late."

She raced out the door, still chewing, her mouth so full she couldn't even call to Billy, who was half a block ahead. When she caught up with him, he grinned at her. He did that a lot lately and she liked it.

"I waited for you," he said in greeting, "but I was late and I thought you'd already gone." He fell in step with her, neither of them hurrying very much.

"I was talking to my dad."

"Heavy stuff?"

"Kind of." Kacie considered whether to tell Billy about her dad and Suzanne. He wouldn't ask. He never did. But she knew he'd listen. "I think my dad and Suzanne are in love."

"Oh, yeah?"

That was as close as Billy ever came to admitting surprise.

"I thought she was staying with you because of that crazy dude she was engaged to."

Kacie shifted her books to her other arm. "Well, she is, sort of. But I think this thing has been going on between her and Dad for a while now. I asked him this morning if he was planning to marry her and he didn't say no."

Billy stared at her. "You just asked right out?"

"So what was I supposed to do, sit back and wait till they got around to talking about it?"

Billy shrugged and pulled a pack of cinnamon gum out of his jeans pocket. "You want some gum?"

Kacie took a stick. "Thanks." That was another thing that had changed. He used to charge her a penny for gum; now he just gave it to her. "I don't know if I'd like it if they got married," she continued.

"Why not?"

Kacie had to chew hard to soften up the gum before she could answer. "Because I don't want to lose Suzanne."

"You'd have her even more."

"But it might be different."

Billy shrugged. "Maybe, maybe not."

They rounded the evergreens at the corner of the school yard just as the warning bell rang. They took off flying for the door. "See you later," Billy called over his shoulder. Kacie smiled as she watched him disappear down the corridor. For some reason, she felt better about Suzanne and her dad. Talking to Billy always helped her make sense out of everything.

THE DAYS PASSED QUICKLY for Suzanne. For the first time since she could remember, she no longer lingered at the clinic to reorganize supplies or take the dog she was boarding for an extra run. She was anxious to get home to dinner with Jed and Kacie and to spend the early spring evenings sitting outdoors with a glass of iced tea watching Kacie and Lucky frolic in the backyard.

Her life was not only good, it was too good, and that was what troubled Suzanne one evening as she took the last tray of cookies out of the oven and laid them on a wire rack to cool. For a week she'd gone to the clinic alone, and now it had become the norm. The time between Jed's phone calls had stretched until he called only two or three times a day, mostly, she suspected, because he wanted to talk to her, not because he was worried. She had heard nothing from Marty, which left her more certain than ever that the dove had been his final act of revenge. Marty was finally gone.

She walked to the back door and looked through the screen at the new green leaves of the oak tree. A squirrel dangled from the end of a branch as he tried to get his footing and climb up. That's what Jed had done after Elizabeth died, and that was what she had to do now. Take hold and go on. She couldn't continue to lean on Jed. It was time for her to go home.

An emptiness swept through her when she thought about it. These weeks with Jed and Kacie had been some of the happiest she'd ever spent. This was part of the reason she had to go now. She wasn't only happy, she had fallen in love. When she and Jed sat on the sofa at night and he held her and they whispered to each other and laughed softly, always listening for footsteps on the stairs, she felt as though a part of her that had been missing had slipped into place. It had become harder and harder to leave him and go alone to the spare bedroom where she slept. She knew he shared her feelings. Some nights he could barely let her go. But what she didn't know was whether he truly loved her or whether he felt responsible for her. She had already made one terrible mistake with Marty. She wouldn't make another.

"Suzanne?"

She whirled at the sound of Jed's voice, feeling naked, as though he might have sensed what she was thinking.

"You look like you've seen a ghost." He took a step toward her and touched her shoulder. "Is anything the matter?"

"No, nothing," she lied. "You just startled me. Kacie isn't due home from the baseball game for at least an hour and I thought you were working."

Jed grinned. "I was, but two things stopped me. The first was the absolutely irresistible smell of chocolate chip cookies." He took one, popped it in his mouth and ate it in a single bite.

"And the second?"

He swallowed the cookie and ate another before he said anything, and even then he didn't answer her question. "Do you bake cookies often?"

Suzanne shook her head. "I haven't baked a cookie since I was in high school."

"So why tonight?"

"I don't know." Rather self-consciously she wiped her hands on the barbecue apron she'd found folded up in the drawer. She had wondered the same thing herself, not only why she was baking cookies but why she was enjoying the process so much. She hadn't come up with any satisfactory answers except that she knew Jed and Kacie would like them and it made her happy to do things they liked. "But you didn't answer my question," she said, overlooking the fact that she hadn't really answered his, either. "What was the second reason you stopped working?"

Looking suddenly uncomfortable, Jed shuffled from one foot to the other, reminding Suzanne very much of Billy when he'd picked up Kacie for the dance. "I got stuck with my strip," he said finally. His eyes were a deep velvet brown as he looked at her. "I thought maybe you could help me."

"Me?" The request surprised Suzanne. Jed had never asked for help before. In fact, he seemed to make it a practice not to discuss ideas he was working on. He'd explained once that talking about them used up the creative energy. "I'll try, Jed, but I don't know if I'll be much help."

"Sure you will." He took her hand and led her into his study where sketches were strewn across his drawing table. She stood beside him with the sense that something important was happening. He showed her rough sketches he had done for three strips. The significant other who had become a central part of the hero's life was featured in all of them. Suzanne still thought the woman resembled her, but Jed had been very clear that while the strip reflected ideas drawn from his life, it wasn't autobiographical.

"I've got these three strips done," he explained. "They're part of what we call a sequence. But there's one more strip to go, and I'm stuck on the punch line in the last box."

He handed Suzanne four sheets of paper. In the first drawing, the man and the woman were in a parked car among some trees with the moon shining down. "But I thought we were going to the movies," the woman was saying. Suzanne turned to the second sheet. The man was holding the woman's hand now. "That was what I told the kids so I could get you alone," he answered.

Suzanne turned to the third sheet. The man was gazing into the woman's eyes and asking, "Will you marry me?"

Intrigued, Suzanne looked at the fourth sheet. It was blank. Puzzled, she looked up at Jed, who was standing behind her with his arm around her waist. "Then what happens?"

He was smiling at her, his hand warm against her back. "That's where I was hoping you could help me. What do you think she'd say?"

At first Suzanne couldn't answer. Was Jed asking her to marry him? If he was, she didn't know how to respond. But maybe it wasn't that at all. She thought about the strip. He'd written it for years about a single man bringing up children. That had been the key to its success. Several weeks ago he had added the significant other. And now he was tinkering with the idea of bringing a wife and mother into the scenario. "I don't know, Jed," Suzanne answered hesitantly. "I think she'd say it would be a big change."

"You mean because she'd be marrying not just a man but a family?" He turned and slid his other arm around her, letting his hands trail slowly down her back. When he did that, Suzanne had trouble concentrating.

"Well, I guess partly," Suzanne began. One of Jed's hands slipped up under her hair, loosening the clips that held it. He touched the back of her neck with his fingers, then moved upward freeing her thick, dark hair until it hung around her shoulders. "Jed," Suzanne began, her voice shaky, "what are you asking me?"

He looked at her for a full minute, his eyes caressing her as his fingers moved inside her shirt collar with infinite gentleness. "I've been wanting to do this for such a long time, but I wasn't sure how. I love you, Suzanne. I'm asking you to marry me."

Suzanne was silent for a moment. She didn't want Jed to think he had to take care of her because of everything that had happened in the past few months. But something he'd said . . . "What do you mean, for such a long time?"

"I've struggled with this since I first met you." He spoke slowly, deliberately, as though the words were hard to say. "But you belonged to someone else."

Suzanne was overwhelmed. "You mean all that time we spent together—"

"I tried to deny it at first," he admitted. "Then I tried to stay away from you, but that didn't work, either."

"But, Jed, I thought we were friends."

"We were, but for me it was always more. Didn't you feel . . ." He wasn't sure how to ask. "Didn't you feel anything?"

She started to say no, but the memories came flooding back. The electric charge that had shot through her when he touched her, the night when she had stayed for dinner although she'd known Marty might come, the excuses she'd found to stop by when there was really no reason at all, the night she'd brought Kacie home from ice skating and tried so hard to come up with an excuse to go in because she missed Jed so much. "I was going to say no, but—" She wrapped both arms around him and clung tight, pressing her head against his chest. "How could I have missed it? How could I not have realized until so late that I'd fallen in love with you?"

Now it was his turn for surprise and a surge of delight as he realized what she'd said. "When did you know, Suzanne?"

She tried to sort it all out. When had she known? Looking back it seemed that it should have been from the beginning, but that wasn't so. Having Marty in the picture had blurred everything. She couldn't imagine how she ever could have thought she loved Marty, but she hadn't known then what it meant to love. "I guess maybe I began to figure things out after Lady died and all I wanted was to be with you. And then these last few weeks—" Her voice broke. "Jed, I was ready to tell you I was going to move back home because I couldn't stay away from you and I didn't want your pity.''

"My pity? Good Lord, Suzanne.'' She was still clinging tight to him, and he held her and stroked her until he felt her relax. Then he led her to the couch and sat down beside her. She reached for him, but he held her away and looked directly into her eyes. ''We need to settle one thing right now. I could never pity you. I love you. That's how Jane got into the strip. She's not you, or any version of you, but since you were all I could think about, I had to come up with a woman for Morgan.'' He stroked her hair thoughtfully. ''And I guess that's how he's ended up asking her to marry him, because marriage was what was on my mind.''

"Oh, Jed.'' She reached for him again but still he held her away.

"You still haven't answered my question, and we're not going to do anything else until you do. Suzanne, will you marry me?''

She smiled and met his eyes. ''Yes.'' That was all she said, because that was all there was to say. She had no doubts, no fears, because whatever happened, they'd work it out somehow. She believed it because she loved him, and she could see in his eyes that he felt the same. His lips found hers, tenderly at first, in celebration of their new life, then insistently as the feelings that coursed through them brought thoughts of things to come. For the first time she wished Kacie weren't coming home and before she could feel guilty about the thought, Jed said it aloud. ''I've never felt so well chaperoned in my life,'' he confessed. ''As much as I love Kacie, I wish she were spending the night somewhere else.''

As he spoke, his hands wandered, lingering on the swell of her breasts, and Suzanne gasped. "Me, too," she agreed, grabbing his hands playfully, "but because she's not going somewhere else, you can't keep doing that." She found herself looking around guiltily just to make sure Kacie hadn't arrived unannounced, but the house was quiet.

"I've been listening, too," he confessed. "We can't go on like two teenagers hiding behind the barn, Suzanne. I want to get married now."

"You mean tonight?" Her eyes sparkled.

"How about tomorrow?"

"You're serious, aren't you?"

He nodded. "Absolutely."

For a moment the sheer magic of it caught her. In twenty-four hours she could be Mrs. Jed Parker. But then she thought about Kacie and realized that wouldn't be fair. They were talking about the rest of their lives and hers, too. "We can't spring it on Kacie that fast, Jed. She needs some time to adjust to the idea."

"Kids are flexible. One week; two at the most." He stroked her hair, then ran his fingers around her ear and down her neck until she shivered. "I don't want to wait, Suzanne."

Neither did she. "Let's talk to Kacie on Saturday," Suzanne suggested. "She's supposed to go to sports day at school in the morning, so why don't we have lunch together? That gives us all afternoon." Taking his hand again, Suzanne rested her head on his chest. "How do you think she'll react to this, Jed? Do you think she suspects?"

Jed chuckled. "I know she does. She asked me the other morning if I was planning to marry you."

"She what?" Suzanne sat up straight.

"She asked me out of the blue. We talked about it a little. I think she's worried that the relationships will change, especially her relationship with you."

Suzanne shook her head. "I like the way things are with Kacie. I don't see any reason why a different title means anything has to change."

Jed grinned. "Well, maybe some things." He leaned down and kissed her and pulled her body tight against him and Suzanne knew exactly what he meant.

KACIE PRESSED HER BACK hard against the kitchen wall and tried to hold perfectly still. They weren't talking any more but she could hear a faint rustling, which meant they were probably kissing each other again. That gave her a funny feeling inside. Not that she minded, really, but she felt sort of left out.

She hadn't meant to spy on them, not this time. She'd left Lucky outside and come in quietly because she was late and she wanted to see what was going on before she announced herself. She'd found the cookies in the kitchen and been about to eat one when she'd heard their voices. From there on, one thing led to another, and she'd found the conversation quite enlightening. It made her feel good that Suzanne wanted to keep their relationship the same, just like she did, and it was also good to know they were going to tell her about their plans on Saturday. It would probably be one of those "little talks" adults liked to have with kids. At least she'd be prepared.

"I love you, Jed," she heard Suzanne say. Then there was more rustling. It was probably time to announce herself. She tiptoed toward the back door and slipped outside to get Lucky. At least she wouldn't get in much trouble for being late. They probably wouldn't even notice.

THE BACK DOOR slammed hard and Lucky let out a vociferous bark. "Wow, chocolate chip cookies!" Kacie's voice carried clearly into Jed's studio. He and Suzanne moved quickly apart, and Suzanne shook her hair and smoothed it down.

"Help yourself, Kacie," Suzanne called to her. "Your dad and I are in here."

Kacie came in munching a cookie and holding two others in her hand. "Billy's team won and he played first base," she announced. "He's really good. Then we stopped for ice cream."

"I'm glad you had fun," Jed told her. "But it's late. You'd better get to bed."

"I'll walk up with you," Suzanne offered. "I'm kind of tired myself." All the way up the stairs she had to fight the urge to reach out and hug Kacie. But Lucky made things easier as he dashed between them and scampered into Kacie's room. "You haven't broken down and let him sleep with you, have you?" Suzanne asked.

"Nope." Kacie looked smug. "But sometimes I get my sleeping bag and sleep with him on the floor. He's nice and warm."

Suzanne smiled. "No doubt he feels the same way about you." And then she did hug Kacie, suddenly anxious for Saturday when she would know their secret and they could begin to plan as a family.

The spare bedroom was cold and empty, but Suzanne pulled on her nightgown and crawled into bed anyway. More than an hour later she was still awake, listening to the breeze rustle the new leaves on the trees just outside her open bedroom window. The peaceful sound should have lulled her to sleep, but it hadn't. As she turned over, the bedsprings creaked and she felt an aching deep inside. If only Jed would come to her. She wanted him in bed with her, his strong arms holding her close and his body wrapped around hers. She didn't want to wait a few days until they were married. She didn't even want to wait a few minutes. She wanted him now. Restlessly she turned over again and hugged the pillow tight against her breasts.

DOWNSTAIRS IN THE KITCHEN, Jed opened one drawer after another, rummaged inside, then shoved the drawers closed. "Damn," he muttered under his breath. The old brass key for the door of the spare bedroom had to be there somewhere. He remembered hiding it years before to keep Kacie from locking herself in the bedroom. Now he needed it to lock her out. Impatiently he dug through a snarl of rubber bands, string and pencils, but with no luck. He slammed the last drawer shut. It probably didn't make any difference whether he found the key or not, he told himself. But he didn't believe that. Despite what Suzanne had told Kacie about waiting till marriage, there came a time between a man and woman when making love was right. He sensed Suzanne felt the same way.

Jed's eyes traveled around the kitchen and finally stopped at the cabinet above the refrigerator where they kept Easter baskets, Chinese soup bowls and assorted Christmas items. That cabinet was his last hope. He dragged a chair across the floor, stepped up and opened the doors. At first he wasn't sure, but all at once he remembered. He fished through a three-pound coffee can full of cookie cutters and triumphantly pulled out the key. "See this?" he said to Lucky who was half asleep on the floor in front of the stove. "This is the key to it all." He dropped the key into his bathrobe pocket, stepped over the dog gate and started upstairs.

SUZANNE TENSED when she heard Jed's footsteps on the stairs. Maybe if she called to him— His footsteps stopped outside her door and she held her breath for a long moment. Finally, after what seemed like an eternity, the latch clicked and the door creaked slowly open.

"Suzanne, are you still awake?"

"Yes," she managed to answer, barely recognizing her own voice.

He stepped inside the bedroom, closing the door quietly behind him. Suzanne heard the key rattle, followed by the firm click of the old lock. She trembled, not with fear but with longing. As Jed turned, the pale moonlight silhouetted him, and she saw that he was clad in a robe, loosely belted at the waist. He was tall and lean and very male. As he walked toward the bed, she trembled again.

"I thought you might be asleep," he told her in a husky whisper.

She drew in her breath. "I couldn't sleep. I kept thinking about you." She met his eyes and saw a desire as deep as her own. Every inch of her body quivered with wanting him against her.

He reached down and stroked her cheek with his fingertips. "I couldn't stay away."

"I'm so glad. I heard you in the kitchen and when your footsteps started up the stairs I wanted to call out to you."

His fingers moved slowly across the side of her face and into her soft, thick hair. "Why didn't you?"

"Because..." Suzanne closed her eyes. She didn't know why and that didn't matter any more. Her whole being was focused on his hands, which had moved downward to caress her neck and shoulders along the lacy edge of her nightgown. His fingers were warm against her skin, and he smelled good. So good. Spicy and musky and masculine. His robe had fallen open above the waist and she knew that he was wearing nothing underneath it. "Oh, Jed—" she began.

She never finished. Her lips parted in an unconscious invitation and his mouth covered hers in a kiss that was at first gentle and exploring and then strong and certain. She wrapped her arms around his neck and pulled him close.

"I love you, Suzanne," he whispered softly.

"Oh, yes, Jed. Yes." She had never known love like this, complete love that held no questions and no doubts. "It seems so right to have you here, to have you touch me, to want to be part of you. This is how it's supposed to be, isn't it?" she asked softly.

He cradled her in his arms, realizing how vulnerable she was and how much she was entrusting to him.

"Yes," he answered. "This is how it's supposed to be." He caressed her gently across the fullness of her breast, down her side and over the curve of her hip before he slipped her nightgown over her head. Then he stood and dropped his robe to the floor. In the next moment he was against her, strong and male, and she yearned to be part of him. She touched his hair, his cheek, the silky hair across his chest, and when she heard his soft sigh of pleasure she let her fingers wander farther to explore the body of this man who would lie beside her for years to come.

As their eyes met they reveled in the wonder of each other. Hard against soft. Angles against curves. Man against woman. She grasped him tight with a strength she didn't know she had, wanting him desperately, not just in the way a woman wants a man but the way a woman wants *her* man, and no words could express that longing.

But Jed's mouth and hands told her he understood more than she could have told him, and he carried her away, far beyond herself, to that place where only feelings and sensations exist. Deep and intense and endless, until she was sure she could bear no more. Only then did he enter her. Finally, at the moment she cried out his name, he shuddered against her, and she knew they had become one at last, their bodies binding them more strongly than any spoken vows.

Long afterward they lay quietly wrapped in each other's arms, awed by what they had shared.

"I love you," Jed told her as the first pink and gold rays of dawn crept through the tree outside the bedroom window.

Suzanne sighed and snuggled against him. "You know I just spent the most perfect night of my life, don't you?"

He smiled at her. "One of many," he told her. "We'll be together until the world ends or we do."

"Promise?"

Jed nodded. "I promise." He'd never been so sure of anything.

CHAPTER SIXTEEN

THE FOLLOWING SATURDAY morning Suzanne awoke early with a warm, complete feeling of being loved. She could still see the hollow in the other pillow from where Jed had slept until an hour or so before, when he had left her to go to his own bed. He had come to her every night that week then left at the first light of dawn. But he wouldn't have to leave her for very much longer.

A quiver of excitement rippled through Suzanne. If everything went well with Kacie, nothing could stand in the way of her marriage to Jed. Absolutely nothing. She'd had a long talk with Kacie's caseworker the day before and Janet had been delighted for her. She'd cautioned that because Kacie's ties to Suzanne were so strong, she and Jed needed to be careful to reassure Kacie that the family being formed was a threesome and that she was an integral part of it. But Jed and Suzanne already knew that—in fact, they were planning to have a foursome because Lucky had become an important part of the family, too.

Suzanne dressed quickly, ate a bowl of cereal and left a note on the refrigerator for Jed and Kacie saying she and Lucky would be waiting to see them for lunch. Once at the clinic, Suzanne found out that waiting was virtually all she was doing. Her assistant had been scheduled to come in, but Suzanne called her and told her not to come. She spent most of the morning day-dreaming except for one scheduled surgery, which fortunately was easy. She watched the clock hands crawl along, wondering if Kacie was having a good time at sports day and what Jed was doing. She tried once to call him, but when she got no answer, she went to check on the little tan cocker spaniel that was recovering from having stones removed from his bladder.

Still groggy from the anesthesia, Buffy barely opened his eyes as Suzanne scratched him behind his ears. But a check of his gums, heart rate and respiration showed he was doing well. Next to her Lucky woofed a few times and wagged his tail hopefully at the cocker spaniel.

Suzanne laughed. "Buffy's not ready to play yet, Lucky, but I can tell you are. Don't you ever wear out?"

Lucky woofed again and lowered the front part of his body to the floor. With his hind end in the air and his tail wagging in double time, the mutt was a comical sight.

"All right, you win. We'll go play Frisbee. I can spare a few minutes."

The instant he heard the word Frisbee Lucky was jumping at the door, waiting for Suzanne to open it and follow him to the backyard.

"Lucky, sit!" Suzanne commanded. If she and this silly puppy were both going to live together, he was going to have to learn some manners.

But, instead of sitting, Lucky barked several more times and jumped at the door again. Resisting the impulse to laugh, Suzanne caught hold of his collar with one hand and patted his rump gently with the other.

"Lucky, sit," she repeated firmly. The puppy rolled his big brown eyes then reluctantly dropped to a lopsided sitting posture. "Good boy! Good dog!" Suzanne praised lavishly, patting him vigorously on his back. Lucky's tail began thumping happily on the floor. Maybe there was some hope that this dog would eventually be socially acceptable, Suzanne thought. He'd never be as perfect as Lady had been, but he was an entirely different personality. While Lady had been a truly gracious dog, Lucky was simply a happy-go-lucky pet and really perfect for a family. Family. Suzanne almost burst at the thought. She was going to be part of a family. She was going to marry Jed and live with him and Kacie—and Lucky—forever. Could anything ever be more perfect? She didn't think so.

She opened the back door of the clinic and followed the puppy out to the yard. The sky was azure blue, without a cloud in sight. Spring-green leaves were bursting out on the trees, and the bright pink azaleas were in full bloom. Lucky took off at a run, sniffing and scratching furiously at every pile of leaves until he finally unearthed the Frisbee. Proudly he came trotting to Suzanne with the bright red disk clenched tightly in his mouth. "Drop it, boy." Suzanne took a firm grip on the Frisbee and waited. Lucky shook his head, refusing to let go. He crouched, dug his front paws into the ground and braced himself for a spectacular game of tug-of-war.

"No, no, no!" Suzanne laughed helplessly. "You're supposed to give me the Frisbee so I can throw it and you can chase it." She pulled as hard as she could on the disk. Lucky growled, a playful puppy growl, and held on tenaciously. Finally Suzanne resorted to prying his jaws open and extricating the Frisbee. She flung the disk high into the air. "Lucky, fetch!" she called loudly. The puppy took off in a run as the Frisbee sailed across the yard. Then, with one magnificent leap, he caught the flying disk in his mouth. "Lucky, come!" Suzanne shouted. Lucky cocked his head to one side as if he was trying to remember what he was supposed to do. A rabbit scampered in front of him. Then it was all over. Lucky dropped the Frisbee on the ground and took off into the woods after the rabbit.

"Oh, no," Suzanne groaned. There was no point in going after the puppy. She'd never be able to catch him. In a few minutes the rabbit would elude him, and Lucky would give up and come trotting back. In the future, she reminded herself, there would be no more Frisbee playing except in Jed's fenced yard where it was impossible for Lucky to get away. Meanwhile she would go clean up from her surgery and wait for the puppy to appear at the back door. She wanted to be ready when Jed and Kacie got there with lunch.

Suzanne checked Buffy, who was more alert now and nuzzled her hand when she patted him. Then she filled her bottle of disinfectant and scrubbed down the surgery table. She was putting her instruments in the autoclave when she heard a noise on the porch. She paused and listened for a moment. Lucky must be back. Smiling, she walked through the clinic to let the puppy in.

"Hi, there fella," she said as she pulled open the door. "It's about time you showed up."

But it wasn't Lucky who greeted her. Suzanne took a step backward and gasped softly. The puppy was no-

where in sight. Instead, she found herself face to face
with Marty.

"Hello, little dove. I've missed you." He opened the
screened door and smiled as he reached out to touch
her cheek.

Bile rose into Suzanne's mouth as a single image
penetrated her mind. The little gray dove, dead on the
floor of the clinic with a bullet in its chest. Slowly, trying to remain calm, she backed farther away.

Marty stepped forward until his foot was just over
the threshold, preventing her from closing the door.
"Don't be afraid," he said softly. "I just want to come
inside and talk to you for a while."

"I don't think that's a good idea," Suzanne stammered. His smile, which had once seemed dazzling, was
ominous. He was impeccably dressed in slacks and an
open neck sports shirt, but his very perfection seemed
plastic and unreal. "I'm very busy right now," she
continued. "I have to finish up before noon." Noon,
she thought frantically. Noon. When Jed was coming.
She heard a rustling of leaves outside. Looking over
Marty's shoulder, she saw Lucky racing across the yard
from the woods. Marty was still holding the screen
door open. Maybe Lucky could divert him just long
enough for her to get away.

"Whatever you have to do can wait." Marty's eyes
narrowed. "What I have to tell you is more important." Giving her a shove he forced his way into the
clinic and kicked the door closed behind him. It banged
against the latch and flew open again, hitting hard
against the cabinet behind it.

Suzanne flinched at the sound. Somehow she had to
get past Marty to the screen door and open it wide

enough for Lucky to get in. She clasped her hands tightly in front of her in an effort to hide their trembling. Her heart was pounding wildly. She took a step forward but at that moment Lucky barked his loud, excited puppy bark and Marty whirled.

"Damn dog," he snarled.

Lucky's bark changed to a deep-throated growl and he slowed his gait. "Lucky, come," Suzanne shouted, lunging toward the door. But Marty was ahead of her. Just as Lucky reached the steps, Marty flung the door closed, and this time it latched. Lucky responded with an earsplitting howl. He threw his body against the door and barked wildly for several moments. Then his protests dropped to a low whine.

"So you got yourself another dog, did you? Well, this one's not going to do you any good."

The sneer on his face sent chills through Suzanne. Slowly, very slowly, never taking her eyes from Marty, she backed up until she was against the stainless steel examining table. Then she forced herself to smile. "What is it you want?" she asked him.

His eyes had narrowed until they were little more than slits. His face was ashen. "Do you remember what today is?" The tone of his voice was melodic, almost a croon. He walked toward her until he was but a foot or so away, then reached out and stroked Suzanne's cheek. Up and down with a single finger. Over and over.

She cringed beneath his touch, feeling violated. His finger trailed across her lips, circling them. First the top and then the bottom. Around and around, endlessly. Only sheer willpower prevented her from crying out. She knew that if she did he would hit her, and besides, there was no one to hear her anyway. Even Lucky's whining had stopped. He apparently had gone away.

Marty leaned so close that his face was hovering directly above hers. She thought she might vomit. "You don't remember about today, do you, Suzanne?" His breath was hot and fetid. Beads of perspiration clung to his forehead. He stopped stroking her lips and gripped her shoulder, pressing his fingers hard into her flesh.

"Remember? Remember what?" Her voice was no more than a hoarse whisper. She wasn't even sure what he'd asked her.

"This is April third, my little dove. Surely you haven't forgotten our wedding day."

Oh, God, yes. Now she remembered.

His fingers dug harder into her shoulder. "You were supposed to be my bride today. You were going to come down the aisle to me, dressed all in white, covered with a veil. And then tonight I was going to take you to bed, and you were going to belong to me forever. No one else. Only me. Do you remember now?"

She forced herself to smile again, trying desperately to stay in control. Slowly, an inch at a time, she began to ease herself around the examining table, trying to put something—anything—between herself and this deranged man.

"Stop moving," he shouted suddenly. His hand lashed out like a snake about to strike, and he grabbed her arm, pinning her against the table. "You can't get away from me. You tried. You told me you didn't want me any more. But I'm not going to let you get away with that." His breathing was shallow and rapid as he advanced on her. His lips were twisted in a perverse smile. "If I can't have you, Suzanne, no one is ever going to have you."

Marty's hand moved slowly toward the pocket of his slacks. Suzanne stood perfectly still, her arm clamped against the cold steel tabletop, her body pressed hard against the metal edge. He was going to hurt her. She knew that. The only ally she had was time. Still moving very slowly, Marty withdrew his hand from his pocket.

Suzanne gasped. He was holding a gun. "No," she pleaded. "Put that down. You don't need to point a gun at me."

"Don't be frightened, little dove," he said in that same melodic voice he'd used before. "It will all be over soon."

She searched frantically for some diversion. Behind Marty the clock hands were creeping toward noon. She had to stall and keep him talking as long as possible. She swallowed hard. "But we're not in any hurry, are we, Marty?"

"No, little dove, we're in no hurry." He took a step toward her, still pointing the gun.

JED PROPPED THE SKETCH of Lady against a chair where it got full light from the window and studied it carefully. He was pleased with the dark brown frame, exactly the color of Lady's eyes, and a cream-colored mat that brought out the gleaming black highlights in her coat. Suzanne would like it, Jed decided, and it was an appropriate present to give the woman he was about to marry. He was certain she'd be surprised. He'd worked on the final sketch while Suzanne was at the clinic, and he hadn't finished framing it until that

morning. He'd thought he and Kacie could give it to
her together at lunch. Jed checked his watch. Kacie was
going to have to get home from sports day pretty soon
if they were going to pick up the submarine sand-
wiches and get to the clinic by noon.

He wandered into the kitchen feeling vaguely unset-
tled, probably, he decided, because of the upcoming
discussion with Kacie. He was pretty sure she'd be
pleased that he and Suzanne were going to marry, but
with kids you could never be absolutely sure. He
checked the cookie jar on the outside chance there
would be a couple of chocolate chip cookies left, but
it was empty. Until Suzanne came, nobody had baked
a chocolate chip cookie in his house since Elizabeth
died. But their succulent smell hadn't made him think
of Elizabeth. It had made him think about finally having a real family again. Which, of course, brought an
image of Suzanne. He was considering her dreamily
when he heard the barking, loud, insistent, and coming closer.

Jed opened the front door just as Lucky bounded up
on the porch, breathing heavily and barking nonstop.
"Lucky, what are you doing here? You're supposed to
be at the clinic." The dog barked harder. "Come in
here," Jed commanded. "We'll call Suzanne and see
what this is all about." Jed reached for Lucky's collar,
but the dog jerked away, whimpering and whining and
moving toward the steps.

"Lucky, what's the matter with you?" He grabbed
at the dog's collar again and this time Lucky growled,
tugging so hard he almost pulled Jed down the steps.
Jed let go of the collar, aware that the puppy wasn't
being his usual playful self, trying to persuade Jed to

run with him. This was different. "Lucky, what is it?"
Barking hard, Lucky ran halfway down the sidewalk
then came back. He did it twice more before Jed realized what the pup was trying to tell him. "Oh, my God!
Something's wrong with Suzanne."

Jed raced for the car and as soon as he opened the
door Lucky bounded in beside him. Jed had never
driven so fast, but the ride to the clinic had never
seemed so long. Lucky whined impatiently while they
pulled into Suzanne's long driveway. Then he started a
fit of barking. Jed didn't even try to quiet the dog. He
barely heard him. His only thought was to get to Suzanne.

He was almost to the clinic door when he heard the
shot, a single explosion from inside. Fear tore through
him as he flung open the door. He had just a split second to absorb the scene—Suzanne lying on the floor
near the examining table and Marty standing over her
with a gun—before Lucky raced past him. With a fe-
rocious growl, the dog charged, sending Marty reeling
backward. The man and the dog crashed to the floor
together and the gun fired again.

Jed stood frozen for an instant in the stillness that
followed. Marty didn't move. Lucky stood over him,
growling. As though in slow motion Jed crossed the
room to Suzanne and knelt beside her, terrified of what
he would find. He said her name, then saw the dark red
stain that was already spreading across her shirt just
below her right shoulder. "Suzanne!" he said again,
but she didn't answer.

IN THE WAITING AREA outside the emergency room at
Cartersburg General Hospital, Jed and Kacie sat star-

ing into space. The place held bitter memories for them both.

"This is just like last time," Kacie said in a small, frightened voice. She looked toward her father for comfort that he was ill-prepared to give. "I remember when we sat here after Mom had the accident. We were here for so long." She stared at her feet.

Jed wished she wouldn't talk about it. He remembered only too well the sudden anguish, the angry, helpless tears he couldn't control. The years had dulled that pain. He felt an overwhelming anger at having to face it again.

"Is she going to die, Daddy?" Kacie's eyes were brimming with tears.

"No, Kacie, she isn't going to die," Jed repeated for the fourth time. He was trying hard to believe it. "The doctor said as soon as he removed the bullet he'd come out and talk to us."

For several minutes neither of them spoke. Kacie picked at some loose threads in the chair cushion. Jed didn't even make a pretext of looking at a magazine. He simply stared straight ahead.

"We were supposed to be having lunch right now." Kacie pulled a thread loose and wound it around her finger. "You and Suzanne were going to tell me you're planning to get married."

"How did you know?" Jed was too numb to be surprised.

"I heard you talking."

"And what were you going to say when we told you?"

Kacie poked her finger deep into a hole in the cushion, burying it in the cotton stuffing. "I was going to give you a hard time," she confessed.

Jed nodded.

"I was going to tell you that I loved Suzanne as my Big Sister and it wasn't fair to turn her into a stepmother." When Jed didn't answer, Kacie continued hesitantly. "I was wrong, Daddy."

Tears were rolling down her cheeks, and Jed reached over and took her hand. "Feelings aren't wrong, Kacie," he told her gently. "You have a right to your feelings. We've always said that."

"But this time I was wrong," she insisted. "Suzanne couldn't be a bad stepmother. She wouldn't know how. Besides, if you got married, she'd be around all the time."

"You'd like that?"

Kacie nodded. "But now we don't know if it can really happen. It's like with Mom and with Lucky. You don't know how much you want something until you maybe can't have it."

Jed squeezed her hand. There wasn't any answer.

"Did Lucky really save Suzanne's life?" Kacie asked after a few minutes. Jed fought to get a grip on his emotions. Every time he thought about what had happened, he felt shaky inside. Kacie was suffering as much as he was. He knew that. But it was just so damn hard to help her. He took a deep breath and began the story one more time. "Yes, Kacie, he did. He came to get me and he whined and growled and made me go with him."

"And then when you got there, he knocked Marty down and the gun went off."

Jed nodded. He'd already told Kacie that Marty was dead.

"Lucky was really brave, wasn't he? He could have been shot, too."

"Yes, Kacie," Jed agreed, "but he wasn't."

Kacie sighed. "At least Lucky's all right."

Yes, Jed thought, at least Lucky was all right. And he could only pray that Suzanne was, too. When the doctor finally came through the double doors at the far end of the waiting room, both Kacie and Jed leaped to their feet. The doctor approached them still wearing green surgical scrubs, but all Jed saw was the expression on his face. He was smiling.

Kacie clutched her father's hand tight as the doctor explained that the bullet had been removed with no complications. He said it was a small caliber, which had lodged in the fleshy part of the right shoulder and had done very little damage. "She'll be sore at first," he explained, "but in a couple of weeks she should be as good as new. I'd like her to stay here tonight, but she'll be able to go home in the morning."

"Daddy! Daddy! She's all right," Kacie shouted, dancing away from him. "Can we see her?"

The doctor's smile broadened. "Of course you can. She's awake and she's been asking for you."

The antiseptic hospital smell was all around them as they walked along the corridor toward Suzanne's room. The doctor's words echoed in Jed's mind. Suzanne would be as good as new, and tomorrow she could go home. Go home. Together they would go home. That was the happiest news he'd ever heard.

Suzanne looked deathly pale against the white bed linen with her hair spread out to one side on the pil-

low. But when she saw Jed and Kacie, her smile was
instantaneous and she held out her left arm as if to hug
them both. Kacie ran to her, remembering barely in
time to be careful of her other shoulder. Jed reached
around Kacie to take Suzanne's hand and found her
grip strong and warm. Relief flowed through him. She
really was all right.

"I'm so glad you didn't die," Kacie told her bluntly.

Suzanne laughed, then winced at the pain it caused.
"Me, too," she agreed.

"Does it hurt much?"

"Not much," Suzanne assured her. "Except when I
laugh. Sorry I missed our lunch."

"That's okay," Kacie told her. "I already knew what
you were going to talk to me about. Dad and I discussed it."

Suzanne gave Jed a questioning look and he nodded. "And?" Suzanne asked, turning her attention to
Kacie.

"And I think you'll make the best wife my dad could
ever find," Kacie announced. Suzanne let go of Jed's
hand and hugged Kacie awkwardly with one arm.
"Thank you, Kacie," she whispered.

"Except I have one question. After you and Dad get
married, what should I call you?"

Suzanne looked at the child she'd already grown to
love so much. She'd been prepared for practically anything else Kacie might ask, but not this. Yet she could
see it was something that was obviously bothering Kacie. "Why don't you just keep calling me Suzanne?
That seems to have worked pretty well up till now."

Kacie seemed relieved. "I hoped you'd say that."
She glanced from Suzanne to her dad and back again.

"Do you mind if I go see Lucky now? Dad says he's still at the clinic."

"I don't mind a bit," Suzanne assured her.

"Did you know he saved your life?"

Suzanne nodded. "Tell him thank you for me, Kacie. And give him a big hug and a puppy biscuit."

"Okay," Kacie agreed, as she started out of the room. "And I'll tell him he was really brave—just like Lady."

Suzanne watched Kacie hurry happily away. Then she turned to Jed. "Did Lucky really save my life?"

"Yes, Suzanne." He moved as close beside her as possible and took her hand. "If it hadn't been for Lucky..." He let the sentence go unfinished.

"I really sold him short, I guess." Suzanne seemed apologetic. "He'd run off after a rabbit before Marty came and then when he tried to get in, Marty slammed the door in his face. I thought he'd just gone off to play and then..."

Jed reached out and smoothed her hair. "You don't have to talk about it, Suzanne." He could see the fatigue etched in her face. "Maybe you should rest."

She shook her head. "No, I want to tell you. It's like a nightmare, like it happened to someone else." She closed her eyes for a long moment then opened them as she began talking. "Marty forced his way in. He was angry because this was the day we were supposed to get married." She saw the stricken look on Jed's face and squeezed his hand. "It's okay. I'd forgotten, too. After a while he took the gun out of his pocket and told me if he couldn't have me, no one could. I knew I had to keep him talking. You and Kacie were coming at

noon and I figured if I could just hold out until
then . . ."

"It's all right, Suzanne, it's over." Jed's voice was
soothing and his hand gentle as he stroked her hair.

"Is Marty . . . did he . . ."

She didn't seem to be able to ask the question. Jed
had wondered whether she knew and he hesitated
briefly before realizing that because she'd asked, he
needed to tell her. "Marty's dead, Suzanne. Lucky
jumped at him, and when he fell the gun went off and
killed him."

Suzanne closed her eyes, feeling nothing, no sor-
row, no hate, nothing. She opened her eyes to find Jed
watching her with a worried look. "I don't feel angry
and I don't even feel relieved," she told him. "I just
feel sad, the way I feel when any human being has to
die. He was like a stranger, like someone I never knew
at all."

"He was sick, Suzanne." Jed stroked her hand,
straightening her fingers then wrapping them around
his own. "I never wanted anything like this to happen,
but now at least he can't hurt anyone."

"I feel sorry for him, Jed. Even after everything he
did. . . ." Her voice trailed off.

Jed didn't answer. He could feel no compassion for
the man who had almost destroyed her life and his
along with it, and yet he could understand what she
was saying. Her kindness and respect for life exceeded
that of anyone he had ever known.

"It's still like a bad dream," she said finally. "It's
like standing on the edge of a storm and everything

behind me is black and in front of me the sun is coming out.''

Jed smiled and leaned over to kiss her forehead ever so gently. "Then let's not look back. The doctor tells me you'll be as good as new in a couple of weeks. How would you feel about a wedding?"

"In two weeks?"

"You want to get married sooner?"

Suzanne shook her head. "I don't know how we can get ready so fast. I mean we have to—"

"We have to what?"

Suzanne hesitated in confusion. Weddings took a long time, what with flowers and food and guest lists.

"We don't have to do anything except what we really want to do," Jed told her.

As she thought about what he'd said, Suzanne's smile turned radiant. "I guess we don't," she said in amazement. "We could get married with just Kacie there, if we wanted to. And we could go for a walk in the woods afterward. Or maybe we could go to the mountains for a couple of days if Kacie didn't mind, and I could make arrangements at the clinic."

"That's the idea. We've got a whole lifetime together, Suzanne. All I want is to begin it as soon as possible."

"Oh, Jed—" She reached for him, ignoring the pain in her shoulder. "Please hold me."

"Are you sure?" He gingerly put his arms around her.

"I've never been so sure of anything in my life." And when he leaned down to kiss her, she was more certain than ever.

THE WEDDING was at the small white frame church on
Oak Street. Kacie, dressed in yellow piqué and carrying daffodils from the garden, stood at the altar with
her father and Suzanne, because it wasn't only a wedding but the beginning of a new family for them all.
Suzanne wore a tea-length, antique lace dress that
Margaret Henniker had given her. She didn't have a
veil. Only a delicate wreath of early blush roses and
baby's breath adorned her hair, which was loose and
curling softly around her glowing face. She carried a
matching nosegay with narrow white satin streamers.

The guests were all special to Jed and Suzanne. His
parents, who shared their son's happiness, had flown
in from Florida for the wedding. Ed and Margaret sat
in a pew near the front of the church, holding hands
and casting furtive glances at each other throughout
the ceremony. Billy, who couldn't keep his eyes off
Kacie, was a little farther back with his parents.

Janet Sawyer and her husband were there, too. The
day before, Janet had revealed they were expecting
their first baby at Thanksgiving time. Several dairy
farmers, including Al Kenner, the owner of Princess
Margaret, had come with their families. Martha
Gresham, the proud grandmother of the three dachshund puppies, was there. And Fred Delaney, the owner
of the Christmas colt, Noel, had brought his wife and
all five of his children.

So much love, Suzanne thought again. So many
wonderful people who cared so much about her, and
Jed, and Kacie. When Jed slipped the plain gold band
on her finger she couldn't hold back her tears of joy
any longer. There was no doubt, no hesitation, no fear.

Only love. She and Jed would live together, laugh and cry together and grow old together. She took his hand and then Kacie's. Her life was complete.

HARLEQUIN SUPERROMANCE®

BSSB

HARLEQUIN SUPERROMANCE®

COMING NEXT MONTH

#522 JUST BETWEEN US • Debbi Bedford
When Monica Albright volunteered to be a Big Sister to
troubled teen Ann Small, she never expected to fall in
love with the child's father. But now that the inevitable
had happened, she and Richard were running the risk
of alienating Ann forever.

#523 MAKE-BELIEVE • Emma Merritt
Marcy Galvan's roots were in San Antonio. She had
her business, her family and her Little Sister,
Amy Calderon. Brant Holland's life was in New
York—his business needed him there. Though love had
brought them together, would their obligations keep
them apart?

#524 STRING OF MIRACLES • Sally Garrett
A lot of slick young legal eagles had made a play for
lawyer Nancy Prentice, but she was saving herself for a
real man: Mark Bradford. The only problem was that
Mark had always treated her like a sister. Well, no
more. Now *she* was going to take the initiative...!

#525 RENEGADE • Peg Sutherland
Former country-and-western star Dell McColl lived up
to his reputation as a renegade. He never backed down
from anything or anyone. Then he met never-say-die
Daylene Honeycutt. Daylene wanted two things from
Dell. She wanted *him,* and she wanted to sing in his
bar. Dell refused to give in on either count. Never again
would he be responsible for a woman's destruction on
the road to stardom.

HARLEQUIN®
Temptation®
the Fortune Boys

A funny, sexy miniseries from bestselling
author Elise Title!

LOSING THEIR HEARTS MEANT
LOSING THEIR FORTUNES....

If any of the four Fortune brothers were unfortunate enough to
wed, they'd be permanently divorced from the Fortune
millions—thanks to their father's last will and testament.

BUT CUPID HAD OTHER PLANS!
Meet Adam in #412 **ADAM & EVE** (Sept. 1992)
Meet Peter #416 **FOR THE LOVE OF PETE**
(Oct. 1992)
Meet Truman in #420 **TRUE LOVE** (Nov. 1992)
Meet Taylor in #424 **TAYLOR MADE** (Dec. 1992)

WATCH THESE FOUR MEN TRY TO WIN
AT LOVE AND NOT FORFEIT $$$

HARLEQUIN®

I N T R I G U E®

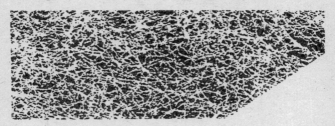

INTRIGUE IS CELEBRATING ITS 200TH BOOK!

Remember all those great adventures you had....

The SHADOW OF THE MOON spills across the stained carpet and the NIGHTWIND howls. You're stuck in a HAUNTED HOUSE in which HIDDEN SERPENTS slither. There's a CALL AFTER MIDNIGHT. It's THE LATE GENTLEMAN ringing to see if that FACE IN THE MIRROR is SUITABLE FOR FRAMING. "What do you mean?" you scream wildly into the phone. But the only reply is WHISPERS IN THE NIGHT.

And the suspense continues! Don't miss Intrigue #200
BREACH OF FAITH
by Aimée Thurlo

Two hundred escapes into suspense and danger with mysterious men brave enough to stop your heart.

IF TRUTH BE KNOWN, a trip through a Harlequin Intrigue can be STRANGER THAN FICTION! HI200